Last Year when I was Young

Monica Dickens – great-granddaughter of Charles Dickens – was
educated at St Paul's School for Girls. She travelled abroad for
a while after leaving St Paul's and then joined a dramatic school.
In 1935 she was presented at Court and soon afterwards found a
job as a cook – an experience described in her first book of
autobiography, *One Pair of Hands*. She has since written two
further books of autobiography – *One Pair of Feet*, which is about
her work as a nurse, and *My Turn to Make the Tea*, a
description of her life on a provincial newspaper – and many
novels. She is married to Commander Roy Stratton and has two
daughters.

Monica Dickens

Last Year when I was Young

Pan Books in association with
William Heinemann

First published 1974 by William Heinemann Ltd
This edition published in 1976 by Pan Books Ltd,
Cavaye Place, London SW10 9PG
in association with William Heinemann Ltd
© Monica Dickens 1974
ISBN 0 330 24803 0

The quotation from *Dedicatory Ode* by Hilaire Belloc which appears
on page 146 is reprinted by permission of A. D. Peters and Company

Printed and bound in Great Britain by
Cox & Wyman Ltd, London, Reading and Fakenham

I

In the afternoons, when the housekeeper was out and Mr Stillman asleep, I used to wander round the empty cheerless house, ruffling the pale pile of the dining-room carpet, dabbing fingerprints on to the polished table, whistling softly, talking to myself in two voices, trying to bring some life into that dead place where the old man lay dying.

The house was in a short pointless street off Fitzjohn's Avenue, halfway between Hampstead and Swiss Cottage stations, and a long walk from both. It has been said that no place in Central London is more than eight minutes' walk from a tube station, but whoever said it did not know Warhurst Vale.

After I got my bearings, I went to Hampstead in the morning and walked down the hill, then went on downhill to Swiss Cottage in the evenings. But there was still that curious seesaw propensity of Warhurst Vale to slant slightly uphill whichever way you were going, like a country road in front of a bicycle, with the wind always against you.

Number twenty-seven was an unwelcoming brick house, blinds drawn cagily to the exact middle of each window, an acorn on the end of the cord. The garage entrance took up most of the garden, and what was left was concrete too, with a few bare bushes and tubs of winter weeds and cat dung.

It was guarded by wrought-iron gates and a low brick wall with an iron fence on top. But who would want to get in? I didn't, that first morning. Small clouds were moving through a bright sky above the Hampstead chimneys, and I would rather have gone up to the Heath. But my patient waited for me, so I fought the stiff gate, and rang the bell over the letterbox.

I worked for the Post Office one Christmas, lugging round sacks of unnecessary greetings for which whole forests had been cut down, so I always notice letterboxes. This one, polished like a coffin handle, was one of those gin-trap affairs that will grab your hand if you don't let go of the letters quickly. I had almost lost fingers in some of those that Christmas when I was seventeen and in a fog half the time, so far behind with delivery by

5

the end of my shift that I used to stuff all the envelopes into one house in a short street, and hope that someone would distribute them.

The woman who opened the door was thin and wary, with bottle-bottom glasses and hair pulled back into a round container like a small string shopping bag.

'Yes.' Her eyes were pebbles behind the thick lenses. People in glasses don't need to blink as often as those with naked eyes, and Mrs Parker could stare for ever without blinking.

'I'm the nurse.'

'Oh. Yes.' There was a sort of north country terseness about her, not unfriendly, but not squandering amenities. 'They didn't say it was a man. I've never seen a male nurse before.'

'Take a good look.' I stepped into the hall with the airline bag in which I carried my white jacket and the tools of my profession. It said Air India, though I had never been east of Antwerp. I got it from a travelled geriatric who would travel no more. Mrs Parker shut the door behind me softly, and I felt the silence of the waiting house.

As we went up the stairs, a cracked old voice called out from behind an open door. 'Mrs Parker? Who's that? Who's that, Mrs Parker?' Fear was in the voice, the helpless fear of calling for ever without an answer.

His bald head was turned to the door as we went in. I saw a mauve old face with lizard's eyelids and a mouth sucked back below the bony nose.

'It's the nurse, dear. Don't be afraid.'

'I'm not afraid.' The weak voice whistled through the dry cavern of his mouth.

'Yes, you are, because you didn't think it would be a man.'

'What man?' Mr Stillman had not yet taken me in, behind the businesslike figure of Mrs Parker, advancing on him with the air of rolling up her sleeves, although she was not.

'The nurse.'

Too big a burden for Mrs Parker, they had told me on the telephone. She may have heard that end of the conversation, for she was a bit tight-lipped about someone coming to usurp the burden. Unsmilingly, she straightened the old man's bedclothes, putting back a knuckly claw that hung over the edge, tweaking his pyjama collar. She stared at him austerely as he shifted and tossed, and flung hands feebly about to undo her work, then bent once more to reshape him.

'I don't need a nurse.' He got himself rumpled again.

'It's all right, Mr Stillman.' I had met this before. A nurse spells serious trouble. That's why families often put it off too long. 'Just to keep you company for a while.'

'I want to get up and get dressed.'

'Tomorrow?' Whoops. *Never make a specific promise*: Sister Rhoda Greencastle, Understanding the Terminal Patient, 2nd Year Psychology, Essex Hospital, London NE18. 'Why don't you stay in bed and rest today?'

He was almost ninety, and his heart was guttering. He shut his deep-creased eyelids and dropped open his mouth, and stopped breathing for a long and scary moment. As I put my hand on the fragile wrist, he suddenly took in a snorting breath.

'He does that,' Mrs Parker said quite proudly. 'Give you a turn, eh? You'll get used to it. Won't he, dear?' She pulled the blanket tightly over his toes, and left me with the old gent.

I sat by him for quite a while and watched him sleep, flat as paper in between breaths, until he gasped and sucked air into his rattling chest. I hoped he would not die on my first day.

*

He did not die that day, nor that week, nor that month. He was stronger than he seemed, the old fellow, and Mrs Parker and I were proud of him. And of ourselves.

'How is he?'

'In the pink.'

'All this good nursing.'

'That's the ticket.'

Every morning when she opened the door with that serious face (she would not give me a key), I expected to hear he had gone in the night. Yet he was always in the pink. Fit as a fiddle. Outlive us all.

But when I went upstairs he looked as ghastly as ever. 'Who's that? Mrs Parker? Is that him?' He could not always remember my name.

'It's me, and it's a lovely day, and two men robbed a bank of fifty thousand pounds, and there's been a plane crash in the Isle of Man and an earthquake in Peru.'

Mr Stillman had lost touch with the world, but he quite liked me to read the worst parts of the paper to him. Just the disasters. If I read about pools winners, or brothers happily reunited after thirty years, he tossed and plucked at himself and smacked the yellow palm of his hand irritably against his head.

The disasters soothed him. A few beastly shocks and tragedies from the *Daily Express*, and he would go off like a baby until lunchtime.

Some days when he stayed awake, I got him up to sit propped with pillows by the bowl of water in front of the gas fire. But although he usually grumbled 'I want to get up', when I made his bed with him in it, after he had been sagging in the armchair for ten minutes he often said, 'I want to go back to bed.'

His small body was thin and wasted. I could carry him in my arms like a child.

'This is very undignified,' he said once. 'I am the chairman of the board.'

Some days he was sharp, and would tell me random things about the furniture business, and the wife in the photograph on the dressing-table, monstrous in a deck chair whose canvas bulged to the ground, and about his three children who hardly ever came to see him. Some days he was, as we say in the trade, quite out to lunch. He called me Robert or Rags, or Mishter Lewish, and saw people in the corners of the room, and did not make much sense. Some days he did not speak at all.

He did not speak to Mrs Parker on any of the days. She communicated with him in terse, rallying phrases like 'upsadaisy', and 'There you go'. But she was fond of our old joker in her laconic way, and was willing to listen for him at night after I left.

She had moved out of her bedroom over the garage into the spare room next to Mr Stillman. Mr Parker, a gritty engineer with dirt in his pores, did not care for this arrangement.

'Hard cheese,' Mrs Parker had told him.

*

After she had brought up the old man's puny lunch, and left my sandwich tray on the hall table, as a fine distinction of how far she would carry what for whom, Mrs Parker went out in the afternoons. Mr Stillman always dropped back into sleep after I had spooned and poured his lunch into him. Then I would wander. When I started private nursing, I thought how great it would be to have time to read. But I was too restless to read. I could not even sit still in that hushed, uncomfortable house.

It did not lower my spirits. It heightened them, by contrast. Instead of dampening my energies, it stirred and challenged them.

When you take care of an old person, it all moves so slowly. We used to hustle them in hospital – we had to, to get done in time – but a private patient is paying, among other things, not to be hustled.

I might get up in the morning feeling that I could push the world over, run down the stairs from the flat, swing along the sunny side of the road and across the common, playing hopscotch with the dog mess, charge down the station steps, canter down the hill from Hampstead, greet Mrs Parker like my cheeriest friend, and bounce up the stairs.

'Who's that? Mrs Parker? Richard – who is it?'

Once into that square stuffy bedroom with the embossed beige wallpaper, the confines of my working day, I had to drop myself down into dead slow gear and stay there.

Into my white coat. 'Just a minute, my boy, before you do anything else, I want you to ...' Any one of a dozen fiddly things, usually involving a token search for something that had never existed. 'Breakfast? I've had that. Haven't I? Well, you say so. Don't bring me eggs ... why do you never bring me eggs?' Strips of pale crustless toast dipped in the yolk, yellow runnels in the chin furrows. The tea in the spouted feeder too hot, too cold, too sweet – 'Ah! That woman could never make tea.'

Blanket bath, passing the soaped face cloth over each skinny limb, dealing respectfully with the flabby genitals. Rub the back, loose goose skin over the knobbed spine. Rub the yellow heels. Clean pyjamas. Make the bed. Set him up for the morn-

9

ing with all the little vital idiocies his world had dwindled to. Handkerchief pinned to his pyjama jacket. Bell clipped to the pillowcase. Watch under the pillow. Teeth in a mug, in case. Peppermints in a saucer. Pills and the glass of water, gullet stretching and retching as if the tiny white pills were golf balls. Blind up. Blind down. Blind halfway. 'Where are my glasses? My handkerchief? My postcard from Australia? My book? What's the time? What's on the wireless? Turn off that terrible racket. I want you to rub my back.'

'I just have, Mr Stillman.'

'No, you've not. My back is so sore. Ouch! Wait. No, wait a minute till I . . . don't rush me. Wait a minute. Wait – ow, that's cold. Go and warm your hands, boy.'

'What am I doing here?' I wondered, rearranging pillows for the eighth time, looking under the bed for bombs. I loved the old person in the way you do when they depend on you. But it all takes so long and goes so slowly, and although it is what you are there for, and there is nothing else to do, the braking of your own tempo, the patience, the plodding repetition build up frustrated electricity.

By the time I had fed him lunch – an endless and messy process, with me opening my mouth at each spoonful, like a mother weaning a baby – I was charged and tingling. I had to move about.

I had to walk, up and down the stairs, making a sharp drill turn at the angle, into the dining-room, round the table, greeting absent diners, touching ornaments, at the mirror sticking out my tongue pasted with the plastic bread of Mrs Parker's sandwiches. Across the polished hall, an ice rink, with small rugs. The ice was thin, with fifty feet of black cold water below. The game was to jump from rug to rug, skidding the last one as far as the door of the drawing-room where the furniture stood shrouded, as if it were dead.

In and out of the little panelled study, whence all traces of Mr Stillman had been cleaned away, as if he also were already dead. Into the scoured kitchen in a vain quest for food, but even the biscuit tin was locked away. Mrs Parker would have padlocked the refrigerator too, if there had been anything worthwhile in it. Cold porridge. Half a cup of pickled cabbage.

Tapioca. I dipped into them all, and rearranged the surface with a finger. Even the spoons were hidden.

Up the stairs and in and out of the bedrooms, the muscles of my limbs fretting like a fit horse. I had made Mr Stillman's room as homey as was possible with that wallpaper and lowering furniture; but in the other rooms, even the one where Mrs Parker slept, a corpse with its toes up on the precise white candlewick would be no more than part of the décor.

In a garden outside the back windows, some children home from school swung and seesawed, laughing. I watched them and waved, and shot the blind up and down to get their attention. When they saw me, they stopped laughing and went indoors. Mum, a man stared at us. Mum, there's a man locked up in that house at the back. We saw him signalling.

Once, on a sunny day, I went round the house and raised all the blinds. The rooms looked quite different. You could believe that a family had once lived here.

When Mrs Parker came home, she trod round in her fur boots and pulled all the blinds down again to half mast. 'In case of prying eyes.'

A peeping Tom would be a welcome change.

When I turned in my staff job at the Essex, for more money and a change of scene, I did not know that nursing could ever be like this. In hospital, there is no time to get restless, and most of my first private cases had been short-term, acute patients who needed enough nursing to keep me busy. But with poor old Mr Stillman there were those long lonely stretches when I paced that silent, polished house.

Sometimes I felt that something very exciting was just about to happen. That was why I could not keep still. My nerves were full of messages. I walked on the balls of my feet, ready to take off into adventure.

When nothing did happen that was any more exciting than Mrs Parker in a plastic hood, hurrying home through the rain with the old man's soda bic., it did not discourage me. My nerves went on getting those messages of something exciting just round the corner, and I went on pacing, round and round that poker-faced house, while the old fellow slept away the last days of his life. Or weeks perhaps. Or even months. Sometimes they linger an amazingly long time in this crumbling half life.

How long would I stick it? Which of us would get tired of it first?

2

The old man was lonely too, although he had me six days a week, and brisk Nurse Rix on my day off, and Mrs Parker telling him, 'Bottoms up' at night.

He was lonely for his family. They did not come very often, but when they did, the visits did not go with a swing. I would tell him, 'Mrs Runyon rang to say she'd be in this afternoon,' or, 'Your son says he'll try and get up here after work.' He would get quite excited. He would toss, and pluck at the lobes of his ears, and ask me the time every ten minutes. But when they came, he did not seem to like them any better than they liked him.

*

Phyllis Runyon was the citified daughter, with skittish skirts over legs thin and wide-set, like cricket stumps with the middle one knocked out, and that kind of squared-off, flared nose that might mean breeding, but usually means trouble.

Marion Sparrow was the country one in a muddy car, fuzz on her veined cheeks, rear end spreading like her late mother in the deck chair.

The moon-faced son Robert stood by the bed, going, 'Well, well,' opened his mouth and stared at the place where the beige wall met the ceiling, but found nothing there worth saying. He was said to be a stockbroker. I would not have trusted him with my money, if I had any.

Perhaps because they grew up in this stiff and stifling house, there seemed to be very little ease or feeling among this family, either with each other, or with their father. They came to visit him from duty, and to find out how soon he would die.

'What do you think?' Outside the bedroom, the face and voice would manoeuvre into interesting combinations of expression designed to convey that it was sad, but we must face the fact that we all must die (a fact that is easier to face about someone else).

'How much –' The slight hesitation was the sad part, eyes slightly lowered. 'How much longer, do you think?' The level look into my kindly brown eyes was the part about facing facts. 'How much longer?'

They hung on my answer. When there is no doctor about, the nurse is oracle. They could see that the old man was almost at the end of what seemed to have been rather a joyless life, but they wanted to hear it from honest Nurse Hayes.

'How much longer, do you think, Richard?' This was a Richard family, not a Rickie or a Dick.

Their solemn voices made mine cheerful. 'It's always hard to say. With luck, he could be with you for months yet.'

They thought I was being too bright. Especially Mrs Runyon. Brightness was one of the things she most feared in nurses. Once when she came at midday and Mrs Parker ungraciously offered lunch, she turned it down, in case she had to have it with me, and I would make bright conversation.

I thought that she was the one who cared most whether the old man lived or died. She had got rid of her husband, or he of her. Her children were grown up. She had bought a piece of land in Portugal and was building a house there. A nice little legacy might make all the difference.

Would there be a legacy? Her father did not like her. He did not want to be left alone with her. He never actually said, 'Don't leave me,' but when Mrs Runyon came, he would wheeze, 'You stay, Richard,' or if he was having a speechless day, he would seek me with the eyes that peered through cataracts as through a fogged windscreen.

I would sit discreetly by the window. If I were a girl nurse I could knit, or something. A man has to pick up a newspaper he has already read and pretend not to listen. Phyllis Runyon made a few abortive attempts to interest her father in conversation.

'Remember the Nixons, Daddy?'

'Never heard of 'em.'

'They sent you their love.'

'Who did?'

'The Nixons.'

'Why?'

When he drifted away into sleep, or his limbo corridor between life and death, she looked at her watch, and saw that the sick-room eternity had been only ten minutes. Too short for duty.

'Richard.' She turned her sleek black head with its effective grey streak – the black manufactured, the grey real – and asked in that smiley voice for buttering up the lower orders, 'Would you be an angel and get me a cup of coffee?'

They don't make a dent with their angels and darlings, any more than their grandfathers ever did with 'my good man'.

Since she was in her own house, she could have got the coffee herself, but she considered that I was being paid the earth, so I could wait on her as well as her father.

'Of course, Mrs Runyon.' My bland voice. You have to be less bossy in private work than in hospital.

While I went downstairs to charm coffee out of Mrs Parker – 'Who does she think she is?' – I wondered whether Phyllis Runyon would try to talk to her father about money.

'Daddy.' Daddy sounded so incongruous from that experienced cantaloupe mouth below the flaring veined nostrils. 'Wake up, Daddy. I want to ask you about the will.'

I imagined that the will was in a locked drawer of the kidney-shaped desk in the study. Wandering in there on my afternoon tours, I used to picture the scene that might take place when Mr Stillman did die.

Early Galsworthy, with the soberly-clad family on the slippery leather chairs, and lawyer behind the desk regarding them through the top of his bifocals. He is very conscious of his moment. He clears his throat. He takes a little key out of a secret pocket in his waistcoat, bends to the curved drawer, and puts the document on the desk. They watch him. He looks at them, clears his throat again, and lowers his eyes to the bottom focus of his spectacles.

I used to sit behind the desk and play the part of the lawyer.

The expensive parchment crackles. 'I, Robert Henry Stillman.' The long legal throat moves like a lizard. 'Being of my right mind . . .'

Or however it went. I had never seen a will. You don't make one at my age and income.

'I give and bequeath . . . and to my beloved daughter, Phyllis Stillman Runyon, the sum of Five, 5 pounds, in token of my –'

Crash. She falls like axed timber on to the harsh Oriental.

*

Everything in that house was stiff, inflexible, unfaded, unused, although the Stillmans had lived in it quite a long time, and Phyllis was married from there, in a rearing hat and a long pleated dress like a Christmas cracker. There was a picture in the shrouded drawing-room of her and Runyon outside the register office, with Mr Stillman natty and spry with a cauliflower buttonhole and quite a bit of hair, and Mrs Stillman in an obliterating hat, gone to jelly already, with swollen legs.

I would never know what happened about the will anyway, because when the old man went, they would pack me off with the cadaver.

While the body lives, they are all over you, can't thank you enough for your kindness and patience, don't know what they would have done without you, will always think of you as a family friend. 'You must keep in touch with us, even after – you know.' They see themselves sending you a little something every Christmas. You'll be on the card list. 'Who's this Richard Hayes?' 'Oh, don't you remember, he was that nice young nurse who took care of Daddy. I always send him a pound.'

But as soon as 'you know' has happened, and the body is gone and you've cleared up a bit, you're out. They don't even want you at the funeral.

'Who's that?'

'I don't know. Some second cousin – Charlie's boy? Who is that, Phyllis?'

'That's Richard what's-his-name. He looked after Daddy.'

'The nurse?' They take another look to see if it's true that all male nurses are queer.

*

The other daughter, Marion, lived in the country. She came up infrequently in a fur hat and Laplander boots, with baskets of things like chicken and apples and celery and home-made cider, that the old man could not eat.

Food was her show of caring. She had done it with her children too. She brought a doughy girl once, with greasy hair and erupting skin, who pouted a fat lip and said, 'Oh mother, *please.*'

She would not stay with her grandfather more than a couple of minutes. She sat on the top stair, kicking the shiny brass rod, and stared at the lozenge of stained glass at the turn of the stairs, as if the tragedy of her life were depicted there.

'Oh, for heaven's *sake,*' she said, and her mother promised that they would stop for a big lunch on the way home.

The other daughter was also overfed. Mrs Sparrow tried to show her father a picture of this dumpling on her pony, and when he would not look, she showed it to me. Little Dee-Dee was a whiz on that pony, and Marion went to all the Pony Club rallies and the shows, which was her excuse for hardly ever coming up to London.

When she did come she chattered about horses and gardens and the jolly doings of her family, and how the house was always full of noisy teenagers – if they were all like the one on the stairs it couldn't have been very jolly – and about people who did not interest her father, nor even remind him of any past interest.

He thought she was a dead bore. While she sat and prattled by the bed, with her florid cheeks and busy pink mouth and kind harmless eyes, he would fall asleep, or pretend to.

His glaucous eyes would turn up, until a slit of yellow-white showed under the loose lids. His toothless mouth dropped open so far that it seemed his jaw would fall off, and he would do the bit about not breathing, until the cage of his chest suddenly heaved in a shuddering snore. The snores grew more regular and louder. For a feeble breather he had a deafening snore, like trains passing in a tunnel.

'There.' Good-hearted Marion stood up, not insulted. 'He's asleep, poor pet. I'll run along back to my brood. Tell Mrs Parker to make the apples into sauce with a little lemon to bring out the taste. He can eat the chicken breast, and she can make a good broth from the rest.'

Outside the bedroom door: 'How – how much longer, do you think?' Clear country eyes anxious under the fur hat.

'You never know. He could be with you for quite a while yet.'

'Well, *that's* good news, Richard.' But she had lost interest as she paddled down the stairs, her mind already on its way home in the muddy estate car to start the pastry for the treacle tart, and see that the dogs and ponies were fed.

*

Even if I had the nerve to instruct Mrs Parker how to cook the apples and chicken, they had disappeared anyway. Mrs Sparrow had unpacked the basket on the kitchen table, but when I went in after she left, the food was gone and the table wiped clean of chicken ooze and earth crumbs from the celery.

I looked into the refrigerator, hoping to be able to take back at least a few eggs and apples to the flat I shared with John Bruce, but it still held not much more than the little dishes of mush and mess that Mrs Parker prepared for Mr Stillman.

'Looking for something, Nurse?' She called me Richard, unless displeased.

'Something to eat,' I said honestly. 'I'm starving.'

'I've nothing for you till I go round to the shops.'

When I came in at noon the following Sunday, there was a car in the garage entrance. Nobody answered the front door bell, so I went up the steps that led to the Parkers' rooms above the garage.

Mrs P opened the door, her nose shiny from eating, her tongue ferreting a gap tooth.

'Go round the front, Nurse. I'll open.'

Before she shut the door, I had a glimpse of Mr Parker with a knife and fork in his fists, and friends or relations sitting round a white cloth, packing away roast chicken and cider.

*

'I think your son is here, Mr Stillman.'

Robert had a key to the front door, which Mrs Parker had not been able to get away from him

Crash – bang – door opens and shuts. Heavy feet cross the

hall, avoiding the rugs. Crack – squeak of sticky door under the stairs. Niagara flush of gents. Crash – double crash to shut sticking door. Hard heavy heels on polished floor. Thud, thud up the stairs. Son Robert moved like an army.

Even the deaf old ears were assaulted, and the furrowed yellow face winced.

I went out to Robert.

'Hullo, Richard.' He spoke heavily too, the voice tilted down. 'All right to go in?'

I opened the door before he could crash it against the commode, and he trod into the sickroom, rubbing his meaty hands. 'Well, well, well. Well, Dad. How does it go?'

He towered by the bed. He had just missed being a case of gigantism. His hands were as big as feet and his feet were like trucks. Mr Stillman looked extra flat and shrunken with his son in the room. He lay as if he were sinking through the mattress, and looked up at Robert without a word.

I pulled up the strongest chair, as inadequate under Robert as a milking stool.

'How goes it then, Dad? Eh? Well, then?'

He got no help from the bed. Mr Stillman turned his head to make sure I was going to stay in the room.

Poor Robert hummed and gaped and tried a few half sentences about the stock market, or his family, or the weather, and looked for inspiration at the edge of the ceiling.

After he left – thud, thud down the stairs, huge heels on the hall boards, creak, flush under the stairs (bit of prostate trouble, eh, Robert?), crash bang of the front door, scrape of feet on concrete path, iron gate swung and slammed, car door slammed, engine raced with the choke out – Mr Stillman would toss and mutter a bit, and push his blue lips in and out at the chair where his son had sat.

'What a fool,' he would say to me 'What a fool.'

*

Once Robert brought his wife, quite a gay woman, normal-sized, but reaching only to her husband's shoulder. Robert stood back while she beamed at Mr Stillman and told him how splendid he looked, and tried to make jokes and hold the old man's hand, but he pulled it away.

When they had gone, he said, 'Who was that woman?'

*

So although we were rather lonely on the empty days, shut in together in this close, unacknowledged relationship of man trying to die and nurse helping him, we were no better off when the family did come.

'You stay, Richard,' he would wheeze, or seek me with his eyes. I tried not to leave him alone with any of them.

Once in a while, some friend would come, or a local acquaintance. I left them in the hall while I asked Mr Stillman whether he wanted to see them.

'Who? Who?'

I had shut the door, so the visitor would not hear the querulous voice.

'Mr Rogers.'

'Never heard of him.'

'Your friend Alice, from the restaurant.'

'Dreadful woman.'

He always refused to see them, whether he remembered them or not.

'I'm sorry, Mr Rogers. It's not a very good day for him. Perhaps another time.' Less discouraging than 'Don't bother.'

'Yes. Well. Do give him my best wishes. I just wanted to see him . . .'

Before he died. A sort of talisman urge, like touching the Saint's toe in St Peter's, to avoid feeling guilty when he did die.

The only friend Mr Stillman would see was the Major who used to stagger up from the old persons' hostelry down the hill, with the ends of his mittened fingers frost-bitten, and ask me to get him a beer.

Mrs Parker would not let such a thing into her stark kitchen. Mr Parker had to go out for his pint. But the Major nudged me, and winked and jerked his head and wheedled, 'Get us a beer, my boy.'

The winking and jerking went on all the time, involuntarily, but the nudge and wheedle moved me to bring in some bottles and hide them in a leather hat box on the wardrobe top shelf. Mrs Parker cleaned voraciously, although I tried to stop her raising too much dust and commotion in the sick room, and the

Major and I could only hope that she would not take a fit to turn out the wardrobe when I was off duty.

She was a bit touch and go some days, with Mr Parker nagging her about getting a place of their own; beer in the wardrobe might set her off. If she left they would have to get a night nurse, even though the old man hardly ever woke. And night nurses cost the earth, as Mrs Runyon remarked, to remind me that I did too.

The Major came up the hill about once a week when he could find the little door at the back of his Gothic building; it was the only one they left unlocked because the old people wandered. His blue fingers dragged him up by the banister, as if the stairs were the last summit of Everest.

I would find him panting on the landing. I saluted him, and he me.

'Good morning, sir.'

'Good evening, my boy' (whatever the time of day). 'How is – er?'

'Not too bad.' I never said 'Very well' about people like Mr Stillman since the time on geriatrics when I said it to a patient's wife, and the old faker was dead before she reached his bed.

'All right for me to –'

The Major, who would still be shorter than me, even if he stood straight, turned his triangular eyes anxiously upwards, lest I might not let him in. Once when he had made this trek up the hill and up the stairs, I had to say that Mr Stillman was not well enough to see anyone.

'Oh dear.' The Major sat down in a straight chair like a bombed-out refugee. 'Oh dear. Oh dear.' He sat and winked into space for half an hour before he could find the heart to start the downstairs and downhill journey home. He dreaded it happening again.

Why not telephone before he started out? They did not let them use the telephone at the Turrets. 'They're afraid we might call for help.'

He had a certain grim humour. He used to tell me fearsome stories about what went on at the home. If they were only *half* true the place would have lost its licence.

'All right for me to –'

'Come right in, sir.'

'Hullo, Robbie.'

'Hullo, Rags.' The dry, cold hands met. I fetched a chair and the beer, and he would sit by the bed and jerk his head and wink and drink his beer between jerks, and entertain Mr Stillman in disconnected half phrases.

'Never thought it. Too bad, you know. When we were at Durham. Never could stand. Nora used to say.'

Sometimes they would both fall asleep, the Major tilted sideways in his chair, his mittened hands folded piously, and his great Napoleonic nose flushed with stupendous hues.

3

'Mr Stillman is going to be ninety in two weeks.'

'You shatter me.' John Bruce's Natalie, an inartistic art stu-dent, was in the cupboard which was our kitchen, dishing up chili.

Strong foods like chili and garlic and curry overrode the basic smells of that sour little space, and made it habitable.

'Yes, ma'am.' I leaned in the doorless doorway, and surveyed the back of her pelvic girdle, twice as broad as it was long in men's jeans cut short in the crotch. 'The old boy will be ninety, if he makes it. Mrs Parker is going to make a birthday cake of blancmange.'

'Dick, you are such a bore,' Natalie said quite fondly, push-ing past me with the bowl of chili.

'All nurses are bores,' John said.

'You've only known me.'

The three of us sat round the rickety table, shovelling in the chili rather disgustingly, with tarnished spoons and hunks of bread. This was one reason we let Natalie come round quite a lot, because she ate like a pig too and did not try to order our disordered flat.

*

I had met John when he came with a compound tib and fib into the ward where I was a staff nurse. After he was discharged we kept in touch, and when his plaster was off, and I had left the hospital, we got this flat together, on the wrong side of Clapham Common.

John had been destined for the Law – by his father, not by fate – but he dropped out of university, and went to work on a building site, then learned to drive a bulldozer.

He made good money, and I was not doing too badly 'on privates', but we stayed on in the crummy little flat, because the rent was fair, and we were both trying to save.

John was an honest, rangy young man, with big joints, and a lot of coarse, sandy hair which he tied back with a rubber band when he was doing something concentrated, like bulldozing or cooking. At other times, it curtained his strongly male face. Natalie used to put it up for him with setting lotion and rollers. Sometimes he made love to her that way. Once, when she had washed her hair in our leaky bathroom, they both went to bed in metal rollers, and crashed about like Martians.

Natalie was worried about me. 'Dick is twenty-six,' she brooded, as the three of us sat round the clutter of the table, rendered lethargic by the chili, and half deafened by John's stereo in the small room. 'It's time he settled down.'

'I am settled down.'

'I mean, with a girl. Your own home.' Natalie's thoughts turned dangerously towards domestic relationships.

I had not told her about Millie. I had not even told John. One of the tragedies about tragedy is that everybody knows it. Your friends, your family, they see you differently afterwards. You are no longer just yourself. You are Dick whose girl was killed, it was awful. You are bereaved Rickie who may or may not want to talk about it, but there's no way of knowing unless he starts first. Everyone at the hospital had known about Millie. She had been in the physiotherapy school there.

When I left the hospital and set up house with John, buying towels and toasting forks like a couple of old queens in Clapham, it was an opportunity to live among people who would neither remind me of Millie nor try to help me forget her.

I did not need reminding. Nor did I need to forget. Millie was just there, at the bottom of my mind, where she had always been when she was alive.

Natalie brought in some girls, artistic and otherwise. I usually did not care whether I saw them again.

'What are we going to do with Dick?' she worried. 'What is going to happen to his life?'

*

Mr Stillman was going to be ninety in two weeks time. That was what was going to happen.

Would he make it? He could pop off at any minute, but the family intimated that it would be rather nice if I kept him going until 14 February, the magic date. Valentine's Day. Rude 'fun' cards and heart-shaped boxes of soft-centre chocolates had been appearing in the shops since New Years Day.

'Well, well, well. Ninety years old, eh? Eh, Dad?' Robert came without his wife, who saw no point in dragging all the way up from Reigate if the old man was not going to know who she was.

'Ninety years old.' Mr Stillman put on a very old voice, pushing out a loose bottom lip, and dribbling.

'Be quite a day, won't it, Dad?' Robert put a hand to his breast pocket handkerchief, thought better of it, and pushed it back. Good Nurse Hayes stepped forward with a tissue to wipe the dribbled chin. 'Quite a day.'

'I don't see why.'

When Mr Stillman did respond to any of his children, he did not make it easy for them. Not having known him when he had all his marbles, physical and mental, I could not know the whole story; but if he had always carried on like this you could see why they did not like him.

'Well, I mean – your ninetieth birthday. And all that.' Huge Robert floundered like a non-swimmer in the deep end. You wanted to put in a boathook and drag him out.

Mr Stillman pushed out stale air with a sound like pooh, and dribble came out with the air, me on hand again with the tissue.

'Of course we'll be here for it,' Robert promised. 'Gwen too, and Michael if he can get time off to come south. Dave will still be in India –'

'I was in Calcutta once.' His father closed the subject. 'I got – what did I get, Richard?'

'Dysentery?' I suggested. 'Blackwater fever?'

'That's right. Lacquer, with lizards curled round it. Kept my cigars in it for years.'

His head went heavily into the pillow. His jaw dropped. He was off.

'See you on the fourteenth then,' Robert told me outside the bedroom, as his weight took him thankfully down the stairs. 'We'll be there for the great day.'

'How nice.'

*

Marion came up from mud country with a panting spaniel with burrs in its coat. She brought it into the bedroom, where it drank all the water in the bowl set by the gas fire to keep the air moist, and woke Mr Stillman by licking the fingers that hung over the side of the bed.

'Who's that?' He pulled up the hand quickly.

'It's Marion, Daddy.'

His father examined the hand for traces of her.

'So you're going to be ninety.' She settled herself by the bed like a hen settling on eggs, and beamed at him. 'We're all so proud of you.'

'Why?'

But you cannot stop people being proud of old age, their own or other people's.

Isn't she a marvel? If she goes on like this, the Queen will send her a telegram.

Yes, my boy. Four score and ten summers I've seen. Something to boast of, eh?

We're all so proud of Daddy. Ninety years old, what do you think of that?

Not much if, at the end, the spirit is trapped in a body that hangs on when it would really prefer to be dead.

In America, they can keep you alive for ever. You have no choice. They catch you moribund, halfway to freedom, and hook you up to machines, and feed you and empty you artificially, and if you are a famous old relic, like a general or an ex-president, they broadcast solemnly stumbling bulletins (doctors are not very good at reading aloud) boasting that they will not let you die in peace.

Marion had brought lambs' kidneys and purple broccoli and 'the little pork pies he loves from our local butcher'. Lucky old Parkers.

She would bake a chocolate cake for his birthday. 'You always liked that. I said, you always liked that, Daddy.'

'He always liked that,' she told me, getting no luck from the bed.

The old man became *compos* again as she was leaving. He often revived when the noise moved away from the bed towards the door. Marion turned back and bent to kiss him in a smother of tweed and warm wool and comfortable furry cheeks.

'I'll see you on your birthday, dear.'

'You will come?' He looked up at her with the eyes of her dog. He liked her the best of his children, and they had all carried on so about his birthday that he was beginning to attach some importance to it himself.

'You know I will.'

As she went downstairs, with the dog flopping ahead on fringed paws, she put the cuff of her jersey up to the corner of her eye. It was the nicest scene I had witnessed on this job.

In the hall, while she was telling Mrs Parker how to cook the kidneys in sherry, the dog lifted its leg on the varnished banister post at the bottom of the stairs.

'And you bring it just to the boil and simmer –'

'Your dog made pee-pee on my newel post,' Mrs Parker interrupted.

'Oh, he never would. Come here, Wallace.'

'Well, someone did.' Mrs Parker went to get a pail and sponge, and Marion got out before she came back.

*

Phyllis Runyon had come with a man, the saturnine type, sexy and hollow-bellied, with a sharp-toothed smile that stood him in good stead when he was not sure what to say.

'You remember Malcolm, don't you? Daddy, you remember Malcolm.'

Mr Stillman was sitting in the chair that day. When I told him that Phyllis was there he had said, 'I want to get up', and kept her waiting almost an hour while he fiddled and fussed and wanted the pillows repacked, and wanted his other slippers, and wanted his finger nails cut before he would let me bring her in.

With private patients like that, it is no good trying to hurry them, or jolly them out of whims and wants. You may think you've won, but they get their own back by messing the bed five minutes after you've cleaned them up.

When I finally went down to Phyllis, she and Malcolm were in the study. Looking for the will? They had found some sherry somewhere and were reading Mr Stillman's collected works from the *Reader's Digest*.

I thought Phyllis would be angry about the wait but she was quite relaxed.

'Oh, look at him. How good to see you sitting up. You look like your old self.' No compliment to the old self. 'Come in, Malc, it's all right. You remember Malcolm, don't you? Daddy, you remember Malcolm.'

If Mr Stillman's old self remembered Malcolm, his present self was not going to let on.

Phyllis at first did not bother to introduce me, then as an afterthought, she did, with the slightly amused air of someone carefully introducing the plumber, or a child at a cocktail party.

'Richard Haynes. Oh sorry – Baines.' Not worth correcting her, as long as the lawyer spelled my name Hayes on my cheques.

I held out my clean, capable hand. Malcolm held out his lean brown one, and lifted the familiar eyebrows. A male nurse could be six foot two with the physique of a boxer and a jaw like a glacial boulder, and the eyebrow would still go up.

'My father is going to be ninety,' Phyllis told Malcolm, who pulled back his lips from his filed teeth and made suitable congratulating noises.

'What shall we do for your next birthday, Daddy?' Phyllis asked gaily, sitting on the rug near his feet with a graceful swooping movement that exposed the broken veins inside her thin knees.

The old man stared down at her. His fingers moved restlessly across the blanket that swaddled his legs.

'Champagne?' Good God, she had on false eyelashes. No, she didn't. They were her own sizeable ones, lavishly touched up. 'I'll bring champagne, and we'll all get sloshed. Richard too –' *Thank you, madam* – 'like we did that New Year's Eve at Basingstoke, remember?'

Mr Stillman said, 'No,' meaning either that he did not remember, or that he and Phyllis had never got sloshed in Basingstoke, or anywhere else.

But she continued to try, I give her credit for that, even after Mr Stillman began to nod, and I had to stand behind him with a hand on his shoulder to keep him from falling into the gas fire.

His eyes were closed.

'Shall we go?' she mouthed at Malcolm.

'All right.'

He had been standing at ease by the door, with his stomach sucked in and his arms crossed. He nodded at me and got out of the room, missing the rifle cracks of Phyllis's knees as she stood up.

She saw the postcard from Australia on the bedside table. As she picked it up Mr Stillman jerked upright with a cavernous snore, and opened his eyes.

'A card from Fanny. That's more than I got. What does she say?'

'Give that to me.' He was going to cry.

Phyllis shrugged and gave him the card, and he pushed it behind the pillows at his back, like a squirrel hiding nuts.

He seemed to set store by this Fanny. When Mrs Runyon had gone, I asked him, as I had before, who Fanny was.

He shook his head. When I got him back to bed, the postcard fell to the floor and he did not notice.

*

'Who is Fanny?' I asked Mrs Parker, after I had fed Mr Stillman some liquid supper and settled him for the night.

'Mrs Runyon's daughter.' Mrs Parker always saw me through the door, in case I tried to get away with an ashtray. 'His granddaughter.'

'His favourite?'

'I don't know. He doesn't like any of them. Not since I've been here, anyway.'

'What's she doing in Australia?'

'I don't know.' She always said that, and then told you. 'She went out there with some people to make a film. She's in what they call the Medium.'

'An actress?'

'I don't know. She wouldn't be that. Too skinny. Like her mother. No legs at all. Not a candle to my niece, the one who's a dancer. You should see my niece.'

Perhaps I had. I thought there had been a girl round that white cloth, going at the chicken and cider, although the dancer's calves would have been under the table.

4

Mr Stillman's birthday drew near and it seemed that he might make it. Cards began to come in from people he had never heard of, although they were signed, 'Your loving niece Alicia and all of us at Kyle of Lochalsh', and, 'From all your friends at Butter's, remembering the good old days'.

The Major came up the hill when the wind was fair and Mr Stillman told him, 'I'll be ninety next Friday,' with a pride he would not reveal to his children.

'You're older than me then, Robbie.' It made the Major's day. 'Only eighty-eight,' he told me.

'A mere boy, sir.'

He was pleased with that. 'A mere boy, eh? A mere boy.' He repeated it on the landing, clapped my shoulder, lost his balance, reeled off the wall, and asked me to lend him a pound to buy half a bottle of Haig for Mr Stillman's birthday.

He never seemed to have any pension money, or social security or anything.

'They take it away and lock it up,' he said. 'Buy cars with it. You should see the cars the staff have outside that place. Asked one of 'em to give me a lift up here once, and she said, "Why are you going out at this time of day?" and shoved me back inside.'

Two days before the birthday Marion telephoned.

'Richard,' she said. 'A most dreadful thing has happened.'

Little Dee-Dee come a cropper over the crupper? 'I'm sorry to hear that, Mrs Sparrow.'

'They've changed the date of the Pony Club Hunter Trials. They've changed it to Thursday. Do you think my father will be terribly disappointed if I can't get up that day?'

'Well . . . he's been looking forward to it.' What did she want me to say? That he didn't care either way?

'Oh dear. I feel dreadful. I have to go, you see, to drive the horse box. Dee-Dee won't let her father do it, because he drives too fast and once the pony stepped on his own foot and cut himself.'

'I'm sorry to hear that, Mrs Sparrow.'

'Oh dear. If we get home in time – these things go on for ever – I'll try and rush up, but don't expect me. Explain to my father, will you? And I'll bring up his present as soon as I can.'

No point in telling Mr Stillman she was not coming, since he might have forgotten that she was.

*

On the great day I got him up into the chair, with his blue cardigan over his pyjamas and the new slippers that Nurse Rix had left for him, with a jolly card, when she was here on my last day off.

Mrs Parker gave him a shawl, which we put round his shoulders, I gave him a silly sort of little good luck figure of a troll, and a paperback called *Murder! A Dozen of the Ghastliest Crimes of the Twentieth Century*, with which I could read him to sleep on his good days.

This was a good day. I read him half a chapter about Neville George Clevely Heath before lunch. When Mrs Parker brought up his tray, with turtle soup and the blancmange with nine candles wobbling in it, he said, 'Let's get the food over with, before anyone comes.'

I had not the heart to tell him about Marion. I waited, hoping she might come later, in Newmarket boots, with pony slobber on the front of her suède jacket.

'When is Phyllis coming?' he had asked me several times.

'Soon, I'm sure.'

'Who was that man? Is she up to something? She's always up to something, that girl. You can't trust her.'

The telephone rang. 'Perhaps that's her.' Phyllis usually rang before she came, to see if he was asleep, or dead.

It was Phyllis.

'Richard.' Her voice was deeper and throaty. Her Malcolm voice. 'Something horrible has happened.'

'I'm sorry to hear that, Mrs Runyon.'

'I told you I was going to Portugal to see my architect. The airline muddled the booking. They booked me today, instead of Monday.'

'I'm sorry.'

'Oh, *so* am I. Will he be very disappointed?'

'He's been looking forward to it.'

'Oh don't. You make me feel terrible. But if I don't take this flight I can't get another for a week. Yes – what is it? Just a minute.'

It sounded as if she opened the door of a call box to talk to someone. I heard background noise and hollow amplified announcements. She was at the airport already, the rat.

*

So when Gwen Stillman rang a bit later to tell me that Robert had suddenly come down with flu – felled like the log of wood he was – I was not surprised.

'I'm sorry to hear that, Mrs Stillman.'

'I hope my father-in-law won't be too disappointed?'

'He's been looking forward to it.'

'Look,' she said defensively. 'He can't possibly come. I told you. He's got flu.'

*

In the afternoon I put Mr Stillman back into bed and he fell asleep after three paragraphs of Haigh and the Acid Bath. I started different stories all the time, because they were so boringly written.

When he woke he seemed to have forgotten about his birth-day and his missing children. It was sad. He did not know it was sad, but in a way that made it sadder.

Mrs Parker's cousin had fetched her in a car to play cards. I did not expect her back until the evening. Sometimes she was not back by the time I was supposed to go off duty. Once, when she was on a winning streak, Mr Parker, who worked outside London, had come home before she did.

'You still here, Nurse?' His belligerent grey hair was like iron filings. He was not used to seeing me except on Sunday after-noons.

'I don't leave until your wife gets back.'

'Well, you can go now, Nurse Hayes.' He used my name like an insult. 'I'm here.'

'I'll wait.'

'I'm here.'

What now? We had confronted each other in the hall, me slightly above him, since I was on the bottom stairs. He made fists, then shoved them in the pockets of his leather jacket, stiff and shiny, like the chairs in the study, the knitted collar and waistband stretched by the thickness of his neck and middle; he turned on a trodden heel and went back to the kitchen.

I did not know whether he thought that I would leave. I stayed, of course. When Mrs Parker came back she asked, 'What did you say to Mr Parker?'

'Nothing.'

'He doesn't like you.' She was an honest woman.

'I know.'

'Hard cheese.'

After she had gone, that day of Mr Stillman's birthday, I walked round the house. Up and down the stairs. In and out of rooms. Staring out of windows. The snow was settling light and dry on dustbin lids, on the tops of walls which divided the shoddy little gardens behind the house, on the seesaw and the branches of the tree where the swing hung. No children came out. There was nothing to look at.

In the street in front, cars slushed away the snow as fast as it fell. Women hurried home with shopping carts, with dogs, with push chairs. Children dawdled home from school, pretending the snow was deeper than it was. Twilight came down early with the thin flakes.

I made faces into the dining-room mirror. I took out a comb and parted my brown hair the other way, but it made one side longer than the other, so I put it back. I walked round the table several times. I drew out chairs and put guests into them, and pushed them back to the table. I sat down at the carver's end near the sideboard, and brought out Millie and sat her smiling at the other end.

Except for her paleness and the thick fair hair that made her small head large, I was beginning to forget what she looked like. When she was alive we had not thought about being married. After she died I began to think that we would have been.

We used to sit at the kitchen table in her house, and laugh. When her mother came in and asked, 'What's the joke? What's so funny?' we would shake our heads, laughing.

'How can you laugh,' she used to say, 'with the world in the terrible state it is? You're so babyish.' She always wanted Millie to be more grown up. 'It's so childish to giggle at nothing.' She said it to Millie, but she meant it for me. 'You didn't carry on like this when you were a child. What is the matter with you?' I was the matter, was what she meant.

But after Millie died she was very nice to me. Even in her most wretched moments, she never suggested that it might have been my fault. It was not, but since I had been with Millie when she bought that lethal gas heater it could have been suggested that it was.

Mr Stillman slept on, exhausted by his birthday. I turned on the light outside the garage for Mrs Parker, but left the hall and downstairs rooms dark. In the patchy light of the street lamps I walked restlessly about, energy going before me. I had that electric feeling of expecting something, waiting for something, seeking something just beyond my reach.

A car stopped outside the house. The door slammed. The front gate opened and shut.

Good old Marion. The Hunter Trials must have been snowed out. I turned on the hall light, and opened the door with a smile, feeling warm to this busy, good-hearted woman, because she had come to her father's birthday after all.

There was nobody there. Footprints in the snow across the front of the garage to the side steps. But Mrs Parker always came in by the front door to let me know she was back.

I stepped outside.

'Hullo?'

I could hear the bell ringing in the Parkers' flat.

'She's not back yet.' I went to the bottom of the steps. A girl was standing at the top in a white raincoat. She had black tights and boots on, but her legs looked pretty good, so I said, 'Are you Mrs Parker's niece?'

'I hope not.' The girl came down the steps. 'The house looked dark, and I saw a light up there, so I thought I'd better come in that way. Who are you?'

'I'm looking after Mr Stillman.'

'Oh,' she said. 'When they said a nurse, I thought it would be some woman.' She looked pleased, not surprised or daunted to find it was some man. 'I'm Fanny Runyon. His grand-daughter.'

'The one in Australia?'

'Yes.' She looked even more pleased that I knew. She had a pleased sort of face. Eager. The eyes curious. The mouth and jaw slightly forward, like a muzzle. Phyllis's thick eyelashes. A red scarf over dark hair. The voice quick. 'I just got back. I went to get my car and came straight here from the airport.'

She might have passed her mother going in the other direction, but I did not say so. I said, 'Your mother didn't tell me.'

'She didn't know. It *is* his birthday, isn't it? He's ninety. How is he?'

'He's been –' I put out my hand to push open the front door as I answered. The door had quietly shut itself.

Fanny laughed. I laughed too, but then I stopped. Mr Stillman was alone in the house, and might wake and call for me.

'When will Mrs Parker get back?' Fanny asked.

'Quite late sometimes, on Thursdays. Mr Parker doesn't get back till about seven.'

'Let's break in.'

We went all round the house trying windows. Mrs Parker had them all locked from the inside, except some of the upstairs ones, which could not be reached. We poked about the small

33

yard at the back, looking for a stepladder, although I knew there wasn't one – I had wandered there when it was sunny and I could not stay in the house.

Then Mr Stillman's voice. 'Richard?' I could hear him thinly through his lighted window. 'Richard, where are you?'

'Oh –' Fanny drew in a breath. 'How awful. What shall we do?'

'Break something. Coming, Mr Stillman!' I shouted up at the window, but he did not hear. He went on calling feebly.

I felt his panic. I called to him again, and a window went up in the house where the children lived. We ducked down behind the shed until the window went down again. I was cold in a thin white jacket. My hands were freezing.

I found a brick. I could not find anything to wrap it in so I began to take off my jacket.

'No.' Fanny stopped me. 'Here.' She took off the red scarf. Her thick dark hair swung short. Snow began at once to glisten on it. I wrapped the brick in the scarf and bashed at a pane in the study window, by the latch. The brick made just as much noise as it would have done without the scarf, and glass fell out with the sound of a car crash.

We ducked down again, but the neighbour's window did not go up.

'Richard?'

I shoved my hand through the glass, cutting the cushion of the thumb, fumbled clumsily with the latch, and at last got it open.

The window-sill was too high. I dragged the dustbin across the stone yard. We did not care how much noise we made. I turned it upside down – the cider bottles, ha ha – and I stood on it and squeezed through the window. I am not fat, but I only just made it. I came through like a cork, diving head first on to a leather chair. Fanny came after me before I got to the door.

'Your hand –'

I was leaving a trail of blood, but there was going to be so much to explain to Mrs Parker that a few bloodstains would not matter. I pressed my other hand on the cut and headed up the stairs.

'Richard!'

'Here I am.' I ran into the room, expecting to find him pan-
icking, the bed clothes flung about, hands and feet hanging over
the edge, fear in his eyes.

But he was lying quite relaxed and neat, one hand making
the sort of rhythmical conducting movements in the air that it
did when he was peaceful.

'I'm sorry you were calling for so long.'

'I wasn't,' he said comfortably. 'I just woke up. Who's that?'

Fanny was in the doorway, not afraid of what he would look
like, but holding her breath. He turned his head. Recognition
brightened his eyes. His empty mouth gaped in a smile. Fanny
rushed forward and knelt by the bed and put the side of her
head against his arm. His other hand went on waving gently,
making the rhythmic movements. Fanny's face was turned
against the top of the sheet, eyes closed. I saw her lips push in
and out a little, thick lashes on her bright cheek.

Usually, even if Mr Stillman did recognize a visitor, he
drifted away after they had been with him a few minutes. But
Fanny sat by the bed and talked to him in her quick voice, with
its rushing starts and breathless pauses, and he seemed to listen.

She told him about Australia. She worked for a producer of
radio features, and they had been out there for several weeks,
putting together a programme about people who had emi-
grated, got homesick, returned to England, seen that it was not
the paradise their nostalgia had shown them, and gone back to
Australia for good.

'I was there.' Mr Stillman stopped conducting. He put his
palms together on his chest, fingers up, tapping them to remember.

'You never told me. Nor did Mum.'

'She didn't know. Did she? Before I ... when I was a boy.
Make my fortune.' He gave a hiccuping laugh and went into a
small choking fit. I propped him up higher, and he said, 'I rode
a horse. They made me ride a cow. Almost killed me.'

'Oh, you are marvellous,' Fanny said. 'Isn't he marvellous?'
she asked me.

I went to the door. Mr Stillman did not say, 'You stay,
Richard,' or seek me with his eyes, so I went downstairs and
shut the study window, stuck a wad of newspaper into the hole,

picked up the broken glass, and wiped my blood off the chair. Mrs Parker would get at the Oriental with ammonia and carpet shampoo.

When I went back upstairs the old man was still talking jerkily. I had not heard him talk so much, except when he was feverish, and mumbled disconnected things.

'A hundred black horses,' he told Fanny. 'They floated flowers down the river. Father's horse. I went with him over the bridge. To the workshop. A woman was crying.'

He drifted away, muttering, his yellow chicken hand clutching the sleeve of Fanny's bright blue sweater.

'Oh, he is marvellous,' she said. 'He remembers all sorts of things I never knew about. Should I go before Mrs Parker gets back? I don't know if she likes me.'

'She thinks your legs are too thin,' I said.

She looked at them dispassionately. 'I don't think so.'

Outside the room, she said, 'Do you – look, could I bring a tape recorder? He remembers things. Imagine, his sister fainted at dances because of her corsets. He remembers Queen Victoria's jubilee. He saw her. I'd love to get some of it on tape before he . . .' She looked at me. Her eyes were not dark, as they had been outside, but a deep blue, brightened by the sweater. 'My mother said he was dying. Is he?'

When the others asked me that, not quite so bluntly, I said, 'Hard to say', and, 'Could be with you for months yet'. Now I said, 'Yes. I'm afraid so. But perhaps not quite yet. He was better with you. Much better.'

'Oh good. I'll come back as soon as I can. I do love him. I was brought up not to.' She whispered, although through the half-open door Mr Stillman was noisily asleep within his hollow skeleton. 'They never liked him. None of them . . .' Her face changed. 'Forget that.'

She went out to the car to get the toy koala bear she had brought from Australia and we put it in bed with the old man and hooked his inert arm round it.

I looked back to make sure we had not woken him and went downstairs after her.

'Oh, this house, this awful house, how could they bear it?'

She jumped down the last three steps, skidded on a rug, and

bounced into the drawing-room morgue. We began to run through the rooms. Her short pleated skirt flew out and whirled, like a child playing. We ran in and out of the rooms, pointing at things, slapping furniture, laughing, and I knew what it was I had been waiting for. The sound of laughter. It was the first time anyone had laughed in this house.

When Mrs Parker came in through the front door and stamped her rubber boots on the mat we stopped laughing.

'Did any of them come?' she asked me.

'I did,' Fanny said.

'Yes, I see.'

'I've got to go.'

'Cheer ho.' Mrs Parker shut the door behind her.

'Come and see what I did.' I put my arm round the waist of Mrs Parker's plastic mac and conveyed her into the study. She drew away from me to be angry about the window.

She saw that I did not care.

'You are not a very responsible person,' she said, 'for a nurse.'

I went upstairs to get Mr Stillman washed and ready for his soup and milk and his pills. Mrs Parker scrubbed the blood stains on the carpet before she would bring up his supper.

5

When I came on duty the next morning, the old man seemed to be all right, but Mrs Parker said he had been restless in the night.

'Had me up and down several times,' she said, 'with his bell. Wanting this, that, not knowing what he wanted. Did you give him his knock-out tablets?'

'Same amount.'

'He was excited. He chattered in the night. It was that girl excited him.'

'Fanny?'

'That's what they call her,' Mrs Parker said, as if it were an alias.

Mr Stillman was rather restless all day. He did not remember Fanny, nor that she had been there, but he seemed to remember remembering. He talked quite a bit of nonsense and, in the middle of the afternoon, he pushed himself upright and said, 'Queen Victoria was a man.'

'That was Queen Elizabeth.' Mrs Parker came in with some medicine the chemist had sent round. 'Are you at it again? Just look at your bed.' She went at him with her tidying and tweaking. She would have done well on the medical ward I was on when I was training, where Sister Purdue checked the angle of your mitred counterpane corners with a protractor. 'That's enough of that,' Mrs Parker said, not sternly. 'We don't want another circus like we had last night, do we?'

'The nights are the worst,' the old man said quite sensibly.

'You're telling me,' Mrs Parker told him.

She did look tired. She had not gone out that afternoon. I took her outside and suggested that perhaps we should talk to the family about a night nurse.

She would not hear of it.

'Are you saying I can't manage?' I knew she would say that.

*

Saturday was my day off. I went to the races with John and Natalie and another girl from the art school, whose future Natalie was worried about too. I should have gone home, but sneaky Natalie had already got the girl into the flat before she asked me to go with them, in front of the girl, so I rang my mother and said I would not be down that weekend.

She did not say, 'Why not?' or, 'What a shame'. She said 'All right, Rickie', which was one of the reasons I did go home quite often to our quiet, unchanging house.

The girl was called Sonia, pronounced Sewnya. She wore a crochet hat pulled down over her eyes and ears and kept it on going and coming, which I took as a hands-off sign. Early sun and a warming wind had melted the snow. We had a good day. Sewnya chose winners from the race card with a toothpick, and we won more than we lost. At home Natalie made lasagne and was disappointed with Sewnya for leaving after supper, and with me for not minding.

'Oh, you are all so bloody casual and *arrogant*,' Natalie stormed. She had begun to be a bit noisier of late. Bad sign. 'You don't give a damn whether you see her again or not. What the hell are girls supposed to do?'

John threw her out soon after that and he and I went down to the basement where there was a silly kind of party going on.

*

When I arrived at Warhurst Vale on Sunday, Mr Parker opened the door before my finger was off the bell, as if he had been waiting behind it.

'It won't do, you know.' He was square, with short arms hanging to the bottom of his jacket.

I got in out of the rain.

'It won't do. She's had three disturbed nights,' he said, 'and it won't do.'

'I told her I thought there should be a night –'

But he did not want to hear anything from me. He wanted to go on saying, 'It won't do', and 'It's not good enough'.

The report from Nurse Rix said something of the same sort, in more professional terms:

'*Patient rather restless during a.m. Housekeeper reported disturbed night. Appetite improved. Beef broth requested, but not obtained.*' She could not write, '*Housekeeper refused*', in case Mrs Parker read the report. '*Calves foot jelly tried, 1 oz taken.*'

Of such thrilling things are a private nurse's day made. I thought of all the hundreds of day and night reports I had written and read in hospital.

'*Admitted with multiple injuries following traffic accident. Plasma infusion commenced. Airway maintained by suction. Intermittent admin. of oxygen. Taken to theatre 1 a.m. for wiring of fractured jaw and insertion of Steinman's pin through knee to immobilize fractured lower end of femur. Returned from theatre 3 a.m. Pulse rate rose 3.30, and profuse bleeding fresh blood from mouth observed. Suction applied and airway restored. Patient returned to theatre for ligature of bleeding vessel. Blood transfusion commenced in theatre, 2nd unit running satisfactorily.*

Mr Bolger, 2 a.m. observed cyanosed, no pulse. Immediate cardiac massage commenced. Resuscitation team summoned. Resuscitation unsuccessful.

Unidentified patient with abdominal stab wounds admitted 5 a.m. For surgery 9 a.m. Mr Dryden . . .'

I used to get hospital nostalgia when I read Nurse Rix's bland reports on the marbled exercise book in which we communicated with each other without meeting.

'Calves foot jelly, 1 oz taken. Slept 1 hr in p.m. Senna pod infusion given. T.97.2 P.60 R.20 Intake 16 oz. Output 12 oz. Albumen present.'

Marion Sparrow came up with an armful of flowers, 'Like a funeral,' said Mrs Parker, who was still rather low.

I asked Marion to telephone Mr Stillman's doctor. He did not like being bothered on a Sunday. He agreed about the night nurse. Marion or I should ring the agency on Monday.

'You do it, Richard.' Capable Marion had a few phobias. Telephoning strangers was one. She had even been nervous about ringing the doctor, and he had made her more so.

That afternoon several customers for Marion's chocolate cake trod up the steps to the Parkers' rooms. I saw the niece's calves at last, like German sausages. I could hear a rumble of voices beyond the closed apartment door, no doubt discussing whether it would or would not do.

I rang the agency on Monday.

'How goes it, Richard?' Mrs Hewlett-Bye called her male nurses by their first names.

'It goes well, H.B., but we need a night nurse.'

'Hditchahd.' She had her own way of aspirating my name. 'You ask the impossible.'

'I ask it, H.B.'

'Blood from a stone.'

'It's urgent.'

'Short of coming myself . . .' She had been a Sister Hewlett for years before she married old Dr Bye, practically on his death-bed.

'If you would, I'd stay on.'

'Then you'd not need a night nurse.'

'You're stalling, H.B. Come right out and admit that not enough nurses will register with you.'

'Only ones like you who can't get jobs anywhere else.'

'Can you find us a night nurse?'

'No, Hditchahd. But I'll do my best.'

I rang some of the other agencies but with no better luck.

Mr Stillman fell asleep early and I was home before John. Natalie was making fish soup. She had moved in with us while she was looking for a flat, but she did not seem to be doing any looking.

'When are you going to look for a flat?' I asked, quite mildly, moving her dressmaking things off a chair so that I could sit down.

Natalie became enraged, with a ladle in her hand. She became enraged more often lately. When John came in while we were fighting, with clay on his boots, she shouted at him, 'And you've got clay on your boots!'

Normally he would have shouted back, or kicked her broad rear with them, but because I was having a fight with her already he took her side.

I went out. I did not want the soup anyway. I went to some married friends and had eggs and cheese, and then walked a bit in the rain, because I thought that when I went back we might get into one of those 'It's her or me' arguments.

When I got back they were in bed. John left for work before I did. Natalie sloped about in a torn grey nightdress with a sallow face and tangled hair. She did not care what she looked like for either of us, least of all for me.

'Are you going to look for a flat today?' I did not ask it until I was on the way out, but she only said, 'No,' and went on reading the paper and poking at her ears with a match.

I had thought of Fanny many times since I first met her but I did not think of her now, in contrast to Natalie. I did not imagine her there in that Clapham flat. There was no comparison.

Mrs Hewlett-Bye telephoned that morning.

'Hditchahd. I have done the impossible.'

'You always do.'

'I have a Nurse Cortland. Quite a nice girl. Though girl may be a bit of a euphemism.'

'Is she coming tonight?'

'Steady. She can't pack up and leave Nottingham at the drop of a bucket. She'll be there in a few days. I'll let you know.'

'Ta, H.B.'

'My pleasure.'

I told Mrs Parker. 'Can you hang on for a few nights?'

'If it kills me.'

She had remained fairly willing and so it was a surprise to arrive the next day and find her and Mr Parker packed up and off to a sister's house near the factory estate where he worked.

Mr Parker was grim, but flustered. Mrs Parker was calm but surprisingly meek. She was too tired now to tell him 'Hard cheese'.

'Look – you can't suddenly decide to go like this.' Mrs Parker was fussing over some string and paper bags in a drawer but I grabbed his arm and made him face me.

'Why not? I decided last Sunday.'

'Why didn't you tell me?'

'None of your business,' Mr Parker said. The taxi came, and he picked up two suitcases and carried them down, a square grizzled man with a long grey overcoat and a bitter face. Mrs Parker followed with carrier bags.

I thought that she was leaving without saying goodbye. I was watching out of the kitchen window, when she turned and came back to the side door. I opened it and she came in. She looked at me through her thick lenses. I looked at her. We had liked each other quite well, and shared the trust of the old man. I moved forward to shake hands. I might even have kissed her, but she stepped back to the door, and with a dramatic gesture, took a ring of keys out of her bag and threw them on the scrubbed counter. They lay there like a token of surrender.

'All the best,' she said.

'Thanks,' I said, 'for everything.'

'Nuff said.'

'Hill – *dur*!'

She made a face towards the brutish voice in the road, and went quickly out to it.

The first thing to do was to unlock all the cupboards in the kitchen and the door that led to the Parkers' rooms.

There was quite a lot of tinned food, fruit cake, which I ate, some wine and packets of biscuits, and a few other items which would have been 'refused' if requested.

I opened a tin of beef consommé and a packet of rusks and took them upstairs with a bottle of wine, for Mr Stillman and me to celebrate our abandoned independence.

Mrs Parker had mitred his corners and said goodbye to him, but he thought she had gone to the shops. I would not tell him that she was not coming back until he got used to somebody else.

With a glass of wine in one hand I rang the agency.

'H.B., old friend.'

'You're drunk.'

'And desperate. The housekeeper has walked out. I need someone tonight. It's a crisis.'

'I read you.' Mrs Hewlett-Bye was up on jargon. 'I'll try again. Expect nothing.'

I rang Mr Stillman's doctor but he was out.

'I'll tell him' the secretary said in a voice that meant: but it's nothing to do with me whether he does anything about it or not.

I rang Mrs Sparrow and she said, 'Oh dear. I wish I could get up. It's all so difficult.' She was supposed to be the capable one. 'Have you talked to my brother?'

'Not yet.' What use?

'Have you talked to Mrs Runyon?'

'She's in Portugal.'

'I think she gets back today.'

Phyllis was back. 'I was just on my way over,' she said at once, defensively. 'You can tell me then.'

I put away the wine bottle, rinsed my mouth with Mr Stillman's mouthwash, and ate some of his peppermints. He had enjoyed his wine, sucking it in, holding it in his mouth, and chewing on it with his gums as if it was food, before dispatching it with a convulsive swallow. He dozed. I did not ring the agency again. While I waited for Mrs Runyon it had come to me what I would tell her. Since last night's fight with Natalie

I had been dully aware of the three-sided argument that would start up again when I got back to the flat. Here was a way to avoid that, at least.

Phyllis came in a red trouser suit, hung about with brass chains and shackles, her shiny shoes banded with metal, like cash boxes. I told her about the Parkers.

She frowned. When she left for Portugal things had been static. It did not suit her to have them in flux.

'So I'll stay here at night,' I said, 'until we can get a nurse.'

'We can't let you do that, Richard.'

'You can pay me for the extra hours,' I said, to make her feel better. I suggested something less than the full rate and she felt worse.

'I never knew nurses were so expensive.'

'Look,' I said, 'Mrs Runyon. It took me five and a half years to get my SRN, including six months' staffing, and two years in MS.'

'What's that?'

'Mentally subnormal.'

'What's that got to do with it?'

'Five and a half years. A man can learn to drive a bulldozer in two months and get about twice what I do.'

'That's why we've got inflation.' She fell back on an easy slogan. 'Everyone is paid too much.'

'Except nurses.'

We had raised our voices and Mr Stillman woke and called.

Phyllis went in. '*There* you are,' she said, as if he had been away, not her. 'I'm so sorry about your birthday.'

'Birthday, what birthday?'

'You know, you were ninety, you clever old thing.' She gave him a very nice cashmere dressing-gown. He never wore it. When he sat up in the chair, he wanted his old plaid institution-type thing, with crumpled handkerchiefs and furred sweets in the pockets.

'Where did he get that?' Phyllis saw the koala bear on the chest of drawers, where I had moved it, because the fluff got up his nose.

'Your daughter brought it, Mrs Runyon.'

'Fanny? She's not back.'

'Yes, she was here.'

'I saw her.' Mr Stillman remembered.

One up to us both.

So her mother invented, 'Oh yes, that's right, she did say Wednesday.'

After she left I told Mrs Hewlett-Bye that we were all right for a while.

'You'd better be.'

I checked with Mrs Sparrow — not wanting another discussion with Phyllis about costs — and then asked Nurse Rix if she could come in the afternoons so that I could get a few hours off.

When I telephoned John, he said, being no fool, 'Are you doing this because of Nat?'

'No, because of the old man. But — look, yes in a way. I don't know. We all need a rest from each other.'

'You and me?'

'I don't know. Are you sick of sharing?'

'I don't know. Are you?'

'I don't know.'

Having agreed that we knew nothing, we laughed, and rang off. Later John came up from Clapham with some clothes and a razor and things, and we shared the rest of the wine.

He wanted to look at Mr Stillman asleep. He had the naïve curiosity of a large, simple man, like an animal exploring. He stood in the bedroom doorway with his workman's hands hanging, and his vigorous hair tied back with a piece of string, his face poked forward, sandy eyebrows raised.

'Is that all?' he said, as we went down.

'What do you mean? I haven't got one of them in every room.'

'No, but this poor old geezer. What a deadly job.'

'It's all right.'

*

It was all right.

Although I disliked that house, I increasingly enjoyed being on my own. Mr Stillman was mine. No one to interfere. No one to complain. We could eat what and when we wanted, and he liked the soups and messes I stirred up for him better than the rigid concoctions which Mrs Parker had assembled according to the directions on the packet.

He was so peaceful that first night that I wondered if the Parkers had invented the disturbed nights as an excuse to flee. I had a hot bath in a decent bathroom, instead of a tepid one in a rusty tub with plugs of Natalie's hair in the drain, and slept so well that I could almost agree with Phyllis Runyon about being overpaid.

One of the keys Mrs Parker had surrendered opened the drawer where she had left the rest of the month's housekeeping money. When Nurse Rix came next day, brisk and on time, with teeth you could see your face in, I walked up to the High Street and bought some food and another bottle of wine.

When I came out of the shop, the sun had burst free of the low-moving clouds, so I went on up to the Heath, hid the shopping bag under a bush, and ran. It was cold, and the only people about were fanatics and dog walkers. If I met someone I ran with my fists clenched, elbows pumping, feet steady, like a training athlete. Otherwise I just ran about, jumping down banks and over ditches, tearing across open spaces above the sluggish haze of London, lying below the wind.

I had bought some steak. Quite a lot of steak. All day I had thought that Fanny would come today, and she did.

I was upstairs with Mr Stillman when I heard her voice.

'Mrs Parker!'

I went down.

Fanny was in slacks and a bulky white sweater, small breasts, small hips, lipstick too bright. Or was that what they were wearing now, in the Medium?

'Where's Mrs Parker?'

I told her.

'I thought it was odd,' she said. 'Kitchen light on. Side door unlocked. Dishes in the sink.' Mrs Parker always put everything away, and scoured and bleached as if the kitchen were never to be used again. 'Food all over the place. Wine. Steak.' She looked at the good juicy meat waiting on a plate. 'A lot of steak.'

'Stay and cook it?'

'Oh good.' She struggled out of the top sweater, and another one under it, as far as a red polo neck. Later, when I went in her car, I found out why she was always in layers. It was an old Triumph with a draughty top, the back window broken and patched with tape.

'How's my grandfather?' she asked. 'I couldn't come before. We've started work on the Australian tapes and I went to the country to see my father. Can I talk to him? Is he all right?'

'Yes. He's had a little wine.'

'That's funny. He would never drink anything. At least, not as long as I remember. He must have gone back to his looser days. He was very tight and stern, you know.' She started to pick at some of the salad things I had bought. 'Did you know that?'

'I don't really know anything about him.'

'That's what's so odd, isn't it? I mean, here you are, tied to him so closely at the most crucial time of his life. So – so intimate with him, and yet you don't know anything about him at all.'

'I don't need to.'

I had learned that, on an earlier case. A man I had looked after had told me something terrible, perfectly horrible. Something he had done, for which someone else had been blamed. When he was very ill, and dependent on me, he had confessed this to me, as if I were a priest. He wanted me somehow to make it all right for him after he died.

'You've got to tell them for me,' he said. 'You've got to make it all right.'

Then he did not die. The growth of the cancer cells was arrested. One of those strange reverses which can be called a miracle, for want of a more technical explanation. He got better. He left the hospital, and there he was with me knowing. He wrote me a threatening letter but I would never have told, even if he had died. Especially if he had died. The death of a patient is the final sealing of the secrets with which they entrust you.

I thought of all that in the space of time it took Fanny's small teeth to bite into a radish, and then she said, 'That's why none of them liked him. Not only because he was too strict with

47

them. They forgot that after they were free. But because he went on being too hard on my grandmother. He made her unhappy, they said.'

'Is that why she got so fat?'

'You've seen? Yes. She went to pieces and ate all the time, and later she got on the bottle. That's why he got off it. But I'm glad he's on again. I never knew much about him. I hardly ever saw him. My mother wouldn't let me. I only, sort of – discovered him last year, when he'd been so ill and was in hospital for ages. I discovered him in the hospital. I went there once, and he was so alone, in a room like a green box, very grumpy. So I took him some books. Mysteries and thrillers, they were all he'd read. Then I used to come and see him here. He didn't talk much, but he liked me all right, I think.'

She took the tape recorder upstairs, and set it up so that the microphone could pick up his fluctuating voice.

I propped him higher to make talking easier, and he said, 'I want to get up.'

'It's a bit late.'

'I want to sit up and talk to her.'

'All right.' It didn't matter. He could sit up all night and sleep all day if he wanted.

I brought the new dressing-gown. 'Fortnum and Mason.' Fanny looked inside the collar. 'Pity she didn't do this sort of thing for him when he was – I mean, when he could have enjoyed it.' He pushed it aside impatiently and groped about for his old plaid relic on the chair by the bed.

We got him up. Fanny was very good with him. Jokey but gentle, and no baby-talk. He sat in the armchair, quite bright-eyed, with a medicine glass of wine at his elbow, Fanny opposite him with a wine glass, and the microphone on a little table between them.

It was surprising what he remembered, with Fanny's help. He could remember nothing of what happened yesterday, or the weeks, months, years before that. He not only did not re-alize that Mrs Parker had gone longer and farther than to the shops. Because he did not see her, he did not remember that she had ever been there. He did not remember Nurse Rix until she was there with her teeth and her, 'Now, what's to be done here, eh?' Had he already forgotten me that afternoon while I was gambolling about on the Heath?

But Fanny led him eagerly back through cloudy images and brief bright patches to glimpses of childhood. He remembered having his tonsils out on the kitchen table. A pair of silk trousers. His father coming home drunk to say that they were ruined. But there were servants always, and a woman called Mossie who took him to London on a train.

'Come on,' Fanny encouraged him, when he stopped, and looked past her vaguely. 'Come on, tell me what London was like. Were there any cars?'

'Yes. Cars. No. Were there? We went on a bus. I can smell it now.' He sniffed. 'No, I can't. Two boys ran away with my hat.' Memory came in snatches. 'Bands on the streets. Yes, the old Queen. Ha, ha.' He laughed, short and dry. 'In black. Very cross.'

Victor Ross, the producer for whom Fanny worked, was letting her experiment with tapes for short programmes.

'If I can get enough good stuff together,' she told me, when Mr Stillman dropped off with his eyes and mouth open, 'Victor and I may produce it as a series. Slices of life. Not special people. Real ones. I just get them to talk. Ramble on. It takes ages sometimes. They dither away in clichés for hours before they say anything alive or interesting. Then I edit and do a sort of background narrative, with the people coming alive through their own words. This will be "Me and Victoria". You'll be famous, Grandpa,' she said loudly, to wake him up. 'Everyone will know you saw the Queen.'

'I didn't. We had mutton for dinner. I don't know.' Mr Stillman's motor ran down. We put him back to bed, and Fanny went down to start the steak.

He was excited and restless. I left my steak three times to go to him. Finally Fanny brought the plates upstairs and we ate on the floor outside the bedroom.

Even with his Seconal he was restless all night. He tossed and mumbled and kept waking and sitting up right out of sleep, like Lazarus. He got very tired and breathless. I did not go to the convex bed next door, with the wooden pillows and intimidating urns on the headboard. I stayed in the room with him.

When Mrs Sparrow came up – with the spaniel, since there was no Mrs Parker – her father was still rather jumpy and excitable, his fingers tattooing the small mound on his slack stomach under the bedspread. She had insisted that I talk to his doctor.

I telephoned from the study, with the door open. Professional discretion, but no conspiracy.

'Do you need me? I'm up to my eyes.'

'I don't think so. Not really.'

You often have to protect a busy doctor from the family. He will come if the nurse insists, so the nurse does not insist for nothing.

'He'll come if there's any change.'

Marion was in the hall, making an anxious face under a green jersey turban. 'You'll be sure to let him know,' she fretted, as if a bit of worry at the end could compensate for years of indifference.

'Of course.'

'Thank you, Richard.'

'Thank you, Mrs Sparrow.'

Her dog favoured the banister post again and I forgot to wipe it up.

Phyllis Runyon came when Mr Stillman was awake but deep in his mind and unaware.

'Why won't he talk to me? Fanny told me he'd been talking a lot to her. What's he been telling her?' she asked suspiciously.

'About the old days.'

'That's what she said. She thinks she can make a programme out of it, or some such thing.'

'She's making tapes.'

'But I mean,' said Mrs Runyon dismissively, 'who would listen?'

*

With Mrs Parker gone, and her mops and brushes static, and her noisy vacuum cleaner silenced at last, the house began to deteriorate quite quickly. The polish dulled in the damp days. Rugs stayed askew. The kitchen was a comfortable mess. There was a stain on the hall floor where I had forgotten to expunge

Marion's dog. A light film began to appear on ledges and table tops. Now, when Mr Stillman slept and I roamed through the house, I could trail a finger in the dust.

When Fanny came on Sunday she lit a fire in the dining-room. It smoked before we found out that the damper was shut, and she wrote on the dusty table top, 'Stephanie Runyon is a girl.'

'Is that your name?'

'It was.'

'Are you married?' I asked, although I knew she was not. She would have told me.

'*Married?*' She laughed. She laughed often, any time there was a chance. Not vacantly, or silly giggling. She liked to laugh, curving her long red mouth and contracting her diaphragm. 'I meant, they christened me Stephanie, and then never called me that.'

'I was Eric and they called me Rickie. So people call me Richard, or Richie or Dick.'

'What shall I?'

I shrugged. It did not matter. 'My last patient called me Dixie. They make the nurse into a sort of joke sometimes. They don't quite know what to make of the intimate stranger relationship, so they make it a nice safe joke.'

'Intimate stranger.' Fanny was alert. 'That's good. Can I try you on tape some time?'

She was always wanting to get people on tape. Me, Mr Stillman, the man at the delicatessen where she bought our lunch. When the Major came crabwise up the Vale, going dot and carry because he had hurt his ankle in a swing door, she wanted to tape him too, but he would not have it.

'Too risky.' He sat down in the hall to wink and jerk, the knee of his good leg going up and down in ragtime. 'If they got hold of that at the Turrets I'm done for.'

He had gone to the kitchen there to help carry trays for the immobile members, and the cook had shut the door on his ankle. Deliberately. With Fanny, a new audience, watching him bright-eyed, he elaborated on this theme, until Mr Stillman heard his voice and called out, 'Who's there?'

Fanny and I helped the Major up the stairs, two feet on every step, panting and grunting and throwing us watery, despairing looks across his monumental nose.

'Hullo, Robbie.'

'Hullo, Rags.'

'Missed your birthday.'

'Did you?'

The Major sat down and slapped vaguely around his pockets. 'I was going to buy you something, but they took all my money.'

I took off his boot and his sock, and we inspected his bluish-purple ankle with clucks of sympathy, although it looked no worse than his other extremities. I rubbed it with surgical spirit and put on a crêpe bandage, which pleased him, but he worried, 'They'll kill me when they see it.'

'Say you put it on yourself,' Fanny said.

He shook his head, jerking it so hard that it nearly flew off over his shoulder. 'They know I couldn't bend that far.'

'Say the chemist put it on.'

'All right my dear.'

He and Mr Stillman had a bit of a chat. 'The time of life. Nora said. That was the way of it.'

They did not put each other to sleep. Mr Stillman was quite bright today. He had a slight fever, I thought, but he did not want me to take his temperature, so I recorded his quick light pulse, and left it at that. In hospital, I would have had to take his temperature if he was dying. That was another reason I liked being on my own.

The Major was in better muster too. He did not limp any more, and when Fanny said she would take him home in the Triumph, he said, 'Oh, hot dog.' We shoe-horned him into the low little car and he drove away with his long woollen muffler waving in the draught like Isadora Duncan.

'He made me put him out at the corner,' Fanny reported. 'And when he got within view of the place, he limped.'

Nurse Rix did not come on Sundays. We got the old man up for a bit more Victoriana, and he stayed up for supper at the table by the fire. He did not want any supper, but he wanted not to have it at the table, rather than in bed.

He had a little wine, and talked a bit, but rambling. Fanny was going to have to edit brilliantly, or her mother would be right. Who'd listen? But she kept telling him that he was marvellous, and feeding him little bird-sips of wine, and I think he did get the idea that he was being special, perhaps even that he was being loved.

It was quite late when I settled him back in bed. I had sat up in the room with him the last two nights. I was tired, so Fanny said that she would stay the night and relieve me at half time.

She went to bed in the cold room that used to be her mother's and at ten minutes after two Mr Stillman died. He died while I was looking at him. He was doing his pseudo Cheyne-Stokes breathing, with long pauses between snoring breaths which sometimes choked him awake. This time he just failed to take the shuddering breath.

I went to tell Fanny. She came out of her mother's room barefoot, with her clothes and hair tidy, as if she had not been to sleep.

'He died,' I said.

'Oh –' She took in a breath. She had told me that it would be stupid to cry, but she did cry anyway, until she went in to see the old man, and then she stopped, as people do. The surprise of your first dead body is that it is just that. A body. A box, a container, a shell. A most heartening thing to realize so clearly that whatever made this human being unique had nothing to do with death.

*

She cried again later when grey dawn silted down the uncaring trough of Warhurst Vale and found us both at breakfast in the kitchen, looking crumpled and plain, and older than our years.

'Don't say no, because it's true. I killed him.' She would have liked to find some way of making that less dramatically egotistic, but there wasn't one. 'I got him excited. I killed him. It was too much for him, making him talk.'

'Perhaps. But it made him happier. He lived a bit.'

'He died.'

The tape recorder was on the cluttered counter, with her bag and notebook and the grapes she had forgotten to give him. Crying, she pulled the tape out of the machine, lit some newspaper in the dining-room fireplace, and watched the tape flare and melt, with her arm along the mantelpiece and her forehead on her arm.

*

After the undertaker had removed the old man, I was clearing up the bedroom when I heard someone open the front door. Phyllis and Marion and Robert had all been in for rueful viewing. I went to the top of the stairs and saw Mrs Parker looking round the hall with an eye for dust and lack of lustre.

'What's going on?' she asked.

'Nothing. Mr Stillman is dead.'

'Hard Cheddar,' she said. 'I knew I shouldn't have gone.'

*

I went back to the flat in Clapham and found Natalie away, and John pleased to see me, and I him. Fanny rang me that night and asked me to go to her grandfather's funeral with her.

'I don't know,' I said. 'I don't think they –'

'Please come.'

'All right.'

She met me at a tube station and took me in the gusty car to the crematorium chapel in the suit I wore for getting jobs, conventional and slightly out of style, but you could take me anywhere.

When we arrived her mother was there with Fanny's father. He had Fanny's eyes, very blue under white hair, a chance combination that somehow looked contrived. Phyllis took Fanny's arm, and she had to sit at the front with them. I sat at the back. There were several people, none of whom had visited Mr Stillman while I was there.

Afterwards I waited outside to see if Fanny would be able to leave with me. She was standing by one of the big black cars, talking to some elderly people inside.

'Who's that?' I heard a woman ask Robert.

'Where?' He turned, met my eye, but did not recognize me in the suit.

'Who – oh yes.' He gave me one of his blank nods, and turned back to say something to the woman.

'The nurse?' She took another look to see if I was queer.

6

When I told my father I was going to be a nurse, he said, 'A what?'

I was nineteen. My childhood had passed in a kind of dream. I had never been good at anything, work, games, acting, music, art. I never finished anything. My end of the garage workbench was littered with abandoned projects. Dried-out paint sets, broken ship models, one bookend, and the wreckage of a fretted pipe rack that fell apart as soon as I laid a varnish brush on it. I did not know anyone who smoked a pipe, but when Mr Begley, with sawdust in the ends of his sad moustache, asked me what I would like to make, I said, 'A pipe rack'.

He did not nag at me to produce the finished article, any more than other teachers nagged me about homework. They had all given up, I think. My father thought I was my mother's job, since she was the one who had suddenly produced a baby, ten years after her first, with the small clothes given away and the pram wheels rusted. She understood about starting things. Her drawers were stuffed with unfinished knitting still on the needles, dresses cut out with the patterns still pinned to them, and peaceably abandoned, as if that was all you needed to do to make a dress.

My friends were peaceful too, and undemanding. My brother called us the Dream Club. We wandered about, poking at things in hedgerows and ponds, and sat against the roots of the big tree in the middle of the village, watching the slow life with slow eyes, like old men.

I was good at nothing, but content. And so my parents granted me their biggest favour. They left me alone.

'Leave him alone,' they would say, when my brother came home from college, bored with us in the first five minutes, and grumbled, 'What are you going to do with this boy?'

'Leave him alone. He'll be all right.'

'When?' My brother was not happy being busy and ambitious and overworked. I had no right to be happy doing nothing.

'In his own time.'

I left school with none of the right credits and drifted into a sort of technical college, which seemed easier than going to work. I could have boarded, but I chose the long train journey and lived at home, although my brother fretted, 'He should be got out of the house', like a smell of cats.

My father was an industrial chemist. My mother was secretary to a man much younger than herself who made small parts for something. It was not a very good job, but she liked the people, and the view of the river from her office window. And as we had always done, we all three came confidently home to each other in the evenings.

That was what I missed most when I first went away from that quiet house. Later, when I started to read and discover other people's ideas, Millie and I shared that poem by Belloc which starts, 'From quiet homes and first beginning . . .'

It was like that.

I studied engineering at the technical school but did not understand much of what we learned. The dreams of childhood had clogged and clouded into a sort of ground fog which protected me from the harsher realities of life. Knowing that I would never pass any exams the Principal threw me out, but kindly.

'What shall I do?'

'You could train to be a nurse.'

I thought I had heard wrong.

'Nursing. A fine profession. You could get into Greengates.'

'Greengates?' It was a huge place over the hill that we knew as the nut factory. 'Why?'

'Because it's about the only place you could get into,' he told me in his kindly way.

'Guess what happened today?' I said, when we came together at supper.

'What, Rickie?' My mother began to smile for one of the fables I used to construct for her out of things that had or had not happened.

'Today I got thrown out of the college.'

'Oh dear.'

'Mr Vance said I should go to Greengates.'

'Oh look.' My father put down his knife and fork. 'It's not as bad as that, surely?'

'Not as an inmate, Dad. I'm going to be a nurse.'

'A what?'

*

At Greengates the fog cleared. It got me out of the house, and it got me out of the dream. From that first morning when the head nurse took me round, and a horde of adolescent boys came charging at me across a stretch of grass yelling, 'Mithtah!', I was shocked into reality.

The boys called everybody Mithtah. They yelled at you, and you yelled back. It was the only way to be heard above the racket. Some of them could be given some education. Some could be given hardly anything but total custodial care. With endless patience a few of those might be trained to sit down when told, dress and feed themselves, and not mess in their pants. But if the training was stopped for lack of time and staff, they would revert to squatting in corners, and standing on the table kicking greasy plates into people's laps.

Most of the nursing students were older than I was, ex-service a lot of them, some of them drifters like me who had come to Greengates in an unambitious fog. The days of asylum brutality were over, but when you struggled those long hours with the mess and boredom of it, and the illogical aggression of psychopaths, inevitably people cracked.

'Mithtah! Mithtah! Lenny's doing 'is nut!'

'Get George.'

Some of the men and large boys like fighting Lenny could only be controlled with a shove in the chest, or even a crack on the jaw, which ex-Marine George did not think twice about dealing out.

The students like George and the drifters drifted out of Greengates. I was the only one of that class who stayed the three years and got my MS.

They wanted me to stay. With patients coming in faster than they went out, dead or alive, they were chronically short of trained staff. I might have got stuck there, married, had a house in the grounds, and become as institutionalized, quirky and lost to civilization as the inmates.

My brother had been saying for some time, 'He's crazier than the patients', and there were times when I thought I was. And I was getting hard. Things were not funny any more. Feeling was disappearing to wherever the dream had gone. Sometimes it was not Corporal George RM who dealt out the crack on the jaw. It was Nurse Richard Hayes, RMSN, and no guilt feelings.

I did two years of general training for my State Registered badge, then staffing, and a Charge Nurse job at the hospital where I met Millie.

Less than two thousand pounds a year, Phyllis Runyon, in case you think Charge Nurses get too much of your money. But that was not the only reason why I got out and into private nursing. It was Millie. I did not want to be there without her, or in any hospital.

I would have told Fanny some of this if we had started putting the 'intimate stranger' talk into her tape recorder. But she never got any of it on tape because Mr Stillman died and I left Warhurst Vale for ever.

7

'Mr Hayes?' It was a doctor I had worked for before. 'I've got a surgery patient at the Alexandria who needs a special. Are you free?'

'For about a week.' I had another case booked, a mongoloid boy whose mother was going away.

'That should do it. Partial gastrectomy, quite straightforward. Just a – just a spot of trouble.'

'Infection?'

'No, with the – er, with the nurses, I mean.'

'What kind of trouble, Dr Ballentine?' I felt cagey.

'Will you take the case?' He felt cagey too.

'All right.' I had been sitting around for three or four days waiting for Fanny to telephone and say, 'Let's go to India. Let's go to the cinema. Let's go and do something marvellous.' If she was not going to, I might as well get back on the job. I had not meant to be lured back into hospital, but the Alexandria in a riverside suburb was small and easy going, not like the high-powered, ordered imbroglio of the Essex. 'What's the trouble?'

'You'll see.'

*

I saw.

Walter Pomfret was a heavy, jowly man, with coarse eyebrows specially cultivated to beetle. He was weathering the operation well, but he did not care to hear that.

He liked it best if I said, 'My God, you look rough, Mr P. Must have been a wild night.'

'You'll never know.' He groaned like a loaded bedspring. 'I pealed that bloody bell and nobody came. You could die in this rotten hole for all the buggers care. When I did drop off for a moment, that bitch who barges round with that bloody great torch comes charging in and shines it right in me face.'

The face was spread broad and disgruntled against the pillow, eyes baleful under the brows, mouth set with vertical straight lines at the corners, like a post and rail fence.

Each morning when I came in, I stood at the end of the bed and let him rave at me.

'Worst night of me life. How can a man live without sleep? They get you in here and carve you up, then starve you of food and sleep until you lose your mind. This place is a flaming scandal. I'm writing to the Minister. Tell Ballentine I want to see him. Get Wrigley. I want you to get Wrigley here. That bloody butcher – agh!' He clapped his hand to his incision as if he were being bayoneted. 'It's killing me. I've been in agony all night.' And so on and so on.

I had looked at the night nurse's report on the way in. '*Good night . . . Slept well for long periods.*'

The nurses, all glad to see me except one wide probationer, who elbowed and hipped me bossily about in the kitchen and sluice, had told me that Mr Pomfret had given trouble ever since he came in, before his operation. He complained about the room, the food, the noise, the bed, the staff. Even when he was still mobile, he had rung his bell constantly, shouted if it was not answered at once, and stormed up and down the corridor in orange pyjamas, terrifying an Indian cleaning lady who took the lift to another floor and never came back.

After he lost half his stomach he was worse than ever. At first, he insisted that he had not been operated on, a common delusion after anaesthesia. He tore off the dressings to check, did not like the size of the wound, demanded to see the surgeon who had gone away for the weekend, and pulled out the needle of his intravenous drip.

When I went in on my first morning, he had just pulled it out again. The houseman and a Bahamian nurse were preparing to replace it. The arm was taped to a splint but the other was waving about with the fist clenched.

'Hang on to his arm,' the houseman told me, without looking up.

'Who are *you*?' Mr Pomfret looked at me. I held down the arm and looked at him, and we exchanged battle messages, like stallions.

'Your special.'

'I don't want you.'

'Dr Ballentine –'

'Ballentine's an incompetent fool. Agh!'

The needle slipped easily into a nice firm vein and he yelled as if he were being torn apart by wolves. I held him more firmly.

'Let go of me.'

'Just a minute, Mr Pomfret.'

'Don't worry.' The Bahamian nurse gave him her wonderful white smile. 'Everything is going to be all right.'

That sort of talk enraged him. He liked everything all wrong, with himself prime victim.

'Let me go,' he snarled at me, 'you long-haired sadist.'

Natalie, with a pursed mouth and her dressmaking scissors, had just trimmed my hair, which I had let grow a bit at Mr Stillman's.

When the needle and tubing were taped and the nurse had the saline drip adjusted, I eased up on Mr Pomfret's brawny arm and grabbed it again just in time as he swung it over to try to pull out the needle again.

'Mr Pomfret.' The houseman was nervous of him, so he raised his voice, for authority. 'We'll have to tie down that other hand if you won't keep still.'

'Get Wrigley,' he told me, ignoring the young houseman. 'I've got to see Wrigley.'

'Mr Wrigley will be in to see you on Tuesday,' the Bahamian nurse said.

'I'll be dead by then.'

'Good,' the houseman muttered to the nurse, as she picked up the intravenous tray.

'Why is she grinning like that?'

'It's her natural face, sir.'

'I don't want it in here.'

'Don't worry,' said the nurse, and went out.

'I don't know that I want you either.' Sprawled on his broad back, one hefty hand splinted and the other clutching the edge of the bed, Mr Pomfret beetled at me. 'But at least you're white.'

That had been part of the trouble. When he declared the first day that he would not be nursed by wogs and chinks, he got a tongue-lashing from the Sister, who advised him to take himself out of the Alexandria and his ulcers with him. Dr Ballentine, who wanted to get the operation done with, and Mr Pomfret and his ulcers out of his curly grey hair, had won her over with the promise of a special nurse. Mr Pomfret had not agreed to that but his wife had.

He was not going to give in without a struggle.

'You're too young,' he grumbled.

'I'm older than I look.'

'Your hair's too long.'

'I've just had it cut.'

'Thank God I didn't see you before.' Weak as he was, he could keep up this kind of repartee indefinitely, like breathing.

He felt rotten. He was in pain. He had probably had grey nagging pain for years with the kind of sour temper that grows along with ulcers. His surgeon was off playing golf. He would not see his doctor until tomorrow. He was a stranger in the strange world of hospital, where everyone knows what's going on except the patient.

But when he added malevolently, 'I don't think I like you,' some lucky, unprofessional instinct made me reply, 'I don't think I like you much either.'

He did not smile. I never saw him smile until the end of the week when he said goodbye and gave me a five-pound tip. But he did let go. He let the anger go out of him on a breath, sagged a bit into the bed and said feebly, like a normal sick person, 'I'm very uncomfortable.'

I got a nurse in to help me lift him, and rubbed his back and changed his hospital jacket for a pyjama top; I made his bed smooth and gave him his injection, and soon he was asleep.

He woke with a bellow of pain and started to thrash about. I checked the drip and put my hand over the taped needle.

'Get that bloody thing out of my arm.'

'Not yet.'

'Get that spotty young man back who put it in.'

'He'll see you this evening.'

'I want him now.'

'He's off duty,' I intervened.

When I tried him on some diluted milk and glucose, he knocked the glass out of my hand. I brought some more.

'How can I drink when vultures are tearing my guts out?'

'Sip just a little. It will help.'

He knocked the glass out of my hand again. He called me a clumsy fool. I called him a stinker and he drank a few swallows of the milk and glucose.

By evening I had managed to make him realize that if he would drink his prescribed amounts we would be able to take down the saline drip tomorrow. He began to take fluids suspiciously – 'What's this filth?' – and even a little arrowroot – 'What's this muck?'

When his wife came in he was fairly docile.

'What have you done to him?' She was not a cowed victim, but a composed lady with an amused tolerance for the monster with whom she had chosen to live. 'Dr Ballentine told me he was giving a lot of trouble,' she told me. 'What did you do?'

'I gave it back to him.'

I offered it to her as a joke but she said seriously, 'Yes, that's what I do.'

'Well.' Mr Pomfret had been glowering quietly at her since she came into the room, with the health and fresh air that visitors bring, as if from another planet. 'You've done it now. You and Ballentine. You've got what you wanted.' He talked like a character in an old Orson Welles film.

'You agreed to the operation.'

'You made me.'

'It had to be done, Wally –'

'They all say that.' He made that ugly sign with the fingertips that means money.

'– and Mr Wrigley is very satisfied.'

'He's not lying here with red-eyed rats eating out his innards.'

'Poor Wally.' His wife sat down beside him and put her too fine hand over his coarse one. 'You've been marvellous really. It's a horrible thing to go through. I'm so sorry for you,' she said very kindly.

He pulled back his hand and turned away his head. 'Your breath smells,' he told her.

*

He was a stinker all right, but his wife had grown used to him and I did too.

In the mornings, I would stand impassively at the foot of the bed and let him blast off complaints at my inscrutable face.

I left the door ajar so that passing nurses could pause on their busy morning way to listen to the saga. One morning nobody listened. There had been a bus accident in the early hours. Some of the injured had been sent up here, and they were on the run. Doctors, relations, policemen – the quiet private wing was in crisis. A young fractured skull had died.

Mr Pomfret was aware of all this, but he had still worked himself into a rage. Nobody had answered his bell and I was ten minutes late, because I had helped a porter take a patient with a blood drip to the operating theatre.

'Do you have to die to get some attention here?' Mr Pomfret fumed at me.

'It would help.' I stood at the end of his bed and contemplated the crags and furrows of his disgruntled face. 'My God,' I said, 'you are a bastard.'

'Aren't I?' For a moment I thought he was going to chuckle. 'Since no one came,' he said rather grandly, 'I peed in the bed.'

After I had washed him and changed the sheets, there was not much to do. He did not need me in the room all the time so I helped the busy staff.

I made beds with the Bahamian nurse and we had some laughs with the patients who were not ill. She laughed a lot. She was a funny girl, her jaw and lips and teeth constructed for laughter, as well as other things. Her silly cap bounced on the back of her ball of hair. Her long black knock-kneed legs seemed to start at the waist instead of the hips. I thought of Fanny. That evening when we laughed and ran through 27 Warhurst Vale, making terrible faces at the furniture, her short pleated skirt had whirled over black tights on the legs that could not hold a candle to Mrs Parker's niece.

When Mr Pomfret realized what I was up to his bell began to ring, and he wanted to know who was paying me. While he slept after lunch I helped with urine-testing and sterilizing and setting up trays and trolleys for the two overworked probationers.

'You've come down in the world,' said the wide one, sailing into the sluice with a full bedpan to find me cleaning the rectal tray.

'Yeah.' I blew into a rubber glove, and popped the fingers out. 'To your level.'

*

Fanny had my telephone number but I heard nothing from her. She had shared quite a lot with me at Warhurst Vale – her feeling for the old man, jokes, her tears when he died and she burned her precious tape. But that was it, apparently, as if I had died along with her grandfather.

On my day off between Mr Pomfret and the mongoloid boy, Bobby Baxter, I rang the BBC. I had planned to do it in the morning before she got too busy. But John was at home, on strike, laid off, or something. We usually shared girl news, both good and bad. We knew each other too well for pretence but somehow I did not want him to hear me getting a gay brush-off from Fanny.

'Aren't you going out, John?'

'It's raining.' In his bulldozer he cheerfully devastated landscapes in storms and torrents of mud, but he stayed in the flat all morning, reading and eating toast.

'What's for supper?' When Natalie was not about we took turns to cook.

'What do you want?'

'Not sausages again.'

'That's all there is.'

Our conversation was as boring as any married couple. 'You could go out and get some fish.'

'So could you.'

'It's your turn.'

'We'll go to Mei Ling's.'

'I don't want Chinese food.'

'Don't come then.'

Perhaps we were both sick of sharing. It sounded like that.

I went down the dark stairs, turning round the central shaft which convected pickled fish and cabbage from Mrs Odessa's ground floor flat and ran through the rain to the telephone in the tube station. The call box smelled of urine and cigarettes, with a slight metallic hint of old blood.

'BBC.'

'I want to speak to Stephanie Runyon, in Features. She works for Victor Ross.'

'Victor Ross's office.'

'May I – would it be possible – can I speak to Stephanie Runyon?'

'I'm sorry.' The voice was nice, but negative. 'There's no Stephanie Runyon here. Just a minute and I'll check with the switchboard.'

'No. I mean, I thought she worked for Mr Ross. Or has she left?'

'I don't know of –'

'Perhaps you call her Fanny?'

'Oh.' The voice became positive. 'Fanny Warren?'

There was a small mirror in the wall above the telephone. I looked at my face. Plain. Ordinary. Swatch of wet brown hair streaked over uninteresting forehead. Brown eyes looking blankly into blank eyes. Why should she have told me she was married? It was none of my business.

'Who wants her?'

'Oh,' I said, 'it's all right. I just –'

'No wait. She's here. Fanny?' And she was on the telephone before I could ring off.

I had rehearsed what I was going to say to her. 'I wondered if you –'

'Oh, it's you. How marvellous. I am glad to hear you. What have you been doing?' She was prattling a bit, this bright, married Fanny, swivelling in a desk chair at Broadcasting House, while I was in a fetid phone box with my collar turned up and my face glum.

I decided to scrub all my rehearsed dialogue, but then she said, typically – she would often interrupt and change the subject, and then drag you back, as if *you* had stopped – 'What were you going to say?'

'I wondered if you still wanted me to talk about nursing.' I had rehearsed that as a fair excuse to see her again. Now it sounded insulting to be offering an excuse.

But she said, 'Oh I *do*. I thought you didn't want to.'

'I thought you –' My face began to lift.

'Let's do it as soon as we can. How about this evening?'

'All right.' I looked better when I smiled.

*

I did not want to meet Fanny's husband. But that was absurd. If she was married, she was married, so what difference did it make if I met her husband or not?'

'Come to supper,' she had said. And this Warren would be a bit too nice to me, since I would be there on business, as a nurse rather than a person. After supper, when Fanny dragged out her trusty tape recorder, he would probably go out, or into another room, so as not to have to listen to this boring nurse drivelling on with the kind of stuff Fanny thought was a slice of life.

Perhaps he tolerated her work, but without enthusiasm. Perhaps he hated her to bring it home. Perhaps when she had told him I was coming this evening, they had had a row, and he had gone out, and Fanny would be alone, but flushed and hectic. Perhaps she had said, 'It'll be boring for you, darling. Why don't you go out?' and so he was determined to stay. In which case, he would turn out to be knowledgeable about wine, and would accept, but put away the bottle I bought on my way to the tube.

I got out at Gloucester Road, the oldest station in the world, where cold winds whistle round the grimy tiles, and the lifts are so slow that people hurrying to work run dizzily down the deep spiral stairs, briefcases and overcoats flapping.

Waiting in the underground gale by the empty lift shaft I not only did not want to see Fanny's husband, I did not want to see Fanny as a wife.

'This is my husband, Peter.' Peter, his name would be, or Tony. Tony Warren. He would be in television, in white denim slacks cut to draw the eye to the crotch, black polo-neck with a Hindu medallion, fluffy sideburns tarting up a rather immature face.

'Glad to know you, Dick.' Mid-Atlantic over diminished north country. The hand would be cold and dry. He would wear a wedding ring – *Bless, O Lord, this ring, that he who wears it and she who gives it* . . . her eyes and cheeks glowing against all that white – although theirs would be one of those free and independent marriages that can be more dependent than the other kind, since you depend on each other for your freedom.

If I had known how to get round to the other side of the lifts to the trains, I would have gone home. I was going to turn back into the wind that had blown me up the steps and tunnels from the platform, when the floor of the lift came into view, and settled on to the centuries of filth and cigarette stubs at the bottom of the shaft.

The lift lady wore a wig and bright red lipstick – so BBC fashions had reached London Transport.

'Thank you, dear.' She liked me. But she said that to everybody who gave her a ticket.

We waited for more trains to give us our quota and rose slowly. I sat on the bench which Fanny's skirts had helped to polish, and looked at the obscene advertisements for men's underwear that Fanny looked at morning and evening. At the top everyone went out of the gate marked, 'Other Side Out at Top Landing'.

Gloucester Road looked much gayer than it used to when I was a child and my mother and I came up to see my grandmother, lonely and critical in Cranley Gardens. Restaurants. Painted pubs. Shops open late. Many more young people than there used to be in my grandmother's day of old ladies and senile dogs.

I crossed the thunderous traffic of Cromwell Road and walked up to Fanny's street on the side of the road where she would walk in the evening, to get the lowering sun through gaps between the houses. In the morning she would be in the sun on the other side. Her house was one of a high white terraced row, painted and come up in the world since its dog days when my mother and I walked up here to the park to get the smell of Gran's flat out of our country noses. Elaborate roof façades against the evening sky. The towers of Imperial College and the Natural History museum dwarfed by a crane so tall, it had radar at the top to get its bearings. The rain had stopped and you could smell blossom from Kensington Gardens.

On a square balcony, over the portico of one of the houses, some men and girls were out with glasses in their hands. Blue jeans and sweaters, and one of the girls in a brown sort of burnous with the hood up, but it was a far cry from the wrong side of Clapham Common where, if you sat out on a promising spring evening, you perched on the mouldering front steps and Mrs Odessa's knickerless children ran over your legs.

There was a stack of bells by Fanny's front door, mostly with unreadable cards. I rang the top one as she had told me, and her voice came ghostly through a grating.

'Come up. All the way.'

Good. If Tony Warren had come through with a hollow, 'Who's that?', 'Dick Hayes', '*Who?*', pretending not to remember what Fanny had told him, I might have turned and gone.

I did not use the tiny lift. Walking would get me to him slower. The stairs deteriorated as they went up. The first bit of carpet was quite decent. Successive flights became more worn and faded. One flight of ratty linoleum, and the last one, which went off at an angle to what must once have been the servants' attics, was bare wood.

There were voices and music behind doors and good smells.

Not Clapham Common smells, although the ingredients may have been the same, curry powder and garlic and chili pepper and soy sauce. Two black boys passed me going down, with a jingle of neck chains, and a girl in velvet shorts and long red socks. A door opened as I trod on the last bare landing and a girl in an orange dressing-gown looked expectantly out and then said, 'Oh sorry,' and shut the door on the noise of a baby. It was the kind of place where Fanny might live, but it was not quite where I had expected Fanny and wine-tasting Warren might live.

It wasn't.

After I went up the last wooden flight and she clattered down some steps inside and flung open a flimsy door which almost knocked me backwards down the stairs, it was obvious that there was no man in this flat.

It was one long room which ran from front to back of the house, with the ceiling sloping on both sides, so that you had to stay more or less in the middle of the room, unless you were in bed or sitting down. There was a gabled window at each end of the room. The front one looked over a box of failed tulips across the broad street to the attic windows of the terrace opposite and the fantastic elegant balustrades and cornices and swags of carved plaster favoured by the merchants who built up this part of London. The back window, above the bed made into a sofa with purple cushions, looked across the mews roofs at the backs of another terrace, the skyline even more fantastic.

Chimneys short and stout, tall as organ pipes, crooked, straight, whole banks of them like bowling pins. Cowls like candle snuffers, metal fans turning high in the sky, two cowls like bent stovepipes turned together to blow smoke into each other's mouths. Lift shafts ran up in odd places between roof angles and blackened brick buttresses. A network of iron ladders and catwalks ran from house to house, where oppressed servants must once have run back and forth at night for liberating orgies in the stuffy attic rooms.

Lights were on in frosted glass bathrooms stuck on as afterthoughts and in uncurtained windows where you could see flat life. A girl at a sink. A man writing at a desk. A woman brushing long grey hair. Backs of heads in front of the blue glare of television. Under the roof of the mews houses beneath Fanny's window the top half of a hayloft door was open and a woman with a face like a turnip poured tea from an enamel pot on to a rose in a tub below.

There was a lot of colour in Fanny's room, cushions and curtains and rugs, and posters stuck on the slopes of the ceiling, since there was not enough room on the low walls. Paintings which I did not understand, unless they were only meant to be design and colour. A blown-up photograph of a brown man riding surf. A glow of daffodils which she must have bought on the way home and stuck into a blue jug without taking off the string.

I was glad I had brought wine, not flowers. I gave it to her. I had chosen the same kind I had bought with Mr Stillman's housekeeping money, a sneaky memory that I had thought Fanny and I could share, even though Tony Warren put the bottle away under the sink and brought out something better.

Fanny came back from the kitchen with a corkscrew and glasses and I opened the wine. Deftly. If T. Warren had been there, I would have crumbled the cork, or pushed it into the bottle with the shaft of the broken corkscrew still in it.

The air coming in was nice, so we did not sit in the chairs draped with Mexican blankets, or the big cushions on the floor. We sat on either side of the small table by the window and said, 'Well,' and smiled, and she said, 'You look better. Not so tired.'

She looked the same as before, eager, brightly coloured, her hair cut in a square fringe over the dark blue eyes and squared off at the ends.

I did not know what to say, so I said, 'Are you married?'

'I was once.' She spoke as if she were quite old. 'Not any more. But I didn't bother to change that name at work.'

'What was –?' Why was I asking what Warren was like? I did not want to know.

Fanny did not want to tell me. She said, 'Let's not talk about that. I want to talk about you.'

But we were both hungry, so before she got out the tape recorder, we ate the supper she had cooked, and then we shut the window and sat on the cushions on the floor and finished the wine, and she began to talk about her marriage.

'My mother never liked Andrew.' Andrew Warren. You'd only have to say one W. And he was in journalism, not television. 'So when he walked out, it proved her right, so she was nicer about it than if she'd been proved wrong. My father liked Andrew but he hardly saw him. He doesn't spend much time with anybody. He never did with my mother. It seemed hardly worth his walking out on her. When Andrew disappeared she told me, "Well, we've got one thing in common now. We've both been ditched."' Fanny laughed. 'It hurt though. I mean, it's pretty humiliating, when someone walks out on you, even if you're glad afterwards they went.'

So then I told her about Millie, and how the gas heater we had been so proud to find so cheap had set her room on fire, and she had woken to flames and jumped out of the window and broken her thin neck. Fanny's eyes filled quickly with tears and she got up and took the glasses and cups out to the kitchen.

I thought it was unfair to have told her. I did not need to talk about it – I never had – and it did not make me cry any more.

When Fanny came back, still rather red in the face, she said, 'How could you let me moan about my stupid marriage when that abysmal thing happened to you?'

But in a way her loss had been greater than mine. She had been smacked in the face with rejection. But Millie had always steadily loved me.

*

Fanny never did get out her tape recorder, and I did not talk about nursing.

'Let's do that another time,' she said. There would be a lot of other times. We both thought that we would be friends.

Friends was the word we thought of. I mean, we kissed, because that's what you do when you love someone, but it was with love, not passion.

'What's she like in bed?' John asked once, after Fanny had been to our Clapham flat and surprised Natalie by liking her.

'I don't know.'

'Cut it out, Dick.'

'We're friends.'

'You can't be friends with a girl without screwing.'

71

'Can't you?'

'No. It's not natural.'

'Then we aren't natural.'

'You can't really be friends with a woman anyway,' John said.

8

I never did make the intimate stranger tape about nursing for Fanny. The next time I saw her, when she came to Windsor to see how I was getting on with Bobby Baxter, she told me that she had only pretended she still wanted it because she thought that was the only reason I had telephoned her.

'It was an excuse, not a reason,' I said. 'I didn't want to do the tape.'

'Nor did I.'

She had given up the slice of life idea after she had made tapes of a woman policeman, and a ticket collector, and a jolly man born without forearms, who played the piano with his elbows, and her boss had said that even edited, they sounded like the nineteen-fifties. Victor Ross had sighed, and got up without hearing the whole tape of the jolly pianist – '*Better than trying to play with me shoulders, ha ha.*'

'Couldn't you find anyone who wasn't a walking cliché?'

'He thinks people are only interesting if they're eccentric and weird.' Fanny crouched on the floor to try to coax Bobby out from under a low table which fitted him like a shell. 'But eccentric people can be so boring because they work too hard at trying to be different. I mean, why shouldn't people want to listen to my ticket collector droning on about "You see it all, in my line of work?" If they recognize him, perhaps they recognize themselves.'

There was something surprisingly simple about Fanny. When you first met her, the bright colour and quick voice and

pleased laughter dazzled you into thinking she was more unusual than she was.

No, that's wrong. She was unusual. She was unusual because
she did not try not to be simple. Millie and I, both products of
plain and rather inarticulate backgrounds, had self-consciously
rejected the sayings of home, like 'It's a small world', and 'Take
your mac', and 'Mind how you go'. If Fanny wanted to say,
'It's a small world', she said it like a discovery.

So she had made unoriginal tapes – mine would have been
the most unsubtle of all, I suspect, full of old nursing saws like
'You're as old as your tubes', and *'You never get used to seeing
a kid die'* – and Victor Ross had said, 'Fanny, dear, couldn't
you find *anyone* who wasn't a walking cliché?'

'I don't care anyway.' She got up and dusted off her knees (I
was supposed to do some basic housework at the Baxters', but I
was going to do it just before they came home). 'I'm on to
something new now.'

Her eyes were excited. She told me, with the breathy eagerness with which she greeted any new project, 'Victor wants to
do some programmes about ESP. Talking in thoughts. The
new communications industry. I've got a marvellous tape of a
woman guessing what someone else is thinking of in another
room. You can tell it's genuine because they both sound so
surprised afterwards. And I'm going to see a faith healer. And a
man in Wales who can teach you to understand your dreams.
When I've found out, I'll teach you. "Bring me your dreams",
he said on the telephone, so I'm writing them down. Wasn't
that marvellous? Bring me your dreams.'

She had a free afternoon so we decided to take Bobby Baxter
to London. Bobby was a six-year-old mongoloid boy, shut into
his own limbo from which, although he would cling and
nuzzle at times, or hit out and scratch at others, he would not
speak or listen, or ever look you directly in the eye.

His mother, a tough and cheerful character, had always
looked after him at home. She made her life round his non-life,
and would not have any more children, which was a good or a
bad thing according to how you looked at it.

One day she had forgotten to shut the gate at the top of the
stairs. Wandering about the rooms in his aimless way, dragging

one foot – from inertia, not lameness – Bobby had fallen down the stairs with a roar and broken his arm.

He had hated the hospital – the only time he had shown such a normal reaction as screaming was when his mother left the ward. So when the poor woman, who seemed to be getting all that life could invent, heard that her mother was ill and her sister hurt in a car crash and she and her husband must go to Cornwall, she hired a nurse to take care of Bobby in his own home.

Taking care of Bobby meant trying to guess when he needed to go to the lavatory and cleaning him up if you guessed wrong, giving him fluid in paper cups, a sip at a time, with a towel poised to catch it running out, spooning into him the strained baby food, which was all he would take, and mopping up the trails of saliva his fingers left all over the house.

His hands were always in his mouth, always wet, and producing more spit as they worked and turned, stretching and bruising his lips. He favoured both hands equally. It was pathetic to see him bent double, contorted, all his dislocated energies straining to get the fingers at the end of the plaster cast into his mouth.

We decided that he would like to go to London, so we took him to London, sitting on my knee in the front of the Triumph and dribbling down my shirt. It was a lovely day, so we had the top down. Bobby's funny stiff hair, always wet and sticky from his fingers, blew forward round his face. When he leaned sideways to get more breeze round the windscreen, his dribble streaked back over his reddened cheeks and flew away.

You could not make him smile but he seemed to be content. He looked almost like a normal boy. At a traffic light two girls in another open car waved to him and he gave them back his blank, unstaring stare.

We gave him a bit of a tour round Piccadilly and Westminster and the Palace, in case it was possible that something could get though to an intelligence imprisoned within the mongolism. We held out his hand to the spray from the Trafalgar Square fountains and dragged him across to feed the pigeons. He would not walk properly holding your hand. You had to carry him or drag him. He lay on the bird-limed pavement and masticated his fingers while Fanny and I threw out the grain. A pigeon sat briefly on his messy hair and we laughed, but a woman said to her interested child, 'Don't look.'

Bobby's trousers were wet by now and it was time to feed him, so we went back to Fanny's flat.

As the lift was broken I carried him up the stairs while he beat me about the head with the plaster cast which never stayed in its sling, and Fanny ran ahead with the bag with his food and clean clothes. She always ran up and down stairs as if a treat awaited her.

As she opened the door of her attic flat I could hear the telephone ringing. I puffed up the last angled flight of bare stairs with Bobby. She was saying, 'Yes ... if you can ... All right, I'll wait. I'll wait for an hour. Got to go. Bye.' She rang off abruptly as she always did. She could be in the train of a breathless conversation, and then suddenly stop in her tracks – 'Got to go. Bye' – and be gone.

'Who was that?' I panted in and kicked the door shut behind me.

'Nobody.'

I changed Bobby on the floor of the little bathroom that smelled so strongly of Fanny and the soap that lingered on her fresh skin, but before we were ready to leave he was wet again. I had no more dry clothes. We put him into a pair of Fanny's shorts, pinned round the waist. He bellowed like a yak and tried to tear them off – he did know certain things, like his own clothes, with the smell and feel of himself – but then he fell asleep under the table, in the unheralded way he did, anywhere he happened to be.

It was on the way out that we got saddled with Maud, or rather Fanny saddled us.

As we came down the front steps under the pillared porch, a man with strands of hair larded over a narrow scalp came out of the door to the basement flat, carrying something wrapped in a dirty towel.

Fanny looked down through the area railings and let out a little yelp.

'It's Maud.'

The man was carrying a moth-eaten brown dog, head hanging limply over one arm, a tangled scruff of tail over the other.

'I thought she went with the Dixons.' Fanny opened the iron gate and ran down the area steps.

'So did I,' the man said dourly. 'But when I went to show the flat to someone this afternoon, there it was, lying just inside the door.' He was a flushed, underfed man with a gristly eye and a rather unsteady step in old grey gym shoes.

'The Dixons left more than a week ago.' Fanny put her hand on the wiry fur of the dog's head and the tail moved slightly. 'Why isn't she dead?'

'Smelled like she was.' The caretaker screwed up his pocked nose. 'But they left the lid of the bog up. She must have drank out of that.'

'Where are you taking her?' Fanny asked.

'Dogs' home.'

The dog's dull eye glimmered recognition of the word dog.

'Oh no.'

'Fanny –' I shifted Bobby's sleeping weight to my other hip and called down over the railings. I guessed what she was up to.

'I'll take her.'

'All right. You take her there.' The man handed over the ugly dog to Fanny who clutched her like a baby, the grubby towel hanging down like a christening robe. 'Save me a trip on the bus.'

'I mean, I'll keep her.'

'Not in this house, you won't.' He put his hands in the pockets of his loose trousers and hitched them up over bare ankles.

'The Dixons did.'

'They paid me,' the caretaker said, with degraded honesty.

'I'll pay you too,' said Fanny, not regally, but eagerly.

If she had said it regally, I would have kept quiet, but the eager, grateful grin with which she favoured this degenerate bloodsucker made me call down, 'Bring the thing up. I'll take it to Windsor.'

'It's Maud.' Fanny ran up the steps with the dog, which was even uglier at close range, sharp nose, harsh ginger fur and small cinnamon eyes between uncoordinated ears.

I did not want a dog. We had never had one at home, and

since I left, I had lived mostly in hospitals. Some of my friends had dogs but if you haven't got one of your own you ignore other people's, or kick them surreptitiously if they get too familiar. Maud was the last thing I wanted, but I did not think she would live very long.

We shut the roof of the car and took Bobby home, still asleep on my lap, with Maud asleep or passed out in the small space at the back.

We played at being a nice Windsor couple, going home with the baby after a day's outing.

'I thought the little chap was quite good, didn't you?' Fanny drove fast, whether she was in a hurry or not, her little jutting profile as serene as if the car were on rails.

'Your mother didn't think so.'

'What do you mean, Mum's ever so fond of him.'

'She thinks he takes after my Dad.'

'Oh well, nuff said.'

'What do you mean, nuff said?'

'Shall we have the cold pork then, or the macaroni?'

'Your cousin looked rough, I thought.'

'What can you expect? They took out all she had. We could finish up the beetroot.'

'Let's go and lay down first, eh?'

'Not till baby's asleep, dear.'

'He's asleep now.'

'I'll wake him up. I don't fancy it.'

'You never fancy it, Muriel.'

'It was three times last week.'

'Four times too few.'

'Men are all the same.'

'If they weren't, you'd have to have adjustable women, ha ha.'

'Don't be dirty, dear.'

When we got to the Baxters' house with the gay door above high front steps at the bottom of the hilly street I tried to make Fanny come in, but she said she was going out to dinner.

'Who with?' The bugger on the phone who was planning to keep my proud Fanny waiting for an hour?

'Nobody you know.' She had taken Maud to the top of the steps and got back into the car.

'None of my business?'

'Don't be dirty, dear.'

She leaned out to give me a quick peck as I stood on the pavement clutching Bobby and the bag of wet clothes, then drove off fast.

I toiled up the steps and put Bobby down at the top, a pool of limp limbs in Fanny's tennis shorts, while I found the key. Inside the house the cat had made a mess in the fireplace. Bobby had made a mess in Fanny's shorts. A poem from his speech therapist had been pushed through the letter box:

Did you forget today?
Ring if tomorrow OK.
E. Mercer

The draught from an open window had blown out all the pilot lights and the kitchen was full of gas. When I gave Maud a bowl of milk she brought it all up and then ate the cat food in a dish alive with ants.

I plodded through the jobs like a woman. It was as if I were the female drudge, shoes taken away to keep me in the cabin, while Fanny, the male adventurer, rocketed off in her red sweater and noisy blue car.

Of course she was none of my business. I did not want her to be. I loved her, but I wanted to be free, like this, on my own to work or not work, take jobs when and where I wanted. *Once I get my SRN*, we had dreamed as students, in the long tunnel of hospital training when the end was not even a speck of light, *I'll be free.*

Bobby woke while I was cleaning him, and he stayed up for hours and was a terrible bore. I could not make supper, or go to the pantry for a beer, or even have a bath, without hauling him along with me, flipping a loose piece of linoleum endlessly up and down, sprawling in the bathroom with his face in a cake of wet soap, going burble, burble above the radio music.

Five and a half years to get my SRN, and the loss of my aimless dreams. Lying in the Baxters' narrow coffin bath, admiring my short compact body and the nice way I kept my feet, since a nurse is sunk without them, I wondered, as I occasionally did, whether I was in the wrong job.

*

But the next morning, after one of Bobby's short nights, I woke feeling marvellous. I could push a bus over.

'I feel marvellous,' I told Bobby. 'Marvellous, do you hear?'

I went all round the house singing. That was one thing about living with Bobby. You could do anything you felt like. He didn't mind. He didn't even notice. I went all round the house with no clothes on, singing, making up songs, childish, babbling, 'mad with devouring ecstasy to make joyous hymns for the whole earth'. It was a good thing E. Mercer did not come to the glass panelled back door. She might have reported to Mrs Baxter that things were in a worse state here than in Cornwall.

*

I stayed with Bobby Baxter about two weeks. Maud did not die. She got better. Her eyes grew brighter under wiry orange brows. Her rib cage filled. She tolerated torture from Bobby's double-jointed fingers, her harsh coat always wet with his saliva.

She was even uglier on her feet than off them, since she moved with a curious stilted gait, narrow-chested and feet paddling far apart, but she was a fairly decent companion. Present, but not cloying.

She and Bobby were almost the only company I had. Fanny had gone to Wales. She rang once.

'It's marvellous. Wait till I tell you what my dreams mean.'

'What?'

'Tell you when I see you. Can't talk now. 'Bye.'

Why? Why couldn't she talk? Was she in Wales with the nobody man who kept her waiting? Was she sleeping with the dream doctor? Was she sleeping with Victor Ross? I knew almost nothing about what she did when she was not with me. But when she was with me I knew all I wanted to know. Her presence. The present moment. We liked being together but we did not try to possess. Free, you see? That was what we both said we wanted. I reminded myself of that, to banish the small melancholy that was the aftertaste of the joy with which I had heard her voice on the telephone.

*

John came down once, with a new girl, but only because they were on their way somewhere, and they did not stay long. When the girl saw Bobby mashing a peanut butter sandwich on the table and sucking it off his fingers, which was the way he ate peanut butter sandwiches, she said, 'I'm sorry, but it makes me sick, it really does.'

Bobby slithered off his chair with peanut butter and mashed bread all over his face. He went into his best corner behind the sofa and came up with fluff and grit stuck to the peanut butter.

John said, bending forward to Bobby with his curious, exploring look, 'The Baxters must be fools, or saints.'

'I hate to say this,' the girl said contentedly, 'but I think children like that should be put away.'

'Put down?' I inquired, wiping Bobby off with one of the damp towels I kept on hand in all rooms.

'How can you stand this job?' She wrinkled up her quite considerable nose, which had coarse broad nostrils and looked better smoothed out.

'It's all I know.' I made a moronic, thick-tongued face at her, and John took her away.

He did not expect me to like his girls and I almost never did. They came and went but they did not manage to come between us. They found that quite annoying and pushed off in the end, as Natalie had.

*

Apart from E. Mercer and people in the shops where I took Bobby, in a wheelchair for convenience, I saw no one else, except for a few children in Windsor Park. It was quite near the house and I used to push Bobby there and leave him on the grass with a pebble in a pillbox to rattle, while Maud and I galloped about near him, high-kneed and splay-footed, to get our lungs going. Or I would tie him into the wheelchair with the belt of my raincoat and bump him round in circles, with my coat flapping, Maud barking at the wheels, and the wet breeze bringing colour to Bobby's flat face.

A bunch of small boys on their way up to the Copper Horse stopped for a serious look.

'Give us a ride.'

I left Bobby on the grass with Maud, who had learned to grab his clothes if he crawled too far, while I gave wheelchair rides to the boys, shrieking with joy over the bumpy grass. When I sat down to get my breath they tried to get Bobby to notice them.

'Look at me!' The bossy one with red crimpled hair shouted into Bobby's faraway face. He punched him, not hard enough to hurt, and it could have been good contact therapy. Maud growled and sneered her lip in an unattractive way she had but Bobby did not respond.

'He won't look at me!' the child stormed. He ran off with his friends, touching, bumping, tripping each other up, throwing away a cap, shouting, to reassure their slighted egos.

9

We did not see the boys again, nor talk to anyone else.

By the time Mrs Baxter, saint or fool, came back, still tough and cheerful, with wet shoeboxes full of Cornish primroses, I thought I might be ready to abandon this cramped and lonely business of private nursing and go back to the crowded world of hospital. I looked at some advertisements for charge nurses, but they were all quite far out of London, and I did not want to go provincial yet.

Private nurses were still in fairly short supply, even not very good ones like me. I had only been home a few days when Mrs Hewlett-Bye telephoned me in her honeyed voice, so different from the one in which she had prostrated the probationers in her far-off days as Assistant Matron at the Cumberland Royal.

'I've a lovely old man for you, down in Epsom, so pretty at cherry blossom time.'

I did not want any more geriatrics for a while. I told her where she could put her lovely old man, and the cherry blossom with him.

'Have you got another job, Hditchahd?' Her voice sharpened with the suspicion that I was getting work through another agency.

'I'm resting,' I said grandly.

But then my friend Bernie, who was also in privates, asked me if I would help out with a case for a few days while he finished a course of lectures in neurology, so I left Maud with John and went off once more with my airline bag and white jacket to General Sir Bertram W. V. Noakes, KCVO, CB, DSO, MC, *hors de combat* with a fractured hip in St John's Wood.

He was at the walking stage, the old white warrior, but precarious. My job was mostly to let him just beat me at backgammon and to pace with him slowly up and down the long dark hall of the flat, into which he had moved so that he could come home to lunch from Lord's, after a fight with the manager of the members' restaurant about unskinned tomatoes in the salad. His goal was to be able to walk back and forth across St John's Wood Road as soon as the cricket season started.

On good days we took a taxi to Regent's Park and walked very slowly along the paths, with people and prams making detours round the two-headed top-heavy creature which was the six-foot-two General towering sideways, with me supporting him like a pit prop.

When he met anyone he knew he introduced me puffily. 'This is me orderly. If he moves out from under, I'll be down like timber.'

We would walk to the Castleton Arms and have two drinks and then walk back, a bit faster, because oiled, but less steadily, while the General made terrible observations to me about the girls we passed.

When Bernie came back to take over the General he was enthusiastic about the neurology course. They were repeating it the following week so, as I had no other job, I signed up.

*

Fanny came home. Walking from the Middlesex Hospital at

lunchtime, I was crossing Portland Place in front of a car at the lights, when a head came out of it and yelled.

Fanny was in the car with Victor Ross. I had not seen him before. He was centuries too old for her. Hooray. He smiled at me with slightly crooked teeth but not with the grey eyes, and managed to make me feel instantly callow and peasantish. He looked ahead, foot on the clutch, one hand on the gear lever, the other tapping the wheel, while Fanny and I gabbled at each other in the few seconds before the lights changed. Then he shot away while I had my hand on the door, and I just stepped back to the kerb in time to avoid being run down by a following taxi.

Through the back window of the grey Jaguar I saw him turn his head to her with a question: Your boy friend? Fanny swung her hair round, but she neither nodded nor shook her head.

She had told me with her face out of the window – not wanting him to hear? – 'Come tonight.' So I went. Gloucester Road Station was now one of my favourite places. The short walk to Fanny's flat, cutting diagonally through Queen's Gate Gardens and Gore Street, was the forest path through which Siegfried Sassoon's girl moved through earth's adoring darkness to discover the paradise of her imperfect lover.

We were not lovers. But Fanny was beginning to colour life for me as if we were.

'Hurry up,' she said, through the grating by the buzzer.

I pushed the door and ran up the stairs past the good smells, but stopped two steps from the top of the last bare flight as Fanny flung open the door of her flat with her usual risky abandon.

'I bring you my dreams,' I said in what I thought was Welsh. I had brought her a bottle of wine and an avocado pear.

'Oh good, but let's not talk about that now. I'm on to something new.'

'Didn't the dream thing work out?'

'Oh yes, the tapes aren't bad. Victor's fairly pleased with them. I think,' she added, going before me into the long room between the dormer windows.

'What did your dreams mean then?' I sat down on the purple

bedspread and pushed off a shoe with the toe of the other foot. I was tired from using my brain all day, an exhausting novelty for a nurse.

'It's not what they actually *mean*, Dr Skully said.' Fanny stood against the window, clasping the bottle, with a row of pot-bellied chimneys sailing through streaked clouds behind her. 'It's what you programme them to mean long before.'

'How's that?'

'I told you, I don't want to talk about that now.' If she was disappointed with the outcome of the dream project she was getting over it in her usual way, by leaping ahead to something else. 'Put on your shoes and get off the bed. We've got to go out and buy the *Psychic News*.'

'What for?'

'I'm going to do a medium. Victor wants me to research it by myself. Find the right person and go through a sitting. Several, perhaps, before I get them to trust me enough to let me bring a tape recorder.'

'It should be you trusting them.' I put on my shoes.

'No, but they always suspect people are trying to expose them. I'm not. I mean, this is a serious study.' Fanny made her face serious, her long fluid mouth straight but dented at the ends. 'We're making no judgements. We're not saying, This is real, or This is fake. We're just saying, This is what happens if you go to a medium.'

'Am I coming?'

'Of course. I'm not going alone.'

'Who are we going to?'

'I don't know yet. It's got to be a random choice. Victor says I'm to be a typical person who knows nothing, and neither believes nor disbelieves. That's all part of the programme. The story starts from' – she looked at her watch – 'now!'

She ran down the stairs and I went down in the lift, and we hit the worn stained mat by the front door at the same time.

The newspaper stall at Gloucester Road was closed, so we went down with the lift lady, who had a bright new wig for spring, and got into a train for Piccadilly Circus. I had never been in the tube with Fanny before. We played at guessing who would get out at which station, and concentrating on people to make them look round and other childish games I had been playing all my life, and found that Fanny had too.

We bought the *Psychic News* at Piccadilly. We were both excited, but I folded the small paper and put it in my pocket, and we made ourselves wait until we got back to the flat and opened the wine before we looked at it.

Fanny lifted her glass. 'I like having adventures with you,' she said. That was the way I felt. But it was because Fanny made things into adventures that they were adventures.

There were several advertisements for private sittings, mostly on the outskirts of London, or farther. We tried with a pin but Fanny did not want to go to Watford. In the end she chose the medium with the plainest name.

Jack Judd.

'No one called Jack Judd could be psychic.'

'We'll see.' Fanny became businesslike, but her thin fingers were a little unsteady as she dialled, and at the last minute, as the ringing stopped, she handed me the telephone.

'Judd speaking.' The voice was any Londoner's, not young, not old, a bit hoarse.

'I – er, we – er, we saw your advertisement. In the newspaper.'

'Oh yes?'

'Do you – I mean, we'd like a sitting.'

'Oh yes.' Surely it was his move next. But this Judd seemed rather slow, or cagey.

'Make an appointment.' Fanny was breathing all over me, and trying to pry my fingers off the receiver.

'Can we make an appointment?'

'Is it a group?' Jack Judd began to cough.

'Just two.' I found myself adding, 'Me and my wife.'

'One minute. I'll put you on to my secretary.' Pause. 'My sister.'

Pause. Murmuring, '. . . wants a sitting.' 'A sitting?' Had I used the wrong word? A girl I knew who went to an Indian seer had been laid out on an altar, although nothing had happened to her, to her secret disappointment.

I heard Judd cough again, more distantly. Then I was aware

that something came quite softly and breathed into the telephone.

'You want a sitting?' So I had said the right thing. 'Next week?' The voice of Jack Judd's sister sounded tentative and somehow strained, as if the telephone were on the wall and she were a child standing on tiptoe to reach it.

'Which day –'

Fanny snatched the telephone from me. 'Can we come on Monday evening? Six o'clock? All right. The name? Oh –' She thought of our weird-looking dog in Clapham. 'Maude. Yes. Mr and Mrs Maude.'

'Why did you say we were husband and wife?' Fanny asked me.

'I suddenly thought perhaps you had to be married to have a sitting together. Like at the sauna baths.'

I had gone once with a big lusty girl who had a roll of fat over her hips. An old lady in a wet white overall had beaten us with a clothes brush and poured a bucket of ice-cold water over my head when I wasn't looking. It had nearly killed me.

Fanny did not ask, 'Who did you go to a sauna with?' She was not curious about other girls I knew. I wished she was.

*

Mr and Mrs Maude.

We were Frances and Dixie Maude. After Monday's session at the Middlesex on Intensive Nursing Care of Acute Infectious Polyneuritis, I picked Fanny up at the BBC. She gave an affectionate farewell to a doorman with one arm and one eye, who she said was her uncle, and we took a bus up that endless stretch of Edgware Road, Maida Vale, Kilburn, on and on through drearier reaches to the north. Frances Maude was wearing a plain dark suit, with a yellow scarf over her hair and large gold rings in her ears, a discreet mixture of gypsy and modest housewife. Dixie Maude was in his grubby raincoat because it was raining. They got off the bus at the Odeon lights and walked back to where a short street ran off at an angle to nowhere except the blank black wall of a railway.

Number thirty-nine was an ochre door between a dry cleaner and a shoe shop gone out of business. It was very depressing. The Maudes held hands, and let go guiltily when bolts were shot and the door opened by Jack Judd in socks and loose grey slacks, a tomato pip on his yellowed white sweater.

He was plump and squat, with thinning gingery hair shaved into stubble all over his pink scalp, and an air of being glad that we had come. He called Fanny 'my dear', and me 'old thing', and went before us up the steep stairs to his flat over the shop, with a wide expanse of rather womanish grey hips, and a gait like a duck.

He took us into a sitting-room, where the television set was on without the sound. Desperate people waved their arms about and opened their mouths, signalling for help. We sat down and wondered what to do next. Jack Judd seemed to wonder too. He was rather vague. He looked at the door as if it had the answer. He called me Francis and Fanny Dixie. Even when we adjusted this he never got it right.

Conversation was thin. Fanny took off her yellow scarf, remembered that her hair needed washing, and put it on again. Jack Judd looked at us mildly. I could not think of anything to say. Fanny was too nervous for more than a few stabs at the beginnings of rushed, breathy sentences. Inside the electric fire a metal fan rotated over an orange light, creating no semblance of flames. On the mantelpiece the clock had cardiac arhythmia between vases of dried flowers. The prisoners in the television besought our help. The stiff material of the settee pricked through my trousers.

At last the door opened and a thin woman with dark grey hair plaited over her ears in two coils came in with a tray of coffee cups.

'My sister Ireen.' Jack Judd looked more at ease. We were all more relaxed, as if Ireen had come in with drinks.

'This is Dixie and Francis,' Jack told her, pointing to the wrong people.

'Is it an exorcism?' she asked Fanny.

'No, I'm sorry. It's not as exciting as that.'

'That's all right.' Ireen handed round gritty coffee.

In her long indoors face her eyes were set deep in lids that were as dark as if she had been in a punch-up. Puckers in her pale mouth showed her to be older than her brother. She had one of those long squashy noses with a blob on the end, that spread a bit with age. Her clothes were colourless and centuries out of date. She looked like someone's unmarried aunt. Perhaps we could hitch her up to Fanny's one-eyed amputee uncle at the BBC.

'We're not in this business for excitement,' she said.

Too true. That stuffy room, with the death glow of the television and the rotating orange flicker of the fire travelling over us like lights at a dance hall, was soporific, stultifying. I began to feel trapped. I wished we had not come.

I looked at Fanny to see if we could get out of it, but she was still sitting upright on the harsh settee, making her eager young researcher face. She would not look at me.

Nothing happened. We were suspended in an airless limbo in which nothing would ever happen again.

Then Ireen suddenly cleared her throat with a noise like a blacksmith's file, and Jack Judd put both pudgy hands (he bit his nails) on his knees and said, 'Time to get to work.' He stretched his sweater unsuccessfully down over his paunch and we got up stiffly and followed him down a passage, past a bathroom with the door open and the lavatory seat up, past a kitchen where two frowsty cats watched something fishy on the stove, and into a little room opposite, with a sign on the door that said 'Place of Peace'.

As we went in Fanny grabbed me, and would have taken a step back if Ireen had not been right behind her with the coffee tray. She had seen a bed. Why a bed, for God's sake, in the seance room? It was a divan covered with a tartan rug. On the wall above the bed some spidery writing on lined paper was hung in a frame stuck with seashells and chips of coloured glass.

'You're looking at my automatic writing, Dixie,' Jack Judd said, although Fanny was actually looking at the bed. 'Or rather, the Doctor's writing. Dr Eisenberg, one of my guides. He used to treat royalty in the days of Europe's glory. Remarkable gentleman. Invented Eisenberg's Infusion. But the formula passed away with the Empire.'

He coughed and sat down, a bubble of saliva on his lips. Touch of emphysema, it looked like, by the shape of his chest under the shrunk sweater. He was a bit wheezy, and his teeth did not fit well.

Fanny and I sat down opposite him with our backs to the bed. 'Everything all right?' Ireen came in to adjust the blind and the shade over the single lamp. She rubbed her dry hands together with a rasping noise, advised Jack not to overdo it, and went out to the fish.

Jack Judd screwed up his eyes and began to tell us some things about ourselves. In spite of his name he was quite psychic. He guessed or 'saw' with some accuracy the kind of work we both did, the divorce of Fanny's parents, her preference for her father, a mutual bereavement (Mr Stillman), and Fanny's trip to 'the other side of the earth'.

'That's amazing,' Fanny said.

'No, no Dixie. Clairvoyance is quite natural. Anyone can do it. You could do it. You just have to learn how to exercise the gift, like playing hockey.'

We liked him even more. He was so nice and normal and modest about everything. It was not getting us anywhere, telling us things we already knew, but it was fun. I began to be glad I had come.

'The only thing I can't seem to get any results with,' the medium said, 'is your marriage.'

Fanny looked at me and smiled.

'Everything – excuse me – everything all right in that department? Of course, of course. What is it you are seeking?'

'We don't know.'

'Surely there is something? You didn't come to me for fun, you two, I can tell that.'

Fanny did not want to tell him about the radio programme yet, so she took a breath, leaned forward and said, 'We had a baby, and it died.'

'That's more like it.' Jack Judd closed his eyes again, set his feet squarely, and put his hands on his knees as if posing for a civic statue.

'Mmm. Mmm.' He made a pained sort of humming through closed lips. 'Mmm.' His wide rib cage lifted in a series of deep breaths. Then he was still, twitching a little. I thought he was asleep but after a while he said, 'Doctor? The baby? Can you tell me about the baby?'

A long silence. Across the corridor the kettle whistled, but it seemed miles away and irrelevant. I stared at Jack, but from the corner of my eye I could see that the calves of Fanny's legs were trembling. The palms of my hands were sweating and I realized that I had my eyebrows raised.

'Doctor Eisenberg?' Jack Judd said into the silence. His lips moved, and a voice, different from his own, but with the same sibilant wheeze, said, 'I vant to spik viz you.'

Fanny and I were transfixed.

'Spik viz me, isn't it?'

We could hardly breathe, much less talk.

'Ze baypee ...' The voice was Judd's and not Judd's, the accents of a thousand Ruritanian screen gems. 'Zere iss no baypee.'

'Ul–*lo*.' Jack Judd opened his eyes and shook his head like a diver breaking the surface. 'Something happened there.' He was more surprised than we were. 'What was it?'

'Don't you know?' I let my eyebrows down and relaxed.

'No. Was there speech? If the guide speaks through me, I don't know it.'

'But it was your voice.'

'Well,' he said reasonably, 'they've got to use something, haven't they? I'm the instrument.'

He was so obviously not trying to fool us that Fanny blushed and said, 'That was right. There was no baby. I made it up.'

'Why, my dear?'

'I was testing you,' Fanny said.

Instead of being annoyed Jack Judd laughed. ' 'ave I passed?' he said, and laughed himself into a cough.

'Yes.' Fanny and I laughed too, and Ireen put her coiled grey head round the door to see what was up.

'Can they try the transfiguration?' her brother asked her. 'If they don't laugh.' She brought in a lamp with a red bulb and a deep shade and set it on the floor between our shoes and Jack Judd's socks.

'Aren't you going to stay and give me the extra power?' he asked, rather anxiously, as she went to the door.

'If you wish.' She turned out the other light and sat down. There was only the glow from the lamp on the floor, red light and shadows on the face of the medium.

'Relax,' Ireen told us. 'Receive. If someone comes through, answer them.'

'I won't dare,' Fanny whispered.

'Yes, you will,' Ireen said coldly.

Jack did his deep breathing, which was good for his chest condition at any rate – or was it the cause of it, like a trumpet player? He began to snore a bit. Ireen had her shadowed lids hooded down over a slit of eye, and a straining constipated look on her usually passive long face. After a while Jack's face began to twist, the lips to move. It did not look like anything except Jack Judd twisting his face and moving his lips, but Ireen whispered, 'Look – the transfiguration.'

'Where?' I whispered back.

'You must help,' she said. 'Half close your eyes.'

Well, all right, anyone looks blurred and different when you slit your eyes out of focus, but Fanny and I did it because we had decided we would go along with whatever happened, and also because we were both infected with the atmosphere of this little room with the man and woman who were either crazy, deluded, or cheats. At the moment it did not matter which. The red light made deep shadows of the valleys between the plump folds of Jack's face. His half-open eyes were turned up to the white, like a dead man. His mouth was pursing in a horrid sort of simper and a womanish falsetto voice (still his) came out.

'Hul-lo,' it said timidly. 'I'm . . . glad . . . to . . . be . . .'

It did not sound like any woman anyone ever knew, but then what would a dead woman sound like, supposing she did choose to come back to a flat over an abandoned shoe shop in Cricklewood?

'Thang . . . kew . . . for letting . . .'

It was absurd, and yet I could not laugh. Fanny was staring, rigid, not pretending. Jack's hands lifted and reached out.

'Take the hands,' Ireen said. We did not know who she meant. Fanny licked her lips and was beginning to move her hands forward when the medium's hands moved sideways and out to me.

'Take the hands.'

My spine bristled. I leaned forward and held out my damp hands. Without opening his eyes Jack's fingers felt for mine, curled round the ends and pulled them towards him.

'Hul-lo,' the horrible high voice said.

'Answer,' Ireen said curtly, with her eyes closed.

I opened my mouth but nothing came out. I was not self-conscious. I was tensely beyond that. But I could not say any-thing.

'Don't you know me?' the voice asked.

Fanny gave a little gasp, and whispered, 'Who is it?'

And then I – my *God*, why hadn't I thought of this? If I had thought of this I would never have come. The whole thing had seemed so far removed from any supernatural possibility that I had never thought of this.

And now it was – in that dreadful room with its smell of camphor and its bed and its crazy brother and sister – it was obscene to think of Millie now. Filthy even to let it drift through the back of a corner of my brain that she could . . . that she could *ever* . . . this paunchy, catarrhal man.

And yet, for the fraction of a second, in the illusion of a shadow, the sweetening of the cheek line . . .

I roughly pulled my hands away and stood up and switched on the light.

Jack Judd opened his eyes and looked startled, hands still held out. Fanny sat back with a jerk and blinked at me. Ireen's face remained strained, eyes closed.

'What is it?' she asked.

'I've had enough. I'm sorry.'

Fanny did not ask any questions. I went down the stairs while she paid the Judds. I tugged at the bolts on the door and got outside and away from that nowhere street into the main road, lighted now, with cars swishing home through the rain.

'What happened?' Fanny came running and pulled me into the doorway of a closed shop.

'Nothing.' I rested my chin on the yellow scarf. 'I thought about Millie.'

'*Oh*.' Fanny stepped back and looked at me. 'I never thought.'

'Nor did I. If I had I wouldn't have got into it.'

'You thought about Millie. Oh *don't*. In that place? It's obscene.' She used the word I had felt.

We waited a long time for a bus, and went back to civilization without talking much.

At Kilburn I roused myself to ask, 'How much did you pay them?'

'Two pounds.'

'Not worth being a fake at that price.'

'I don't think he is,' Fanny said. 'Ireen said I could take the tape recorder another time and see what I can get from Dr Eisenberg. Will you come?'

'I don't think so.'

*

When the neurology course finished at the end of the week I had planned to find an undemanding temporary job in London, so that I could stay on the medium project with Fanny, and also give poor old Maud a bit more of my time. Clapham Common was a wonderland of delights to her. She liked it better than Windsor Park, where the smells had been more diffused by nature.

I had my hand out to ring the agency when the telephone rang.

'Hditchahd.'

So I was psychic too. 'I was just going to ring you, H.B.'

'Great minds.'

'Yours and mine.'

'Hditchahd, my dear. It's a little matter of a poor old person.'

'I don't want a –'

'Jenner's emphysema, cardiomyoliposis.' (Showing off, H.B.) 'You know the sort of jazz.'

'Male or female old person?'

'Male, of course,' Mrs Hewlett-Bye said sharply. 'The ethics still stand.'

'How long?'

'How long do you want?'

'A temp.'

'It's a temp.'

'In London?'

'Well, almost.'

'How almost?'

'Maidenhead.' Then as I drew breath, 'A lovely spot, I've always thought. The pictuwerdesque hdivah. And you'll quite enjoy the journey up and down. Cottage gardens in bloom. Cdisp, bdight laundahdy on the lines . . .'

'Half my time travelling.'

'Bdoarden the mind.'

'Geriatrics are narrowing.'

'Hditchahd.' She sounded tired. The agency must take more out of her than the Cumberland Royal, where she had sent people scuttling about in fear at the lift of a cuffed wrist. 'Anyone would think you were doing me a favour, instead of the other way round. What are you living on?'

'All right,' I said. 'I'll take it.'

'Phew,' said Mrs Hewlett-Bye, and rang off.

*

I did not want to go to Maidenhead but it would keep me from going back with Fanny to the Judds until I had got my breath back about it, so to speak, and settled Millie again into the place where she belonged. Undesecrated. At peace. Gone for ever, but securely loved.

John did not want to keep Maud while I was away from the flat so early and home so late. Natalie was gone for ever, but he had taken up with a sharp humourless girl with a hard little mole under one eye that begged to be flicked off with a finger nail. Maud did not like her either. When Maud took an aversion to anybody her bristly ginger hair rose along her spine like a dinosaur, and she gave out a strange sour smell like sputum and old rags.

I smuggled her back to Fanny's flat under my coat, in case the caretaker was watching from the basement window. Fanny was planning to sneak her in and out of the building in a huge straw bag that her mother had brought back full of native loot from Portugal.

We put Maud in that to take her down from the flat for a run in the park. As we stepped out of that precarious little lift, wiping our mouths with the backs of our hands so that anyone in the hall would know we had kissed in the lift, which was all it was good for, the caretaker came up the steep basement stairs on all fours. He stopped with his hands on the top step and his head poked round the corner of the doorway.

'Hul-*lo*, Mr Ewing,' Fanny said, with a voice and a smile that would not sober you up if you were tipsy, but might make you tipsy if you were sober. 'How are *you*?'

'What have you got in that bag?' He nodded at the heavy straw bag in which she had rested the lumpy body of Maud on the floor.

'Empties,' Fanny said, and the caretaker said, 'Lucky you,' and drew back his head like a tortoise.

In the park we saw a man with a shoulder camera, a man with a big light, and a group of people hunched round.

'Oh look, they're making a commercial.'

We walked over and Maud ran off. Just off the Flower Walk, behind a curving bank of azaleas and heather, they were making a dirty film. A ring of men in anoraks and leather jackets were more or less screening a man and a kneeling girl from early morning nannies and children, and the ladies with toy dogs on coloured leads.

'If I'd dreamed about *that*,' Fanny said, as we ran away, 'Dr Skully would have been more pleased with me. He complained that my dreams were very middle class.'

We ran over the slippery London grass, and round the Round Pond, while Maud barked harshly at the toy boats and ate the soggy bread thrown for the ducks. We both had to go to work, so we ran back through the elm pods that had blown down Queen's Gate, put Maud into the straw bag before we turned into Fanny's street; then Fanny drove me to Paddington and I went unwillingly to Maidenhead.

IO

Back to the geriatrics.

I had not particularly wanted to nurse another old person, but in privates there are more of them than anything else, and they are all right as long as you don't stay with them all for life. Their life, I mean. I know nurses who move from terminal case to terminal case, each one ending the same way: 'We shall never forget you, Nurse.' But who is that at the funeral?

Helping people to die is just as much a nurse's business as helping them to stay alive, but too much of it can be very depressing, like living permanently underground, and with no triumphant recoveries to balance out the constant weight of loss.

I walked from the station to the Snows' river house, garlanded with early blown roses, a heavy old clematis smothering the front porch. When she heard me at the gate Mrs Snow opened the front door and came down the path between mixed-up beds of rioting flowers, grey and toddly in an apron, like a Beatrix Potter field animal.

'I'm so glad you've come, Nurse.' She wrinkled her face at me, and I was glad too. 'I've been having the District Nurse to him, but the doctor said he should have someone all day, and you can't find anyone round here for love nor money.'

She had mouse feet in canvas strap shoes, a little fluffy moustache and a furry chin. She looked like somebody's grandmother. Not mine, who lived angrily in Dover, complaining that no one came to see her, and then was foul to them when they did.

She took me into the house, which was cool and shadowy, smelling of the river and of roses. The furniture was polished on top under the dropping petals but cobwebbed underneath, and old spiders lived lavishly in all the ceiling corners.

'He's better today.' She took me upstairs. 'Less restless. His breathing seems easier and he's not so red. I expect you'll think we're terrible frauds, to get you to come all this way, but the doctor did say, and I want to do everything that's right.'

She opened the door of the bedroom where her husband lay in a high double bed, with pale light filtering through yellowed white curtains, and roses fraternizing with the sick room smell.

'He's asleep,' she whispered.

I need not have been afraid of being stuck in this job too long. Mr Snow was dying. He was in a coma, his breathing shallow and infrequent, cyanosis round the mouth and in the fingers inert outside the white counterpane, the pinched high nose of a Roman senator.

'He hasn't woken up yet.' The wife stood by the high bed with her hands flat on the counterpane, as if it were an altar.

'Mrs. Snow,' I said, 'what's your doctor's number?'

'Oh, it's all right. He left instructions for you. So did the District Nurse. Mrs Penny, her name is, such a nice woman. They give them a car, you know, these days, I think it's wonderful. Let's see, where did I put it?'

I put down the old man's wrist and went over to where she was rummaging on a table by the window. 'I'd like the doctor to come.'

'But he's better.'

'I'm afraid not.'

'Oh.' She turned with her hand to her mouth and stared at the mound of man on the bed. 'You don't think he's worse?'

'Mrs Snow.' It was insulting not to tell her. 'I think he's dying.'

His doctor was away. The answering service referred me to a 'patient sitter', one of the mercenaries, fledglings or fossils, who answered calls from unknown patients with varying degrees of luck or competence.

This one was a fossil.

'I can't possibly get there till tonight,' he said, either with his mouth full, or his teeth loose.

'That may be too late,' I cupped my hand round the mouthpiece since I was outside the room where Mrs Snow attended at the altar on which her husband was offering up his life.

'What's that? I can't hear you.'

'I'd like you to come at once.'

'I'll see what I can do.'

Mr Snow had been written up for coramine. I rode fast to

the chemist on his wife's bicycle, which had lettuce leaves in the basket. The pulse improved slightly after the injection but he was still in deep coma.

When the doctor came at last Mrs Snow ran down, pulled open the door, and said at once, 'He's dying.'

'Who says so?' He was a stooped, meagre man, his wiry eyebrows the strongest thing about him, his mouth embittered by the slavery of National Health.

'The nurse.'

'The nurse does, does he?' The doctor nodded at me on the landing and went past me to the bedroom without speaking.

I followed, but he said, 'Thank you', and shut the door.

I opened it again to tell him what medication I had given, and he shut it again without comment. Mrs Snow and I waited on the landing, holding hands spiritually, if not actually. When the doctor came out he jerked his head for me to follow him downstairs.

'Why did you tell the wife he was dying?'

'Because he is. You saw it.'

'The nurse doesn't say that to a patient's family.'

'Well, I did.' One of the advantages of privates is that you are free of the medical hierarchy of hospital.

'Are you SRN?' Sharp, sour doctor, with whiffs of malpractice in his past.

'Yes, sir.' Crisp, correct nurse.

'I may have to report this.' The eyebrows threatened me.

'Go ahead.' I felt quite relaxed.

While we were talking Mr Snow had quietly died. I ran down to call the doctor back, but he had driven off angrily down the river road, and I had the pleasure of telephoning a message to his home for him to turn right round and come back.

Mrs Snow behaved very well. She did not cry.

'I'll cry tomorrow,' she told me, 'when my daughter comes. She always cries a lot, especially when it's too late to do any good.'

After the doctor had returned to certify death, as suspiciously as if I had brought it about to prove myself right, I laid out the dead man, whom I had not had time to know alive, and made some arrangements with the undertaker. Mrs Snow asked me if I would like to stay the night. She meant that she would like me to, so I did. She made us scrambled eggs on toast with chives mixed with the grass that grew among them, and talked to me about her marriage, and her son who had been killed in the last week of the war, and her daughter who had married a man they did not like.

She wanted to sleep in the big bed with her husband, where she had always slept.

'I'll make you up a bed on the couch, Mrs Snow.'

'Why? I'm not afraid of him.'

I don't know whether she did sleep on the couch or beside him. In the morning she had made the bed quite tidy, put white flowers into his hands and surrounded the stiff grey head with the pale roses that blew outside the window.

I slept in the son's room, with schoolboy books and pictures of rowing crews. I could not hear the river but I could smell it every time I woke in the night, seeping, brown and unfamiliar, in at the window. After a lot of rain, the water had risen over the bank at the end of the lawn. I went out in the morning barefoot on the sodden, squashy grass, throwing in twigs to see them bolt into the scummy harbour of a tree root, until Mrs Snow called me in to breakfast.

She gave me bacon and eggs and fried bread in the kitchen.

'What will you do?' I asked.

'Stay here as long as I can.' She put her hands on the back of a chair, stroking the smooth worn wood like a familiar pet. 'If I get lonely and feeble there's a place just outside the town where you can have a nice room and some of your own bits of furniture.'

When the telephone rang, it was cheering to hear Fanny's strong young voice which suggested laughter, and the promises of life.

'Can you talk?' she said on a rush of breath. 'Oh good. Look, how long – I mean, how much longer will the job there last?'

I was talking in the kitchen, leaning back in my chair to the telephone on the wall. 'It's over,' I said, and Mrs Snow, pouring more coffee, patted my shoulder as if the loss were mine.

'Over? It's only just started.'

'The patient died,' I said quietly. Mrs Snow was running water into the sink.

'Already? You can't be a very good nurse.' Fanny struggled with a laugh. I shut her up and she said, 'Sorry. But look, I've got another job for you.'

'Who with?'

'Well, it's Victor.'

Had a stroke? Ruptured himself? I would not nurse him if he paid me double. Or would I? And ram Fanny up against the wall outside the sickroom, where he could hear.

'Not him. His brother. He had an accident and broke both legs and he's at home in a cast and they've had such bad luck with nurses and the one they've got now is walking out. Victor asked me if I thought you might help.'

'How does he know I'm a nurse?'

'I told him.'

'Oh.'

Why should I mind? I was proud of being a nurse. But I did not like my image of the conversation: *What's your boy friend do? He's not my boy friend. What's he do? He's a nurse. A nurse?* And up would go the eyebrow over the cool grey eye, and Victor would dismiss me as no threat.

'Oh please,' Fanny said. 'They're awfully nice people, and they've got this lovely old farmhouse –'

'In the country?'

'You like the country.'

'I'd have to live there?'

'You'll love it.'

'Don't programme me.' She had learned to do that in Wales from Dr Skully who had told her she could tune into dreams like a radio. 'I'll see.'

'Shall I tell them yes? Got to go. Bye.'

'Another job?' Mrs Snow turned round, drying her pink hands on a dish towel printed with pictures of the Churchills' golden wedding roses.

'Perhaps.'

'I hope it will go better than this one.' She smiled, the smile turning inward, since I was already out of her life.

'Did you mind,' I asked her, 'me telling you that your husband was dying?'

'I'd have killed you if you hadn't.' She hung the towel neatly on the front of the stove, and I saw her toughness, and that she would be all right here in this cobwebby damp house, or in the nice room with her bits of furniture.

II

Harry and Georgina Ross lived in a large stone farmhouse, which had sat for centuries in the middle of its own burgeoning land.

The retiring nurse met me at the station in a fogged-up Land-Rover.

'Three cars,' he said laconically, as I climbed on to the hard front seat with my feet in what looked like a chicken's nest. 'Nurse drives the Rover.'

'How long have you been here?'

'Too long.' His profile was laconic too. He looked through the smeared windscreen, his face and voice telling me nothing.

We drove in silence through banks foaming with cow parsley. I wanted to ask him about the patient, but he would only answer, 'The usual', or, 'Normal ortho care'.

'Why do they have trouble with nurses?' I asked.

He shrugged a shoulder as if I were only making conversation.

'Got another job?' I asked chattily.

'Not yet.'

'But you don't want this one?'

'You can have it.'

'Why?'

His small fastidious hands, which did not look as though they could do the things that nurses do, tugged the stiff wheel. He trundled the Land-Rover over a cattle grid on to the rutted road that ran between the wide fields. Bright green wheat. Dark leaves of sugar beet. Aromatic flowering beans. Beyond a fold of pasture where yellow cows lay in the wet grass, farm buildings came into view, old tile roofs, the tin roof of a high Dutch barn, wandering old walls, and then the many gables and chimneys of the house, its thick tiles chequered with moss, a long, low, lovely place. As always, when I saw something like this, I wondered what the hell I was doing in Clapham.

'Why can I have it?' I asked the wooden profile again.

'You'll see.'

'What's wrong with him?'

He did not answer. He drove round to the back of the house – small deep-set windows, mullioned bays, random stone porches and outhouses stuck on as periodic afterthoughts, a garden full of glorious trees – and stopped in a yard outside the back door.

As he got out he turned and looked at me for the first time.

'It's not him,' he said, his lips sucked in, his eyes deadpan. 'It's her.'

There are several reasons why people hire male nurses for male patients (they can't hire them for women, alas. A male nurse is not allowed alone in a room with a female patient, or even in the back of an ambulance, even if he's queer). One: as a companion. Two: they can't get a female. Three: a man is stronger. Four: less irritating (questionable). Five: old ladies fear a female nurse will seduce the old man into leaving her his money. Six: to service the wife.

I never heard of number six working out satisfactorily, but they are always hoping.

Had Mrs Ross had a go at Deadpan? She must be in dire need.

She greeted me affably, assessing me with sideways looks through dark glasses on a grey day as we walked down a cool passage and across a stone-floored hall with an enormous fireplace you would need every inch of in winter.

'Victor said you were young.' She cultivated a husky voice, or booze and fags had done it for her. 'But not as young as this.'

'I'm older than I look.' I always said that when people said that. It was not true. Perhaps one day it would be. If my unremarkable young face in the crowd did not grow seared and singular as I matured, I would grow a brown beard and force my sideways forelock back to show the noble bones.

'How old are you?' Mrs Ross gave me an amused look, shoving up the glasses into the thick hair, which was at the crossroads where she would either have to let it go grey, or do something about it.

'Twenty-six.'

'He's twenty-six, Harry. That should make you feel about a hundred.'

She opened the door of a room that had been converted from a library to a bedroom for the injured man. Books and panelling and a fireplace with a carved stone arch. A cushioned seat in the three-sided bay looked out to where the land dropped down a slope of orchard into the patterned greens and yellows of the valley.

Harry Ross lay on a hospital bed, naked above a full cast that encased both legs to the waist, exercising his arms and shoulders on an overhead bar. He let himself down with a grunt, wiped a hand on his chest hair, and held it out to me.

'Welcome to the pest house.' He was a strong, agreeable man of about forty-five, an outdoor face fading from enforced indoors, clipped hair on a square head, none of Victor's cool wariness in his friendly eyes and mouth.

'Richard Hayes.' I got my hand back.

'Sorry. My top half's got stronger. Good of you to take me on at such short notice. Where's Fletcher?' he asked his wife.

'Fled.' She made a face.

'He fill you in on me?'

'Not much,' I said, 'but it seems straightforward.'

'Straightforward helpless,' he said, 'in most of the ways that matter. What shall I call you? Richard? I had a Mrs Richards before Fletcher. Great beefy arms. And I've got a Dick. He's away at school.'

'You can call me Richie, if you like.' I had not been Richie yet to a patient.

Seeing that we liked each other Mrs Ross put a hand that looked more like town than country on top of his brindle hair and told me, 'This ridiculous creature thought he could climb all over the roofs like a boy. "Mending some tiles, Georgie," he calls down to me. Crash. Mending his femurs now, he is.'

'It's bad luck. Fanny told me.'

'Ah, Fanny,' said Mrs Ross mysteriously.

'You know her?'

'We know *of* her.' She slitted her eyes in amusement.

How, know of her? What did they know? What did Victor tell them? *Victor's latest. Poor Eileen.* My mind raced off and came back like elastic to Harry Ross saying, 'Another three months in this strait-jacket. I hope you can stand it.'

'I don't know how long I —'

'Oh Christ, they all say that,' Mrs Ross said impatiently. 'Move in, move out. Complain, sulk, make trouble. It's like a bloody circus. I'm sick of it.'

'Try getting used to different nursing every two weeks,' her husband said.

'Try getting used to their different food fads.' She stuck out her tongue at him, a long pointed tongue, with morning fur on it. 'Only the clichés are the same.' Going to the door in the wide tweed pants that hid her feet, she asked me, 'Are you Irish?'

'No.'

'All nurses are Irish. Unless they're black. And even then.'

'Shut up, Georgie.' The man on the bed turned his head wearily sideways. He needed a shave and a bath. He needed a lot of things Fletcher had fled from this morning. 'No wonder they don't stay.'

'Old Rich will.' She turned in the doorway to give me a dazzler. She had marvellous teeth, big and rather prominent, like an American who has escaped the temples of orthodontistry. 'We'll be so good to him. He'll stay.'

*

I stayed longer than I meant to. I had only thought of staying about a week until they found somebody else. But although Harry and his cast were heavy to turn and lift, the nursing was enjoyable, because necessary. Nurses are not really power-hungry. It's just that a helpless patient makes it more worthwhile. He and I got on all right, and one day led to another with things we planned to do, and before I knew it, it was two weeks since Fletcher had fetched me in the Land-Rover and been driven away himself by the farm manager, with Georgina Ross's thumb to her nose as the deadpan profile went past the window.

She gave me no trouble and I thought Fletcher had been fantasizing, if you can fantasize with a face like that. Perhaps he was more her style. There's some to suit all tastes.

They seemed to have a lot of friends, or at least people who rumbled over the cattle grid for a free country weekend, with plenty of gin and incredible food produced by Georgina at erratic hours, depending on the gin. There was a houseful the first weekend I was there, coming in and out of Harry's room with drinks and stories and packs of cards and magazine articles he must see and tales of what he was missing in the outside world.

One of them, a short thick man called Hugo in roll-neck sweaters, who should have stuck to shirts, seemed to be a stand-in. Fetching linen upstairs, I saw him through the half-open door in Georgina's bedroom.

It was a huge room like a banqueting hall, the full width of the house, the roof supported by a vaulted beam which was famous for something or other – being cut from a thousand-year-old tree, or taken from a galleon, whatever it was. Everyone who came to the house had to visit Georgina's bedroom, where they viewed her four-poster with its historic quilt made by ten blind girls in a Victorian poorhouse, and the secret door in the panelling for lovers or priests, that had once led to an underground passage.

Georgina was brushing her hair at the dressing-table and Hugo was sitting on the quilt with his shoes off. I got the impression over my pile of sheets and towels that he was not in there for the ritual viewing.

I had been led in for that on my first day, then she left me alone. She was so used to having a nurse in the house that she hardly noticed me. She introduced me to guests or not, it didn't make much difference. I was the non-person who 'looks after Harry', the original invisible man.

The wives of two of the men on the farm came in to help over the weekend. Dorothea, with a curled hairpiece that almost matched her hair, fed me in the kitchen. When Harry did not need me, or was with the guests, I went out, or watched the children's portable television in my room, which was high up among the jumble of roof angles and charred chimney pots.

Because it reminded Harry of hospital, I did not wear my white jacket with the SRN badge. Meeting me in passages or on the stairs, guests would greet me vaguely. Occasionally someone would offer me a drink, or if stuck with me in a room, talk to me about my patient, or about their own ailments, which they supposed to be my only subject, like a doctor at a cocktail party.

Sometimes Mrs Ross invited me into the drawing-room for a drink before dinner. If I accepted she watched me impatiently, afraid I might ask for another and stay the whole evening. If I refused, because I had had my dinner ages ago in the kitchen, it was, 'Good little Rich. Don't you ever come off the job?'

I usually went to the village when I wanted an off-duty drink. There was a nice old pub there with good dark beer. The local people were friendly, but detached.

'Working up at the farm then?' They knew the unkempt Land-Rover.

'I'm taking care of Mr Ross.'

'Poor chap. How is he?'

'Pretty good. It takes a long time.'

'So I hear. Well, good luck.'

Having established that I was who they thought I was they lost interest. I made friends with two free-wheeling girls called Joyce and Ethel who were camping on the gorse common outside the village. We all went to the cinema in the Land-Rover, and stopped at the Stag for a drink on the way home, while Joyce and Ethel argued about who would get me, or both. It was only a theoretical argument tonight since I had to go back to the farm to put Harry to bed; but tomorrow I was going to the tent instead of the cinema, to keep my hand in.

'Or keep it out,' Joyce had a loud vulgar laugh, 'of your pocket.'

A towny couple from the farm came in to do the country thing of a drink at the local. That yob with the girls guffawing in a corner . . . They knew me, and didn't know me.

Next morning, when they met me coming out of Harry's room with a covered bedpan, they knew me and didn't know me again.

'Good morning, Nurse.' Did one chat to someone carrying a bedpan containing the products of Harry's weekly pipe opener?

'How are you today?' As I went into the gents I settled their doubts with, 'How did you like the Running Stag?'

Ha ha. Great light dawns. 'How did *you*?'

*

'So I hear you have a harem in the Stag, sexy Rich.' Mrs Ross was in the kitchen chopping things that smelled good, while some of her guests prepared for the day with bloody Marys at the round table in the deep stone window. Dorothea clashed and splashed about in the scullery beyond to try and flush them out. I folded my arms and smiled. I was beginning to see why Fletcher had become laconic, if he wasn't before. Things were said to which no answer was required, or desirable.

Georgina was wearing a blue and white striped butcher's apron, with the strings tied several times tightly round the waist. She was in good shape for her age, I had to give her that, and her legs hadn't lost a thing, although she had reached the point where the whole job looked better from the back.

'Mr Ross is tired and would like to stay in bed for lunch.' When people were there, I usually took him on a wheeled stretcher into the dining-room and propped him up to eat on the couch, balancing the plate on the front of his cast.

'But he's got friends coming, dammit. His friends, not mine. Oh Christ, wouldn't you know it?'

The people at the table shook their heads and stirred their bloody Marys with a finger, to show they knew the old story, but Nurse Hayes was not going to be drawn into marriage counselling.

'Mr Ross is tired. He's got a headache.'

'Your fault for keeping him out too long.'

We had gone out early before anyone was up and driven over to see lambs on the other side of the valley. There was a door without a sill or step in one of the little stone porches which tilted in odd places round this old house. I wheeled him out on the stretcher, and his strong arms could haul himself on to the mattress in the back of the estate car. I was allowed to drive that with Harry. Otherwise it was the Land-Rover, with the knob pulled off the gear lever, and usually out of petrol.

'And making a call at the Stag?' jested one of the towny people, not realizing we were having a fight.

I did fight back at Mrs Ross, under the surface, and not in words. I fought for Harry when necessary. Upright, on two good legs, he could hold his own, but laid low with two compound fractures of femur, and a knee that might have to be opened again when the plaster came off, he needed help with Georgina.

She alternated between being impatiently casual about him – 'Oh, don't baby him, he's not paralysed, for God's sake' – and wanting to keep him victim and prisoner. 'That's insane. He can't possibly go to a point-to-point. You look ghastly, Harry. I'm going to ring Dr Lucas.'

His surgeon had recently ordered for him a special kind of trolley, which had big wheels in front with an inner wheel, so that he could propel himself by hand all over the ground floor of the house and the level parts of the garden. This would make all the difference to his life. And his wife's. She would have to readjust a bit when he was mobile.

She scooped up a handful of onions and herbs and flung it into a simmering pan with a rise of aromatic steam.

'Tomorrow,' she said, banging at a veal cutlet with the edge of a plate, 'I want you to keep him quiet all day, so he'll be fit for the party at night.'

'Tomorrow is my day off,' I said. 'Mr Hogg is coming over.'

'That hairy bore. Can't you change your day?'

'I've made a date.' I had not rung Fanny yet because time off was chancy in this house.

'Sexy Rich.' That had never been funny, and it still wasn't. 'Change it, there's a little love.'

'Sorry.'

'All right then, my good man.' She ran her oniony hand up through her thick hair and gave me her wide odontic dazzler, as the bloody Marys smiled their admiration. 'Take tomorrow off, Hayes.'

*

'Take tomorrow off, Runyon.'

After I had given Harry his lunch, and sucked out crumbs from under the cast with a vacuum cleaner, and scratched an itch with a flat wire coat hanger, and rubbed and powdered his back, I rang Fanny at work.

'Victor Ross's office. Can I – Oh, *Dick*.'

Hooray, I was a man again. Fanny's voice did marvellous things for my past, present and future.

'Take tomorrow off, Runyon.'

'Of course.' She always agreed to the unexpected.

'What about –'

I was telephoning from the hall. The silhouette of Mrs Ross appeared in front of the glass door at the end of the passage, paused, moved on.

'What?'

'Victor.'

Even saying his name brought me the unpleasant image of the unsmiling grey eyes and the tilt of his head as he put the Jaguar into gear and almost got me run over.

'Oh, bugger Victor.'

'No thanks.'

Jubilantly, I bounded outside and tore down the slope of the orchard in the long wet grass, jumped over the low wall at the end, scaring a lark into the air, and ran down the grass track with my chest full of air, as if my energy could never be used up. In the little corner wood with low trees dripping, I ran through on the squashy dark path and jumped out over the ditch, shaking water out of my hair like a giddy retriever. I could have run all the way to London.

12

Mr Hogg, the whiskered ex-orderly who obliged on my rare days off, offered to come over that night, so I caught an evening train to London, was first off at the station to battle through the crowds coming up from the Underground against me, and was sucked towards Fanny like small change in a department store vacuum tube.

At the telephone boxes I hesitated. Fanny did not know I was coming up tonight. Should I ring her? No. If she was out, she was out, and I'd go on to Clapham. If she was in, she was in, and I'd hope not to. If Victor was there, I'd make a scene. No I wouldn't. Or would I?

At Gloucester Road, a blackboard said, 'London Transport regrets inconvenience to passengers this morning. Delay was due to person on line at Green Park Station.'

I rang Fanny's bell three times before her voice said, 'I'm asleep.' When I pushed open her unlatched top door she was in bed, but she would not let me get in with her.

I sat on the outside with Maud. 'What's the matter? Are you ill?'

'No, but I've got to stay awake all night. Someone who knows about Victor's programme rang today about a poltergeist. It makes noises at night and he wants me to try and get something on tape.'

'I'll stay here while you go.' Fanny's bed, even without her, would be better than my lumpy cot at Clapham.

'You're coming with me. You'll love it.' Fanny liked to decide, not only what you were going to do, but how you would feel about it.

'And tomorrow we'll go back to the Judds. Victor wants to hear a recording of Dr Eisenberg, isn't it? I vant to spik viz you. We'll be Francis and Dixie Maude again.'

'Not me.' I still could not think properly about Jack Judd's face among the red and black shadows, sweetening for an instant to a memory of the hollow place under Millie's cheekbone.

When that image came back, at night, turning restlessly towards sleep, I felt guilty. I wanted to hold Millie's thinness, bury my face in the thick fair hair that seemed to have drawn all her strength to her head, and beg her to forgive me. Once I had been jerked upright and awake by the terrible thought: Suppose this was the only way she could . . .

But I could never go back to the Judds.

To stop Fanny talking about it, I began to tell her about the job. How much did she know about Georgina and Harry? How much would she tell Victor? I did not care. I told her everything. I always told her everything. I stroked the arm that lay outside the blanket, and told her about Fletcher's laconic hints. About Hugo. The weekend guests. The person I had found weeping in the little sitting-room once when I came down to answer Harry's buzzer in the night. About my alliance with Harry and my unspoken war with Georgina. Even about Joyce and Ethel, who had been a dead loss, because when I got to the gorse common, they had pitched camp, the rats.

Fanny got out to have a bath, and I lay on the bed that was still warm from her body and looked through my feet at the fabulous skyline of the opposite terrace. I tilted my head back to the conglomerate chimney pots and catwalks outside the back window and wished that I could move in here with Fanny.

When she came out of the bathroom in a towel, with small wet feet like a child's, I asked her, 'When I'm through with this job, why can't I come and live with you?'

'You know you can't.'

'Why?'

She slid her eyes sideways in a way she had when she was going to lie, or change the subject.

'Why can't I?'

Instead of answering, she asked, 'Why do you want to leave John?'

'I don't. Yes, I do. We both do, I think. I don't know. Two guys, scrapping over the milk bill and who'll go to the launderette, it's a bit juvenile. I think we've outgrown each other.'

'Where will you go?'

'Here. I told you.'

She had dressed in front of me, not to tease, but to make us seem like brother and sister, dammit. She pulled on a sweater and we left Maud on the bed and went down to the car.

*

The poltergeist's house was the most unhaunted place you could imagine. A newish, suburbanish white house with green trim and window boxes in a long straight road between a country town and the factory district thereof. Nor did it contain the requisite adolescent which psychological fiction has led us to expect. It contained two middle-aged couples (we never did discover who paired with who), who had beaten the cost of housing by mucking in together on the purchase of 302 London Road.

Sensible people they were, factual and practical, the women with a well-ordered kitchen and hair styled for convenience rather than charm, one of the men with a tool bench in the cellar and a lathe for turning chair legs, the other with a darkroom under the stairs where the gents used to be.

It was the enlarger that had gone first. They had not been in this house more than a few months when they all sat straight up in the two double beds they shared with whoever it was, as an almighty crash came from below the stairs. The enlarging machine had fallen into the sink and smashed. It must have been on the edge of the shelf. Not like George to be so careless.

A few nights later the noise was lower down. Clatter in the cellar. Michael's chair legs were rolling about on the lino.

Since then, clocks had shot off mantelpieces, cups flown from hooks, with the handle still hanging, and the manuscript pages of Mary's life's work on crewel stitchery scattered from desk to floor.

Sometimes a shrill whistling sounded through the lower floors of the house. They were becoming a little unnerved. 'But we're not going to let them drive us out of this house,' Michael said, 'whoever they are. If it's them or us, it's going to be us.'

I was scared, and I think Fanny was too. But she looked eager, and said, 'I'm so glad you're giving us the chance to hear it.'

'We thought we should get it on record, so people won't think we're barmy,' Michael said.

'We're going to get someone to come and clean it all out,' George said, as if it were the drains.

Perhaps they would like Jack Judd and the Doctor to do an exorcism, in psychic Viennese.

After they had shown us the house, they all went to bed – who with who? – and Fanny and I settled in the front room. The sofa was new and hard, so we put the cushions on the floor. We listened for ages but nothing happened.

Fanny would not let me talk to her in case she missed anything, so I stopped being scared and went to sleep.

I woke in fright, as the door opened.

'Got everything you want?' Michael's voice in the dark.

'Yes, thanks. We thought you were asleep.'

'Just came down to say make coffee when you want. Heard anything yet?'

'Not a thing.'

'Good luck. If that vase on the mantelpiece takes off again – duck.'

We listened to him going upstairs. A door shut. The house was quiet. We listened, and it listened back to us. Fanny got up and took the vase off the mantelpiece and put it on the floor.

'You make the coffee,' she said, as she lay down. 'I'm not moving from this room.'

'Nor me.'

I turned to put my arms round her but she turned away.

'Why not?' I said to the back of her smooth black hair. 'You can hear just as well with me holding you.'

'It's not that, Dick.'

'Victor?' I made myself say it.

Fanny did not answer.

'You're a fool,' I said. 'A middle-aged radio producer no one has ever heard of, who doesn't give a damn about you.'

That was a guess, but she sighed and said, 'I suppose he does, in his way.'

Then she rolled over and hid her face against my sweater and said, in a gasp, 'I'm so sick of doing it his way. Discreetly. That means hole and corner. Restaurants where he's not known. When he can get away, I wait about for him. Hours sometimes.

Days once, when he was in France, and we were supposed to meet in Antibes.'

'It sounds deadly,' I said.

'It is.'

I thought she was crying quietly. Then her breathing slowed and deepened and we both slept.

*

I woke to the traffic beginning, and the grey light of London Road filtering through the fibreglass curtains. Fanny was still asleep, with her lashes curling, but when I touched her awake she swore she had stayed awake all night.

'What did you hear?'

'I don't know. Nothing.'

She was relaxed from sleep and smiling. I put my arms round her and held her tightly on the sofa cushions. I had never held her like this before. Her body was so different from Millie's. She was strong, firm, not breakable. She —

The door opened and Michael came in looking spruce in polka-dot pyjamas and polished spectacle lenses. He had either shaved at 6 a.m. or did not grow a beard.

He regarded us calmly, while we let go of each other and sat up.

'Hear anything?'

'Nothing, I'm afraid.'

'Wily beggars. But we've never had more than twenty-four quiet hours since it started. Can you come back tonight?'

I said, 'I'm afraid not,' before Fanny could open her mouth. I did not want her lying on the sofa cushions without me.

'Sometimes it plays tricks in the daytime. I was at home once with the flu, felt rotten, stomach upset, nose blocked, throat scratchy, ached all over.' Michael had been watching too many commercials. 'I was upstairs trying to rest when, by God, if the plaster didn't start flaking off the ceiling, all into my hair. "You've gone white overnight," my wife said, when she nipped home in her lunch hour.'

Mary got up in a blue quilted dressing-gown and slippers with clipped pompoms, and made us a beautiful breakfast, and we drove away from the neat, unspooky house, with the hedge trimmed geometrically (Michael), and the fence sparkling white (George).

At the flat Maud greeted us hysterically, as if she thought she had been abandoned again. We both had a bath, not together, and this time Fanny did not dress in front of me. She put on a yellow and orange sweater since we were going to drive up and see the Major, who did not have much brightness at the Turrets.

Maud began to bark again, standing on the pillow with her feet on the window-sill, to abuse a dog in the mews below, her hair bristling along her knobbed spine, her ratty tail going like a maddened metronome.

'Wherever you go after the job with Harry Ross,' Fanny told me, 'you'll have to live somewhere you can have Maud; I can't keep her if she's going to bark.'

We stuffed Maud into the straw bag and took her down. The girl on the next floor came out as we were waiting for the lift.

'How's the dog?' she asked.

'What dog?'

'Look,' she said. 'Everybody knows about it. Including Mr Ewing.'

'He doesn't mind then?'

'He minds.'

The lift came up mysteriously, like a lit coffin. The girl crowded in with us, so that I could not ram Fanny against the scratched metal side and kiss her for half a minute as I usually did.

We found the Major in a long day-room at the Turrets, spryly dressed among the dressing-gowns and shapeless smocks, hooking a rug contentedly. But when he saw us, he pushed the rug into the lap of an old lady tied into a rocking-chair and staggered desperately to the door.

'Thank God you've come!'

He was excited, his nose on fire. We sat him down and chatted for a while.

'My mother said that Grandpa left you something in –' Fanny began, but the Major whispered fiercely, 'Not here!' glaring round the room at the harmless occupants and the two kindly women in blue overalls who were dispensing coffee from a trolley.

'Come on out for a drive then,' Fanny said. 'Would you like to?'

'Would I?' He pushed himself half up, then sank back with a sigh. 'They'll never let me.'

But when Fanny asked one of the women, she said, 'Of course, how lovely for him,' and went at once to fetch the Major's coat.

'They seem all right,' I said, as we went down the passage to the door, Fanny holding his arm, me behind to prop him when he staggered backwards.

'That's because you were there. They're clever at it, you see. Years of practice.'

Maud and I sat in the luggage space at the back of the car and we drove up the hill. At the pond the Major took his watch out of the pocket of his gravy-and-ash-stained waistcoat, snapped open the lid, and said, 'They're open.'

We took him into Jack Straw's Castle.

'Walk behind me, my boy,' he said. 'Cover my tracks.' Inside he looked all round, sighting with his nose for spies, before he would sit down at a table in the darkest corner.

I bought barley wine and sandwiches from the bar, and Fanny asked him again about her grandfather's will.

In spite of my fantasies in the green leather study Mr Stillman had left Phyllis enough to build the house in Portugal. He had left his old friend a hundred pounds. The Major looked round the bar again before he told us this, behind his hand.

'It's in Savings,' he whispered. 'I'm going to leave it there till I've got enough.'

'Enough for what?'

The Major shot a glance at an American couple at the next table, pints of beer among the maps and cameras.

'To buy my freedom,' he said. 'They don't know. If they know you've got money, they take it away from you. Promise to take care of you for the rest of your days. But,' he put a finger along his nose and winked at me, 'what they take care of is that you shouldn't have too many days.'

'How, sir?'

'Oh, come on, my boy, you know how it's done. You're in the profession.' The good strong barley wine allowed him to laugh out loud, and forget to check for eavesdroppers. 'One sneeze, and up flies the window. One cough, and your bed's pushed out in a draughty passage. All the old dodges. You know 'em.'

We hated having to take him back to the Turrets. It was a nice enough place as far as they go, but he shrank into himself and became silent as we went down the hill, and made Fanny stop at the corner so that no one should see the car.

'Why not?'

'They'll take your number, girl.'

'And do what with it?'

'They have their methods.'

We took him one on each arm to the door, where he was greeted rapturously by a blue-black girl with shiny eyelids who called him Uncle Billy and unwound his muffler lovingly. But as she led him away, our last sight of him was the glance with which he reached back for us over his shoulder, one eye searching, the other hidden by the salient of his nose.

When we moved in together at last, we would have the Major to live with us. Perhaps Mrs Snow too, later on, with some bits of furniture. Dixie and Frances Maude. Rooms for old relics.

Coming down into St John's Wood we were going to call on General Sir Richard Noakes and see if he would like to live with us too. But there was a match on at Lord's, and he would be in the members' stand with his hat tilted down against the invisible sun.

As we waited to cross Maida Vale, Fanny said, 'Do you want to go and be the Maudes?' She jerked her head to the right, towards the no-man's-land where the Judds dwelt.

'Fanny, I can't.'

'Were you afraid?' She looked at me closely and curiously, the way children look at each other.

'I don't know. Yes. I mean, I know it's impossible, but suppose it *was* possible.'

'To hear Millie?' Fanny said it quickly, on an indrawn breath.

'Using that — that sort of *unworthy* man.' It was the only word I could think of to describe what I had felt about Jack

Judd in connection with Millie. 'It seems not fair. Like opening a coffin.'

I could not explain properly, to Fanny or myself. Or ever to Millie. What I remembered of Millie.

'It's all right.' Fanny put her hand on my knee. She took it off to put the car in gear and turned safely to the left, away from the Judds. 'I'll go another time.'

'Don't go back there.' I thought of Ireen's dry clasped hands and straining, constipated face, the suffused obscenity of Jack Judd, snoring like a cerebral catastrophe. Truth or trickery, there had been something quite nasty about the Place of Peace, with its red shaded lamp and tartan couch. The poltergeist farce had been much jollier and more sanitary.

'Victor wants me to. He thinks it will make good radio.' Fanny put on her conscientious, career-girl voice, with which she talked about her work. BBC researcher, in conference with Victor Ross. Did he have a tartan couch too?

'I don't want you to.'

'Victor will be angry.'

'Good.'

'All right.'

Gear-changing over, Fanny put her hand back on my knee, and her long, lovely mouth spread into a smile. With the length of her mouth and the jutting shape of the lower part of her face, her smiles spread backwards as well as sideways, round the corners with the most beautiful fluency. 'Where shall we go?'

'Back to the flat.'

I had always known that our first time together had to be in Fanny's flat, under the window with the crazy skyline view of chimney pots and iron steps and catwalks, which had once led the Edwardian underdogs to their trysts of ecstasy.

13

When the grey dusk had deepened into the light night sky of London, we lay on our stomachs with our elbows on pillows against the window-sill, and looked out at the crazy skyline of chimney pots and iron steps and catwalks, which had once led the Edwardian underdogs to their trysts of ecstasy, like ours.

It had been done before in this room, and it would be done again (by me and Fanny, among others), but it would never be done like that for the first time. Often, it's not much good the first time together. This time it was, that's all.

*

When it was time to go to the station we saw that a note from the caretaker had been pushed under the door. It was a bill.

'*To keeping quiet about dog. £5.*'

Blackmail. I would not let Fanny pay. 'I'll take her to the farm.'

'Haven't they got dogs?'

'She'll like that.' Maud was as gregarious as if she had never looked in a mirror.

'Georgina won't.'

'Who cares? It'll be me and Maud or nothing. And she wants me, I'm afraid.'

'Don't be afraid.' Fanny kissed me. 'Maud will protect you.'

We put the big straw bag back on top of the cupboard, and took Maud downstairs on a piece of string. In the street I threw a handful of builders' sand at Mr Ewing's basement window to make him look out and took Maud back to the farm. At the station I couldn't start the Land-Rover. It got fits like that, because everybody on the farm drove it, whether they could drive or not, and abused it beyond its natural capacity for punishment.

It was late and there were no taxis, so Maud and I got a lift with a man who had been on the train. He dropped us at the cattle grid where the farm road wandered off through the dark fields and we walked up to the house.

Maud, who had not been in the country since Windsor Park,

and never perhaps in open country like this, went frantic. She raced off after some night creature and disappeared through a hedge in a shower of shrill urban barks. She would have to learn to go baying after prey, like a proper farm dog.

I did not see or hear her again, but I did not worry. Ugly, raffish Maud had never been a dependent dog, looking back every few yards to check on you. Her trauma in the deserted flat, watching the door day after day with her nose on her ginger paws, had killed her trust in people. Now she did not need them.

As I came over the rise and round the elms by the pasture gate, I saw that the party was still going on. There were lights everywhere, and music.

I could not face meeting a lot of half-potted people, and either being explained away, '... who looks after Harry', and half-heartedly offered a democratic drink, or being dragged in by a tiddly Georgina: 'Sexy Rich! Come and tell us about your date'. Would she know? With girls you can always tell if they've been at it. Would it show on me?

I sneaked under the lit front windows to the side porch. From there I could reach the little back staircase which led through various angles and levels to the old servants' wing, where my room was. Later, when things subsided, I would come down again and risk crossing the hall to see if Harry was all right. Mr Hogg would have put him to bed before he left. I hoped there were not too many people rioting in Harry's room. Because he never complained people treated him like a healthy man who happened to have both legs imprisoned like a mermaid. But he did have a lot of discomfort and pain. He was exhausted by the end of an ordinary evening, much less a party.

A brick path led round the house to the porch. It was dark here, away from the music, under the windows of the room the children used when they were at home. I whistled for Maud, and called her. Maud is an awful name to call. I used to feel like an idiot yelling it over the populous wastes of Clapham Common, but it was the only name she would answer to, and then not always.

I whistled again and listened. I heard her bark, muffled.

She had flushed something behind the brick sheds at the end of the house, where cars and bicycles were kept. I went to the corner to look and with a ghostly rush, something was on me, something swift and silent that hit me in the middle and knocked me into a clipped yew bush, and tipped itself over on to the grass in a yell of laughter and spinning spokes, with Maud scrambling after it for the kill.

Harry swore, beating off Maud as she tried to lick his face.

'What the hell are you doing?' I pushed myself out of the yew and went to pull off the dog.

'My new trolley.' It lay on its side, big shiny wheels in the air. It had tipped Harry unhurt on to the wet grass. 'It came this afternoon.' He put his hands behind his head and smiled up at me as if he were there for the night. 'Old Hogg left me on it for the party. When I heard your voice, I got someone to help me outside, so I could whiz round and surprise you. Then that rabid thing came after me. What is it?'

'It's Maud. I had nowhere to leave her.'

'Georgie won't stand for it.'

'If Maud goes, I go.'

'Then she'll stand it. Get me back on to the bier, Richie, and I'll show you my speed.'

*

Georgina discovered the dog next morning. 'Not in this house.'

'If Maud goes, I go.'

'Don't make issues.' She was hung over. 'I said not in the house.'

There were dogs around the farm, none in the house. Maud won by not wanting to come in the house anyway. She took up with the farm dogs and fed and slept with them, one of the pack. When the man went down for the cows, there was old Maud with her stiff legs and bristled tail, trotting off to work with the slinky sheepdogs.

I got some boards, and made ramps for all the door sills on the ground floor so that Harry could propel himself everywhere on his stomach. The bier was light and silent. It went schwee-ee-ee when he gunned it across the stone flags of the wide hall, but in the rest of the house, unless a board creaked, or he ran into something, you could not hear him coming. Whispering down the cool passage, his head would suddenly appear at waist-level in the kitchen doorway. Georgina would turn from the stove with a shriek.

'Just came for some ice, my dear.'

After the party Georgina worried about her shape and went out to do some therapeutic gardening with those unlikely hands. It was a hot sunny day. Harry had been out to the farmyard, which was rutty, but navigable, and down the road as far as the field where the cows were. I was fixing boards down the steps to the lower lawn, so that he could watch people play tennis. Georgina was kneeling in a nearby flower bed when Harry came rocketing down a path and suddenly stuck his head through a bush above her bent back.

'Scare you, eh?' Harry could be a bit childish, but his opportunities for visual humour were restricted.

'Be your age.' His wife did not let herself look up, but her elegant fingertips were dug into the earth, and I could see her heart beating fast under the tight shirt.

She was out gardening not only because of her shape but because the two children, Dick and Fiona, were home from school with some friends. They were playing records on the other side of the house. The whole valley shimmered and shook in the blast of noise under the brazen sun.

The children were all right, all feet and hair. They did not talk much to Harry and Georgina, or listen. At meals they ate fast with one hand, picking at the skin on their bare toes, then jumped up to go on with what they had been doing before. They were hardly aware of me, except as an appendage of Harry, like his cast, on which they drew daisies and messages of peace and love.

Except for the children, who created their own life, there was no one staying in the house, and Georgina was bored and restless. She worked off chatter on me, but she talked at me, rather than to me. With no audience she had given up teasing me, but she still did not treat me as a person. If she had really made a pass at deadpan Fletcher and those unattractive small womanish hands, I must be slipping.

Thank God. I thought about Fanny. I thought about her telling Victor. He could fire her if he liked. She would ride no more in the grey Jaguar that matched his eyes. She would wait for him no more in dark bars and Indian restaurants. I thought about Fanny most of the time.

Then one night I passed the vaulted bedroom, and saw Georgina sitting on the side of the bed facing the door, with all the top buttons of her dressing-gown unfastened. *Agh-gh-gh!* Was it beginning?

'Hullo, Rich.' She smiled thoughtfully, and did not fasten any buttons. I walked on with what I hoped was a Fletcher profile.

The next day she announced that my hair was too long – it was much shorter than her son's or his friend's – and sat me down on a straight chair in the little back sitting-room, a place of chintzy sofas and small lamps, where guests went for intimate talks, or in secret crisis, like the one who had wept.

While she cut, with her lower lip caught between her splendid teeth, I watched in the mirror between the windows. She didn't do a bad job.

'Thanks, Mrs Ross.'

'*De rien.* I wouldn't want that soft, sexy stuff to be butchered by the local barber on his day off from castrating bullocks.'

To my horror, I saw her put the scissors into the pocket of her poppy-bright overall and move her hand, palm towards me, fingers almost giving out sparks, to run it under my hair and up the back of my head. *Fanny – help!*

I pushed back the chair clumsily and stood up, shaking my head and brushing hair off my shoulders. Nothing was said. Nothing was ever said. But I knew. And she knew that I knew. Would she strike again?

*

I asked Harry what they were doing about getting another nurse. 'I can't stay here for ever.'

'It's not for ever. Just till I get this stinking cast off.'

'I've got another job booked.' I was sitting on the window seat at the other end of the room. I did not like to say this to him, but it was time for me to get out.

'Victor said he didn't think you were busy.'

'All nurses are busy.'

'Don't be like that, Richie. Look, we'll give you more money. Would that help?'

Oh God. The nicest people have their generous ways of thwarting your desires. I looked out over the valley, where bellying rain clouds churned and re-formed in the wind that drove them across the ridge.

'Would it?'

'Would it what?' Georgina came in.

'I'm raising Richie's pay to make him stay,' Harry told her.

'But of course.' Georgina went out.

Trapped. Weak fool. I began to leave notes for myself in drawers and inside my shoes in the cupboard: *Got to get out*, and, *I am going mad*. And *Fanny!* some of the notes said. *Fanny. Fanny.*

*

Georgina was taking the children back to school and staying the night in London with Victor.

'And so what will you and POR do?' Since the hair-cutting episode and the increased pay, I was no longer sexy Rich. I was Poor Old Rich.

'Nothing.'

Harry was low. We had spent most of the day before at the hospital. He lay on a trolley in Casualty, while I tried to ferret the X-ray technician out of the dark room, or lunch room, or wherever he was. But in a hospital an outside nurse carries less weight than even the anxious relations.

Then we waited for the films to be developed. Then we waited for the surgeon to be found. Then we waited until two other patients were finished with the plaster room. Then it took two hours and considerable pain to remove the peace-and-daisies cast, and swathe Harry in a spotless new one. The surgeon and the plaster nurse wrinkled their noses as the shears cut away the old cast.

'Bit high,' the surgeon said, to no one in particular, but was meant for me.

'It's been on two months, sir.'

'I know that. I put it on.'

All right, I was not the world's best nurse. In training I was constantly on the mat, I'd scraped through my exams, and as a

Charge Nurse, I ran a happy but sloppy ward, which nearly fell apart the day they did a spot-check inventory. But a two-months-old cast is going to get a bit high, however careful you are.

I said nothing. The surgeon offered me a few hints on basic nursing techniques. I lit a cigarette for Harry and he saw my face.

'He does all that,' he told the surgeon. 'He's a damn good nurse.'

'I daresay.'

The plaster nurse winked at me, but I did not wink back.

Harry stayed in bed the next day. The children came in to say goodbye and to leave new messages on the pristine plaster. Fiona, who was going to grow up gentler than her mother, wrote, *Remember that I love you*, and drew a heart with an arrow through it.

'Time to go.' Georgina came in and Fiona raised the endless crinkly hair which was spread over the cast. 'Phone call for you, Rich,' Georgina added as an afterthought. 'Some kind of girl.'

It was Fanny.

'I've got to see you.'

'Me too.'

'Get time off.'

'I can't. Harry's alone. Georgina's taking the children back to school and staying the night in London.'

'Can I come there?'

Fanny's voice poured joy into me.

'Georgina would murder me.'

'She won't know. I'll come after Harry's in bed.'

'He's in bed now.' My grin spread.

Georgina called me in a high, peremptory voice, like hailing a taxi. I told Fanny quickly how to get there and to leave her car behind the sheds so that Harry would not hear. *Fanny.* I went through the hall grinning.

'We're going.' Georgina was halfway out of the door. She saw the grin and came back. 'Who was that? Not Fanny, was it?' The amused eyebrow.

'No, a friend.'

'Oh.' Georgina lost interest, beyond a passing surprise that I had friends, or any life at all outside my job, and went out.

14

I was finishing Harry's back, and straightening the bottom sheet, when we heard the engine of Fanny's car, which sounded lustier than it was.

'Who on earth?' Harry was still tired. 'Tell 'em I'm dead.'

I made a show of going out to look. 'Only someone going to one of the cottages.'

'Thank God.'

I had planned to persuade him to take a sleeping tablet but he asked for one anyway. I turned out the light, left on quiet music and a shaded lamp, and went out to Fanny.

Maud had already found her. She had come from wherever she slept in the farm buildings and was sitting in the passenger seat, looking alertly through the windscreen, as if she expected to be taken back to London.

'Maud's pregnant,' Fanny said, after we had blocked out the night, and time, with our kiss.

'She can't be.' But why not? Even beautiful silky sheep dogs don't go by looks.

'Didn't you know? Some nurse.'

'We didn't do obstetrics.' The male students had stood in the doorway of the labour ward and once, when they were busy, a nurse in Maternity had asked me to bind a girl's breasts, if she did not object. She had objected.

It was raining again. The hot weather had broken and it had been raining for days. The damp house sat like a mushroom in the dripping countryside. The side door was swollen and stuck, so we ran round the house to the back door. Maud came in with us, either because she liked Fanny better than me, or because she knew Georgina was gone. We went into the kitchen and I fell upon Fanny with a sigh.

When I said that I loved her she put her hand over my mouth. 'Don't.'

I bit the hand. 'Why not?'

'It changes things. And it hurts too much when it's cancelled.'

'It won't be.'

'It always is.'

She turned away and looked round the kitchen quite sadly. She talked about needing to be free and independent, not wanting me or anyone to tie her down. Now, looking smaller than usual, and uncertain in Georgina's large kitchen with the Italian tile floor and huge clean stove and thick striped chopping blocks, I thought she lied. What she was afraid of was rejection.

I made coffee and we sat at the round table in the window where guests sat with booze while Georgina was brilliantly cooking, and I sat without booze for my meals more opaquely cooked by Dorothea. I told Fanny about the haircutting, and Georgina's creeping hands, and her sadness left her and she laughed, leaning her head back among the window-sill greenery that Dorothea tended, and Georgina took credit for.

Like Millie, she loved to be made to laugh, or to make herself laugh. Millie's mother would have thought us just as silly as she used to think Millie and I were when we sat at her kitchen table with the sauce bottles on it and laughed about nothing.

I washed the bright lipstick off Fanny's mug very carefully, and hung it back on the same hook.

'Would Georgina be jealous?' Fanny asked.

'She could make trouble. It's not really ethical to move in women as soon as the family goes out.'

I thought of my friend Albert Briggs, who had moved in booze, and passed out on the pantry floor, while his elderly patient passed out on the bedroom floor above, and fractured a hip. I thought of that shrieking old queen Greeley Watkins, who had moved in his boyfriend, and kept him for quite a while in the garage flat of the chain-store magnate, to the cheering of whose last days he was supposed to be single-mindedly dedicated.

Albert and Greeley had been sacked, as I would be, if Georgina found out about Fanny. I wanted to get out of here, but not to be kicked out. A thing like that follows you around, professionally. Greeley had ended up, boyless, nursing geriatric psychopaths on the Isle of Man.

I went to look at Harry. He was deeply peaceful, tilted on his side against pillows as I had left him, the face of a younger man renewed each night in sleep.

Fanny came into the doorway and looked at him with her eyebrows raised, making a tender mouth.

'He's better looking than Victor,' she whispered.

'You've never seen him?'

'I told you. Hole and corner.'

In the hall outside Harry's door I held her tightly and whispered, 'Stay here.'

'I can't.'

'The cleaning women don't come before nine and Georgina won't be back.'

'I can't.' Fanny bent her head so that the square ends of her hair swung over her face. 'I've got to be at the office early to work on the script about the hypnotist.'

'Haven't you been sacked yet? What have you told Victor?'

She shook back her hair and kissed me, and I whispered, 'Stay a bit longer.'

'All right.'

We had the choice of the whole of the big quiet house, where clocks ticked thoughtfully and the woodwork made small rustling noises, but we went up the twisting backstairs to my little room. From the window you could see a dozen different crazy roof angles, chimney pots singly, or in uneven lines of four or five, the tops of the dripping elms, a stone path lighter than the dark lawn.

'It's lovely up here.' Fanny always went to the window first in any new room, inspecting out of it before she inspected within it.

'I hate it.'

'Why?'

'I'm trapped.'

'You can leave any time.'

'It's not so easy.'

Maud had not been up here since I smuggled her up that first night. She went sniffing round to check the room. I had not seen her for several days but I saw now that she was indeed going to reproduce whatever species she was.

Fanny poked round too. She always inspected every new room. I had a vision of us together, porters taking tips and leaving, and Fanny poking in and out of drawers and cupboards in hotel rooms all over the world.

'What's this?' She found one of my notes. *I'm going mad.* 'Is it that bad? I'd never have asked you but Victor always said they —'

She crouched on the floor to read the note in my slipper. She froze, looking up at me with her mouth open, as a door crashed somewhere far below.

'Somone's here.'

The crash had sounded like Georgina's way of shutting the heavy front door. I went down to see if she had changed her mind and come back tonight. She had. Worse, she had brought Victor and his wife Serena. They had all decided London stank, and driven down for country peace.

'This is the boy,' Georgina waved a hand at me, 'who looks after Harry.'

Victor turned round from the drinks table. 'I know.' He nodded, tried his whisky with predatory lips, found it more or less acceptable, and turned away to sit down.

'You've met?'

'I've seen him.'

'I see.'

Georgina gave her Fanny smile. 'Serena, that's Rich.' Smile extra satisfied, as she indicates (introduces would be too gracious a word) Serena to the boyfriend of her husband's ex-girlfriend.

'Everything all right?' she asked me.

'Mr Ross is asleep.'

'Why aren't you?' Since the patient was my only excuse for taking up vertical living space.

'I was just going to bed, Mrs Ross.'

Did Serena, fortyish, fluffyish, detect the drums of war beneath the civility?

'We're staying up for a bit. Goodnight.'

Fanny had taken off her dress and was lying on my bed, half asleep.

'Victor's here,' I said.

She sat up, flushed, not from sleep.

'What have you told him?' I asked her.

'Nothing . . . yet.'

'Why not?'

'I need the job.'

'Not that badly. His wife's here too. You ever seen her?'

She shook her head. Since I was angry with her I described Serena as younger and more attractive than she actually was.

'I've got to get out of here.' Fanny swung her legs down and trod into her shoes.

'Not yet. I'd never get the side door unstuck without a lot of noise, and you can't risk the others without being seen.'

'They'll go to bed.'

'They're staying up. And Georgina doesn't sleep well. She gets up and wanders.' Taking hot milk to Harry just before dawn I had once met Georgina in an Empire see-through with splayed nipples. *Ouch!*

'I'll climb over the roof.' Fanny was at the window, her back looking more mature than it was in the chaste white slip. The rain had started again and all the roof angles were steep and streaming.

'Not in this.' I brought her back to the bed. 'Stay here with me and go early.'

*

I awoke confused. I was alone, but the bed smelled of Fanny. I turned and saw her with her dress on, at the window.

'Come on,' she said. 'It's stopped raining. I'd better go.'

There was no moon, but the sky was lighter and the trees were stirring with birds. I climbed out of the window with Fanny and we slid down the tiles, edged round a corner chimney stack, and along a gully between two roof angles. We were making for the end of the house, where we could drop down to a flat level, and then to the gabled top of one of the porches. It was quite easy.

'We must do this again,' I said. Fanny and I seemed to be always climbing in and out of houses.

She kissed me and jumped down from the porch and I watched her run over the lawn, leaving dark traces in the wet silver grass. I heard her start the car.

A light went on in Georgina's room. A window opened. I edged back on the porch gable, and a loose tile fell.

'Who's that?'

'POR.'

'What the hell are you doing?'

'Taking a walk.' I talked down at the ground, hoping that was how you did ventriloquism.

'Is Harry all right?'

'Yes.' I had not checked him again but he had a buzzer to my room.

Georgina shut her window. The light stayed on. I climbed back to my room with more difficulty, cut my shin and bruised a toe, and thought about Fanny zipping back to London to change and be at the office early. Maud barked at me as I came over the sill.

In the morning Georgina said, 'I told you that dog couldn't come in the house.'

'She wasn't well,' I said. 'She's pregnant.'

'Dear God.' Georgina put her hand over her eyes and appealed to Victor.

He looked quite old in the morning light, drinking black coffee with pale lips, in a grey-on-grey shirt, one side of his silvering hair bent up from the pillow. But I was staying here with Georgina and he was going back to London for the day, where Fanny would be in his office, writing a script about a hypnotist who made a woman remember what it was like to be born in a train crossing the Canadian Rockies.

15

So another day started badly, and got worse. Harry woke with a Codeine headache. When I suggested aspirin he called me a pill-pusher.

'You asked for the sleeping tablet.'

'You gave it to me.'

He was sour and difficult over his bath and the various things I did for him each morning.

'I'm sick of being nursed,' he grumbled.

'I'm sick of nursing you.'

We had a good thing going. We could say what we liked to each other, but today I could not jolly him out of his mood with abuse.

'I'm going to treat you like dirt all day,' he announced.

So was Georgina. She had to go into the town for food. After I helped Harry on to his travelling bier, he said he would play billiards with Serena, so Georgina, who hated the town traffic, caused by people she did not consider fit to have driving licences, wanted to play too. Rich could do the shopping. And fetch the laundry. And go to the Town Hall about the water bill.

'The Rover's out.' A private nurse can easily get conned into being a family servant. I was not going to let her start that.

'Take my car.'

'It's not my job.'

I thought she would be angry but Serena was in the room, so she spread her lips into the great smile and said, 'Please, old Rich? Just to be nice?' She sparkled her eyes at me, the bottom lids pushed up.

'Mr Ross isn't feeling too great. I'd like to stay with him.'

'I'll be here.' Big help.

In the end I went because Georgina told Harry to tell me to go; because he felt lousy, he did.

'And on the way back,' Georgina called over the banisters, showing inside the top of her dress, if I cared to look, 'stop at the garage and get them to fix the cigarette lighter.'

I can't stand it. On the way out, I dropped the memo into the hollow elephant's leg which held canes and golf umbrellas in the hall.

*

When I got back they were finishing lunch. With the women's help Harry had got himself on to the dining-room couch, and nobody needed me.

Georgina came out to get the glasses she had left in the car, but carried nothing in. I unloaded the laundry and took the shopping bags into the kitchen, and helped Dorothea to put the food away. She made me a toasted cheese sandwich and I took a beer out of the refrigerator.

Harry's trolley had been pushed into the room across the stone passage which was used for flowers and shoe cleaning and odd jobs. It annoyed Georgina to see it standing about in rooms or the hall. She would pile it with coats or disordered newspapers, or push it out of sight somewhere, even when Harry was going to use it.

I took it back to the dining-room, set the brake, and helped Harry on to it. He had to heave himself up from the low couch with his powerful arms, while I lifted the heavy cast.

'You've had a beer,' he said.

'I needed one.'

The trolley shifted a bit as his weight settled but I caught it with my foot and pushed it back against the couch.

'Is it all right?' Lying on his stomach with his chin on the pad, Harry turned his face to me.

'Yes, fine.' I tucked the blanket round to make a neat red cocoon of the cast.

'I'm going down to the farm.'

I helped him out through the porch with the ramp and went with him as far as the archway which divided the backyard of the house from the farmyard where the barns and cattle-sheds and the dairy were. Propelling himself with his hands on the inner wheels, he crossed the yard among some chickens, and I watched him go through the narrow space by the tractor shed and out on to the back road where the farm manager had his office.

The trolley was too flimsy for this sort of thing but I let him go alone. It was bad enough for him to have to depend on me for so many things.

I went back to the house to take the laundry upstairs since I was household drudge today. I was very bored. It was potty to be a nurse, doing the same womanish things day after day. Why wasn't I an actor, a financial genius, a reporter, a pilot, a politician who swayed the destinies of millions? Because I had trained as a nurse – 'A *what*?' I could see my father now, putting down his knife and fork – and it was all I knew.

I stuck my head out of the linen room window and smelled the cow smells that Maud liked, and thought that I would chuck this indoor lark and live with her and a cow or two and some chickens and whatever else you needed to support life, on a hill somewhere with a view, and a river to wash in. And Fanny.

The linen room was at the back of the house. Through the farmyard archway came a group of shouting people. 'Oh my God!', 'Call the ambulance!', 'Get a doctor!', 'Where's the nurse?'

I ran down the backstairs and outside. A man grabbed me and ran with me through the farmyard, gabbling something about Harry.

'I saw it,' he kept saying. 'I saw the whole thing. I ran, but there wasn't nothing I could do. He was gone by me. I couldn't – "He's over!" I said, and I come round the corner and there he was, Mr Ross, with his head in the mud, and he –'

We came round the corner, and there he was, with a small crowd round him saying, 'Don't touch,' and, 'Get him out of there.'

Harry was at the bottom of the short slope outside the office shed. The trolley had tipped right over with all four wheels in the air. He was lying on his back with his head and shoulders in a ditch and his legs on the stony edge of the road. The cast was broken and he was groaning and swearing.

'Here's the nurse.' They stood back. I felt important. Harry's shocked face lit with relief. I decided to go on being a nurse.

'Something's bust, Richie.'

'The cast.'

'More than that.'

He was in a lot of pain. I sent someone to call the ambulance, and someone else to get my locked drug bag from the bedroom. I did not want to move him without expert help, so I lifted his shoulders and sat on the edge of the ditch, with my feet in the mud and his head in my lap.

He looked up at me. He had not wanted to shave that morning. Blue hairs tattooed his square chin. He drew his lips back from his teeth in a strained attempt to grin and the teeth began to chatter. We had covered him with the red blanket and someone brought a horse rug and put it over that.

My bag arrived and I gave him a shot. He flinched and closed his eyes. When he opened them Georgina had come flying round the corner and was standing over him.

'What on earth have you done?' Bad choice of openers. She dropped to her knees on a corner of the horse rug and amended it to, 'Are you all right?'

'We don't know yet,' I answered. 'The ambulance is coming, and the hospital is getting Mr Jenner.'

'Are you all right?' she asked Harry, as if I had not spoken.

'What the hell do you think?' The shot was taking effect. I could feel his shoulders relaxing. 'Something has bust again.'

'Oh, my *God*.' Georgina sat back on her heels. 'After all these weeks. Have we got to start all over again?'

'*I've* got to start all over again.'

'What happened, Harry?'

I had not asked that. It was obvious. He must have come round the corner too fast and either hit a stone, or failed to brake in time, or both.

But he told Georgina, 'Richie said it was all right, but it wasn't. When I braked, nothing happened. The bloody thing went faster. We hit the corner at ninety, and –'

'You didn't fix it?' Georgina turned to me with the sudden fury of a serpent. I had never seen her like that. She was too careful how she looked to let anyone see her ugly with rage.

'Fixed what?' What the hell were they talking about?

'I told you to look at the brake, that it was slipping.'

'You didn't.'

'I did.'

'When?'

'When you came home.'

I shook my head.

'You stinking little liar.'

The onlookers were enjoying this but the ambulance arrived. The men and I got Harry on to the stretcher, covered him with clean blankets, and slid him into the back. The attendant got in and I put my foot on the step to follow.

'You stay here.' Georgina grabbed my arm, pinching.

'I'm going with him.'

'You're not.'

I shook her off, got in and closed the door. As we drove away, I looked back through the tinted glass and saw her beginning to talk fast, with the nodding head of accusation. The farm manager, who had bent to pick up the muddy blanket, straightened up and looked after the ambulance. She was accusing me.

*

I knew she had not told me to look at the trolley. Or had she? She knew that she had not told me. Or did she?

A dozen times as we drove to the hospital, with the ambulanceman attending to Harry, since it was his domain, I went over and over what had happened that morning.

I had got home. Georgina had come out for her glasses, asked me if I had got everything, grumbled because there were no artichokes, got into the car to look in the glove compartment, found the glasses, got out of the car and went back into the house without carrying any of the bags on the back seat.

She had not been in the kitchen when I went in. She did not speak to me again until she rang from the dining room as if I were the parlourmaid, and asked me to bring the trolley for Harry.

Nothing had been said. *Nothing had been said.* I'd stake my State Registration on it.

But before the day was out it began to be apparent that this was exactly what might be at stake. My SRN. My licence to practise as a Registered Nurse.

Georgina followed us to the hospital. After Harry had been X-rayed and found to have a cracked callus at the original fracture, and been admitted for possible insertion of femoral pin, poor old Harry, Georgina began to talk.

She talked to the surgeon. She talked to Harry's doctor. She talked to the Sister. She talked to Harry when he came out of sedation. She talked to anyone who would listen. She had told me to check the brake on the trolley. I had not done it. I had caused a bad accident. I was not fit to practise as a nurse.

Not even as a ward maid, the ward maid told me she had heard her say, when she paused with a bin of empties to find out what the racket was in Sister's office.

Georgina was in Harry's room when I came upstairs from supper.

'What are you doing here?' she asked.

'Staying with Mr Ross.' I had assumed, and so had the floor nurses, that I would continue to take care of him. They had given me a room in the nurses' hostel and Dorothea was bringing over some clothes for me.

'You're not.' Georgina looked about ten years older when she was angry. I felt like telling her that, to see if it would help.

'Georgie.' Pale and bearded on the bed, with the cast off, and one of his legs in traction, Harry lifted a feeble hand.

'I want you home and packed and out of my house before tonight.'

'Mrs Ross.' I was afraid, but I folded my arms and tried to keep my voice steady. 'You did not tell me about the brake. Neither –'

'I did.'

'Neither did Mr Ross.'

'Because,' Harry said, 'I knew my wife had told you. I said, "Is it all right?" and you said it was.'

'It was, as far as I knew.'

'You said it was fine. You had beer on your breath.'

'Beer?' Georgina had not heard Harry say that in the dining-room. Oh ho, now she had got me. That was all she needed. I was not only a rotten nurse, inexperienced, irresponsible and not fit to lance a boil. I was a drunken liar as well.

I did not think we ought to be having this conversation in Harry's room. He said, 'Georgie –' once again, then he closed his eyes and did not defend me. Why should he? He did not know who was lying.

At this point, I was not even sure myself. Had she forgotten to tell me and was covering up? Had she told me, and I had forgotten, and forgotten that she told me? Had she forgotten to tell me, and forgotten that she forgot?

When she asked me, 'Why did you think the trolley was in the workroom?', I was so fed up, I said, 'Because you like to stick it away where it will be more inconvenient for me and Mr Ross.'

Her quick glance at Harry to see if he believed that showed me that it was true.

'You're sacked,' she said.

'I quit,' I said.

It was classic. I turned and left cleanly. The hospital staff would take good care of Harry. We could sort the money out later, or never.

I found Dorothea sitting in the car park, smoking up a storm with one of the hospital porters, a cyclical brother-in-law, despaired of by the family, because he never kept a job more than three months without disappearing.

'I'm chucking this,' he told me.

'So am I.'

We shook on it. His damp hand was filthy, with long black nails and tobacco-stained fingers. The hospital would never miss him.

'You're not going to leave poor Mr Ross in there?' Dorothea jerked her yellow curls in distaste at the hospital.

'I've quit,' I said.

'She sacked you?'

'Yes.'

'She's sacked me half a dozen times. She'll take it back tomorrow.'

'She may report me tomorrow, to the General Nursing Council.'

'What for? You've done nothing wrong, dear.' Dorothea's pouchy smile and comfortable ways were just what I needed.

'She says I have.'

'It'll blow over. She's a bit edgy. You've got to make allowances.' Her compassion was enormous. I often remembered Dorothea later, when I needed some, and asked myself what she would say.

She took me to the house to get my things. Victor had come back from London and found no one. Serena had driven Georgina to the hospital.

'Where is everybody?' He came into the hall with a glass in his hand as I went to the stairs.

He did not know. What an opportunity. I told him my version, not blaming Georgina, but not blaming myself either. What a scream if it were Victor, of all people, who spoke up for me at the court martial, or whatever the GNC gave you, with medals on matronly bosoms.

When Victor asked me if I would take him to the hospital, I said breezily, equal terms now, 'Sorry. I don't work here any longer,' and went up the stairs.

'Wait a minute. What –' He was not very tall. He was not any taller than me. Furthermore, when he was puzzled, his eyes got closer together.

'Mrs Ross's car is there,' I said. Georgina hated other people to drive it. She had only let me that morning because she hated town shopping even more.

Dorothea helped me to pack and we found Maud breathing stertorously in an unused goat shed and left for the station before Georgina came home. Even with Dorothea's assurances, I took the precaution of leaving a note in Harry's report book.

'... *some damage to callus and possible bone injury. For exploratory surgery in a.m. by Mr Jenner. Accident was caused by defective brake on trolley, not reported to nurse.*'

'She'll tear it out,' Dorothea said, less sure.

'I've made a carbon.'

16

I could not get into the Clapham flat because I had given my key to John for the mole girl to use. It was late, but they were not there. I thumped on the door and told Maud to bark. She would dislike the girl now more than ever. Pregnancy had made her even more censorious.

The noise opened a door on the same landing.

'For Christ's sake.' Audrey, who was married to a Nigerian law student, came out in a dreadful sort of grey track suit, which did not seem fair on the Nigerian. 'Oh, it's you.'

'I can't get in.'

'Nobody there. John gave up the lease. I've got your stuff here. Somone is moving in tomorrow.'

John gave up the lease. Well, he had signed it in the first place, and I paid rent to him. But he could have told me, or asked me how long my country job would last.

'Was that girl still with him?'

'Alas, yes,' Audrey said. 'He deserves better.'

She did not know where they had gone. She offered to let me sleep on her sofa, but their flat smelled of cat, so Maud and I, jolly rovers, left our bags with Audrey, and took to the road.

We walked across the common and along the endless uphill, downhill terraced streets that lead to the river. On Battersea Bridge we had coffee and a meat pie. Two pies each, since Maud was famished. She was not due yet, but she was getting very big. Sometime after the pies, she went on to someone's small lawn and lay down to pant, and I thought she might have a miscarriage, right there in Drayton Gardens.

We rang Fanny's bell. She would welcome us into her soft warm arms, and believe every word we said, and stand by us for ever, even if Georgina and Harry and Victor and Serena all lied at the court martial. We rang and rang. She was not there. Exhausted by the events of the night and the day, Maud and I walked round the corner to the BEA terminal and spent what was left of the night in two chairs in the lobby.

'I'm sorry.'

I awoke stiff and confused, to see a uniform standing over me.

'I'm waiting for a bus.' There were a few other stranded bods slumped like old clothes about the place. Why pick on me?

'You're flying?'

'Yes.'

'May I see your ticket?'

'I'm picking it up at the airport.'

'It's the dog,' the uniform said. 'We can't have the dog in here.'

The tube was running by now. We went to some friends in Putney and slept. I rang Fanny at the office.

'Where were you last night?'

'I went to see my father. Where are you?'

'In Putney. I got the sack.'

'Because of me?'

'No, darling.'

'Victor rang this morning. What happened? He said Harry was back in hospital.'

'Georgina is saying I put him there.'

'That bitch.'

When she came home from work Maud and I were waiting for her on the wooden bench in Gore Street, where the old ladies and gentlemen sit.

The caretaker was painting the hall and stairs of the flats, perilous on a step-ladder, so we could not take Maud and her family in.

I had decided to go home to see my parents but I could not take Maud there. My father was so allergic to anything with fur on it that he almost choked to death the day I brought home a rabbit. I could never have a pet as a lad. I had felt deprived. When my mother explained that it was dangerous, my father might even die, I had thought: 'Then I could have a dog and a cat as well.'

We took Maud to Fanny's new local friend Miss Barrow, who lived in a flat in the building where she used to be the nurse years ago when it was a house. Since then she had hired herself out all over America, with the snob appeal of a British

Nanny, and when she retired, her family here had given her one of their flats.

We had meant just to go in and offer her Maud, but from the welter of photographs in her sitting-room, and seen through the doorway of the bedroom among the powder bowls and lamps and framed children's paintings and other loot and mementos, it was obvious you did not get away from Miss Barrow's in less than an hour.

We had tea and light port, and saw all the pictures of all her babies and some of their babies she had gone back to nurse, and she told us about the Kennedys. She had nannied for some cousin in the heyday of Hyannisport when J.F.K. was President. Everything he had said to her – 'Good morning', 'The baby is growing', 'Going to rain' – was engraved on her mind's tablets. Why not? It would have been on mine.

We told her about Mr Ewing and my allergic father. Would she keep Maud for a while until I found a room? She would, kindly Miss Barrow, with severe thin hair and a signed copy of a dirty novel written by one of her boy babies.

'Is she near her time?' She made a disapproving face. She had only taken babies from the month, and never had to mess with parturition or postpartum affairs.

'Not yet. But I know you'd know what to do, dear Miss Barrow,' Fanny wheedled.

'She'll manage for herself,' Miss Barrow said, 'or not at all.'

That would be all right with the old loner. Maud was the type who would disappear one day and come back with pups in her mouth, rather than make it a public sideshow on the master's eiderdown.

In Fanny's flat I suddenly felt depressed. I had not had time to feel anything but anger. Now I felt humiliated. Georgina had sacked me partly because I had rejected her barbering advances, partly to get herself off the hook about the trolley, but partly because she did not like me.

I brooded on that. I had never been sacked before. It hurt.

'I've never been sacked either,' Fanny said. 'I know how you feel.'

'Have you been?'

'I may be.' Fanny was squatting on the floor, doing what she thought was Yoga. 'That's why I went to see my father.'

'What did he say?'

'He never says much. I thought he might have ideas about jobs but he didn't.'

'I'll help you get ideas.' I sat on the floor with her. 'I don't want you working for Victor any more.'

'You don't own me.'

I felt I did a bit, in my old-fashioned way, but I knew her better than to say so.

'Things are changing.' Fanny bent forward and hung the blunt cut ends of her hair to the floor. 'Victor wants to go freelance, I think, and take some of his staff.'

'Including you?'

'I don't know.'

'Fanny.' I grabbed the hair and made her look at me. 'Have you told him yet?'

'Told him what?' She opened her sea-blue eyes very wide, thick lashes curling.

'About you and me.'

'Yes.' The eyes looked down, although I still held her head up by the hair.

'You haven't.'

'Why do I waste time with lies no one believes? I lied all the time as a child. My mother sent me to a doctor. He said they should call it fantasy, but it was lies.'

'Tell him.' I let go of her hair. 'Tell him tomorrow and get out.'

17

Fanny was going to come with me to see my parents. I did not usually take girls home. Not because of the sort of situation I had heard about from friends, with their father either disapproving or being too gallant and goatish, and their mother either disapproving or being too glad ('thank God he's got rid of that girl with the shawls and dirty toe nails').

I don't know why I did not often take girls home. My mother liked me to, and my father did not care either way. Perhaps I was afraid that the things I liked most about my quiet home, nothing changing, nothing much happening, would bore a girl. Tough luck on her, if so, but I was afraid her boredom might spoil it for me.

Fanny would not be bored. Fanny was never bored, except by things that more passive people find stimulating, like pot and pop.

She was doing her face in the bathroom when the telephone rang. I put out a hand and picked it up.

'Who's that?' Ah ha. Got a bit of a shock there, didn't you Victor?

'Fanny's brother.' She had one, in America.

'David?'

'Yeah.' I put on a brotherly voice. Good old Dave. Harvard Business School's pet limey. 'Can I take a message?'

'Let me speak to Fanny.'

'Hey, Fan!'

She came out with cream on her face. 'What on earth?'

'Some guy wants you.'

'Hullo, yes? Oh, it's you.' She made a face at me. I sat close to her and stared, to put her off. I could not hear Victor's end. He talked quietly. Cool and quiet was his line. Seen it all.

Fanny's end said, 'When? ... No, I've been here ... Well, I did go out for a bit. To get some food. For David?' She looked at my stare and tensed her jaw to keep the smile from her voice. 'Yes, he's here. He's on vacation ... What? Well, it's different from England ... Yes, yes, that was why I didn't come in ... Oh, you are? Where? ... You didn't –' I shook my head. You don't say, 'You didn't tell me' when you have not been told. You pretend you know already, or don't care, or both. 'Me? well, I'll see ... I might. I'll see ... All right. Have fun.'

With a flat verbal wave, she put down the telephone and turned to me. 'He's going to Nicaragua.'

'For ever?'

'His assistant needs a secretary. Victor said I might do that till he gets back.'

I grabbed the telephone and rang Victor back. 'This isn't Fanny's brother.'

I was angry but he was still cool.

'I didn't think it was.'

'And Fanny won't be there when you get back from Nicaragua.'

'Oh well,' Victor said. 'That will save a lot of embarrassment for everybody,' and rang off.

*

We got to my house before my parents were home.

It is a small, untidy house that always carries a faint reminder of the last meal or two. It seemed smaller than ever to me after the farm, where the many rooms and passages and staircases kept people away from each other, and it took twenty steps to cross the cool flagged hall. My mother had not done much washing up recently, and some of my father's clothes were draped over the top of the banisters. The house seemed shabby, without charm. A house to get away from. I wondered why I had been so happy and secure there.

But Fanny liked it. She said, 'I see why you wanted to stay at home,' and the house clicked back into place and I stopped feeling like my brother, coming back with legs too long and feet too big and complaining that nothing had changed.

In the evening, after my mother came home and cooked and Fanny washed up enough things to eat with, we went up the back garden, where someone had left a spade in a half-dug plot, and my mother's white climber had sprawled over the coalshed like an octopus and borne it to the ground. I pulled Fanny through the old hole in the hedge that had grown bigger as I grew, and up the small hill where I had dreamed away a lot of my childhood so unproductively, while other boys were Outward Bound, or building short-wave radios.

We sat against the tree roots at the top that my back knew, and surveyed some of the flatter, duller fields of England, rotating peacefully from crop to crop.

Fanny said, 'You are so lucky to have lived in a place where nothing happened. At home where I was something was always happening. All hell breaking loose every hour on the hour. Crisis upon crisis. Until my father got out and I told my mother I was going with him. That really did it.'

She smiled, remembering. She was quiet for a moment, and then she said, 'Did you come up here with Millie?'

'Mm.' Millie and I had preferred to come to my house when we had time off together, rather than go to her home, where her mother railed at us for laughing about nothing. It was up here after a day of playing with my brother's two babies, and helping my father to cut up a dead tree, that Millie had told me that poem.

From quiet homes and first beginning,
Out to the undiscovered ends . . .

I had not shared it with anyone else, but I told Fanny now.

There's nothing worth the wear of winning,
But laughter and the love of friends.

'We do love each other,' Fanny said, too easily. When she said, 'I love you', it was not a committal. 'And we are friends.'

I remembered John saying, 'You can't be friends with a girl without screwing.' But he had got it wrong. You can be friends and lovers at the same time. But they are not the same thing.

18

Next morning, Fanny stayed in bed, feeling sensuous and sluttish, and I rang Mrs Hewlett-Bye. Since Fanny was out of a job someone had better go to work.

'Where have you been, Hditchahd?'

'In the country.'

'You're supposed to let me know when you're on holiday.'

'I wasn't.'

I knew she would be angry that I had taken a job without

going through her agency, and she was. She told me I was unethical, and she was glad I had got the sack. However, because she was a saintly woman, for whom to forgive came as naturally as breathing, she could fix me up with the best job I had ever had in my short and tainted career, one that I was by no stretch of the imagination suited for in any way, but at the moment, alas, she had no pdefable male nurses fdee.

'That means another old codger with a colostomy and a catheter.'

'No, Hditchahd. It means Mr Budd Malone.'

'*The* Budd Malone? The film star?'

'The same.'

'What's his trouble?'

'He doesn't say. That usually means pdostate,' she added indiscreetly.

Budd Malone was still playing raffish heroes – dead-beat divorcées, sodden chiefs of police in arid mid-western towns, lone widowers, wolfish in dun cottages. Surely not yet prostate age.

'You're to go to his hotel for an interview day after tomorrow when he flies in from L.A. Over the Pole.' Mrs Hewlett-Bye enjoyed being part of the jet age.

'You've booked me? How did you know I'd be free?'

'Great minds, Hditchahd.'

'Yours and mine.'

*

'I'm going to nurse Budd Malone.'

'Who's Budd Malone?' Fanny woke up. 'Budd Malone!' She sat up. 'Can I meet him?'

'No.'

I felt masterful. I felt master in Fanny's flat. I moved the furniture about a bit to prove it. I tore down the psychedelic poster she had had before I knew her and put up the one we had bought yesterday, of a man and a girl running into a path of sunset in the sea. Then I fried some kind of meal and we got into the car and went to see Fanny's father in Hertfordshire. It was time I met Fanny's father.

*

As we came round the corner and stopped in the circular drive, the French windows at the end of the house burst open, and a cloud of coloured butterflies, fairies, gnomes flew out and cast themselves about on the grass, or pranced, knees high, stubby hands like starfish.

It was Fanny's stepmother's nursery school, 'Small World', making its afternoon breakaway. After them came a stout, over-heated person in a brown overall and clog shoes, crying, 'I didn't tell you to open that door, you people. Come back in at once and pick up the chalks!'

It was Mrs Burnham, who did not agree with Fanny's step-mother's belief that small children were in an almost permanent state of fantasy, and could only conform to the grown-up world when it happened to fit into the dream.

After Mrs Burnham came a tall, brown-faced woman with large hands and feet and knobbly bare ankles under shrunk jeans. She bumped her hip on the door handle, tripped over the sill, jumped down the step with her ragged hair flying, and ran across the grass to throw herself down with two tiny boys who were rolling down a bank, wet green stains on her white jeans.

It was Fanny's stepmother, optimistically christened Melody, not skittish or girlish at fifty, just big and clumsy, unmusical, ungraceful, large-featured, content.

Fanny and I got out of the car and went across the lawn. The citizens of Small World had disappeared into the bushes. Mrs Burnham was going back to the house, unbuttoning her overall.

'Hullo, Fanny,' she said. 'They've got away from me again. But what the hell, it's my last day.' She went into the long room beyond the French windows, and I saw her pick up a broom and begin to make stabs at a clutter so endemic, you could hardly see the floor.

'The Burner is leaving?' Fanny asked, as Melody came up the bank on hands and knees, dragging the little boys by her ankles.

'She can't take it any more. She and two of the mothers got together and decided the children should learn to make letters and relate to their peer group. That's what they called it. So Burner is going, and one of the mothers has removed her child, but the other one is leaving it here, because she goes to work and there's nowhere else.'

'Mel, this is Dick Hayes,' Fanny said, 'I told you about.'

'The one who looked after your grandfather? Oh good.' No raised eyebrow here. A rough-skinned hand, an eager, lopsided smile. Something doggy about her. Not a doggy woman, with hairs on her skirt, supervising the mating. She was like a large dog, strong, but not independent, needing to be liked.

The house where she lived with Fanny's father and her son, and tried to make some money with her nursery school, was a comfortable country place on the edge of a small town, not old, not new, brick and grey stone, garden going off in odd directions, a lot of bloom and a lot of jungle weed, an orchard at the back where ancient trees, askew in rough grass and wild flowers, were supported by props so ancient that they themselves had taken root and sprouted and grown bent with age.

When Fanny's father, an accountant in Cambridge, came home, he looked me over benevolently enough, neither anxious nor optimistic, in the same way that my own father had looked over Fanny. They are both quiet, undemanding men, who actually demand a lot: to be left alone. The hardest thing to get unless you live in a shack at the end of a sheep path.

While Melody was crashing round the kitchen, burning her fingers and dropping glasses, he was having a drink with Fanny and me. The gravel crunched. He looked over his shoulder and saw a car stop and two women get out. Fanny went to greet them and by the time she brought them into the drawing-room her father had gone, and taken his drink with him.

A local friend had brought in her shy young neighbour when she heard that Melody needed someone to help with Small World. Mrs Turner's husband was 'building a cinema in a hayfield'. The quotes were censorious. They had just moved into a cottage in the next village and the wife was looking for a job with children.

'One out, one in,' Fanny's stepmother said happily, engaging the silent young woman on the spot. 'I knew I'd find someone right away. I always do.'

'That's because you take just anybody,' Fanny said, and Mrs Turner blushed. 'Sorry – I didn't mean it for you,' Fanny said quickly, but the girl's blush stayed on her neck, and she sat looking down at her hands in her lap and spoke less than ever.

Melody, in a baggy apron crusted with old flour, wanted to go back to the kitchen. Something was beginning to burn.

'So if you could start tomorrow, Mrs Turner – oh, I can't call you that, it reminds me of the Burner.' The blush rose again, like mercury in a thermometer. 'What's your first name?'

'Marigold.' The girl put her small feet side by side, toes together, calves of legs together, knees together with hands pressed between.

'See you tomorrow, Marigold. About eight-thirty. Excuse me.' Everyone stood up and Melody went out, ricocheting off the doorway like Nixon going in to lunch at Buckingham Palace. She clattered down the hall and gave a yell, 'Fire!' as she reached the kitchen. Taps gushed. 'Fire out!'

Fanny paid no attention. 'How's Robin?' she asked the woman who had brought Marigold. 'Still in hospital?'

'Yes. I wish we could have him home, but he needs a lot of care. They've finally decided what it is. Poly-what is it – poly-radiculo-neuritis. Somebody's syndrome.'

'Gullain-Barré?' I said.

'How on earth did you know that?' Robin's mother, who had not registered me any more than people do register someone who is vaguely introduced as 'Fanny's friend Dick', turned to regard me with surprise.

'Dick's a nurse,' Fanny said.

'A nurse?' She took another look, and saw that Fanny had taken my hand. I suppose it was sticking out all over us. I could always tell whether people were sleeping together or not, although Fanny was unsure, and used to poke me in the tube to ask what I thought about this or that couple sitting opposite, or hanging from straps in the rush hour, with their armpits in our faces.

'How nice,' said Robin's mother, and I wondered whether Robin were old enough for her to enliven his sick bed with the extraordinary news that Fanny Runyon was sleeping with a male nurse.

*

While we were having dinner – messily served but marvellous – the front-door bell rang. Fanny's father looked up from his chop like an animal disturbed at its prey, and Melody went out with her mouth full.

We could hear her talking to a man in the hall.

She came back to the dining-room and said, 'That girl's husband is looking for her. The hayfield one. Where did she go? When I said I didn't know he sat down and said he was tired.' She looked at her husband. 'Shall I bring him in for a drink?'

'No.'

Fanny got up and went out. I went too, since I was in the habit of going with her in and out of rooms.

'I'm Jeffrey Turner.'

He was sitting on a hard chair in the hall, with his feet stuck out in filthy frayed gym shoes and his hayfield head against the wall, a desperate-looking man with a long crooked nose and eyes hung lopsidedly in pouchy lids.

'My wife was here. I've lost her.'

'She left with Mrs Dent.'

'I tried their house. Ever been there? Christ!' He stuck his hands under the arms of his stained sweater, although it was warm, and sweat was gathering along the top of his ragged moustache.

'It's late shopping night,' Fanny said. 'Perhaps she went into town.'

Jeffrey Turner said, 'Shit,' and bit his nails. 'I want her to drive me somewhere.' He brooded for a moment and then got up and loped down the hall.

'Mrs Dent said you were building a cinema,' Fanny said. 'Is that true?'

'If I live. Classics. Foreign films. Whatever people want. If they want it.'

'How exciting.' Fanny went with him to the door.

'No, it isn't.' Her voice went up. His went down. 'It's disaster.'

He lurched down the steps and across the gravel to where a bicycle lay on its side in a low juniper bush. He dragged it out, got on, and rode fast out into the road, no lights, passing car hooting, squeal of brakes.

*

The gears of Fanny's car had been rough for some time. It always came back from servicing worse than when it went away, like people who go into hospital for a minor operation and come out with pleurisy, so she had done nothing about it. It seized up completely on the way to get my clothes. We abandoned it to a breakdown lorry and I took the tube the rest of the way to Clapham.

New people had moved into the flat I had shared with John. The smells were different already. More on the Scandinavian order, like that time John got the girl from Göteborg to come round with her pickled fish.

Audrey said she missed us. She gave me my suitcase, apologized for having given two of my shirts to a destitute friend from Uganda, and I took my things home. Home was Fanny's flat. I would have run, if I had not been weighed down with two suitcases and a shoulder bag full of books.

Life was wide open. Excitement moved in all my being. When I put down the bags and waited for the train, I could not stand still. I paced between the cigarette machine and the poster of the girl with hair pencilled on in likely and unlikely places. I felt enormous with energy, blown up and ready to take off. When three or four boys clattered down the stairs I moved away from the edge of the platform, in case they went berserk and charged me on to the line. I had too much to lose.

At Gloucester Road station, the blackboard said: '*London Transport regrets inconvenience to passengers yesterday. Delay was caused by person on line at Holborn station.*'

They kept the writing on the board, and filled in the name of the station as appropriate.

I was still a bit supercharged when I left Fanny and walked across Hyde Park to the hotel where Budd Malone was staying. I was nervous too. Having seen him on the screen, it was hard to believe he actually existed.

He didn't. The hotel knew nothing of him. Two girls looked at me over the reception desk as if I were the victim of a peculiarly pitiful fantasy. Budd Malone! As if he could be here in London without a foyer full of P.R. men and press photographers, and if he was, as if I could have an appointment with him.

I telephoned despair to Mrs Hewlett-Bye.

'Oh, didn't I tell you? He's not calling himself that, of course. He's here in strict incog. Name of Joe Hdiley. Service entrance, baggage lift and what have you. You're to go round to the staff door and ask.'

I gave my name to a man in a glass cage by the time clocks.

'I'm expected.'

'Who by?'

'Mr Joe Riley.'

He made a fist with the thumb up, and took me in a large lift with cabbage leaves on the floor to the top of the main part of the hotel where he directed me to a corridor which led round three sides of a tower to a smaller lift to Mr Riley's suite.

In the lift I put on my SRN badge and my name badge. I expected to have to fight my way past secretaries and hatchet men, but it was the great one himself who opened the door in dark glasses and an old towel dressing-gown too short over bare legs rather bandy, proof that the horse in his Westerns had not been ridden by a double.

He had come to London alone and in secret.

'Richard Hayes.' He read my name badge. 'This is between thee and me. They told my doctor I could trust you. If I can't, say so now and leave.'

'You can.'

'Richard Hayes. Man of trust.' He observed me all over. He had the advantage. I could not see his eyes, but I liked his deep voice and the rest of his face. 'Come in, my boy.' He stepped back on long bare feet with manicured toenails. 'And I shall share my secret with you.'

We went into the fabulous sitting-room which looked out over a view of roofs and trees and church spires that took away your breath at what London really was.

'Drink?'

'No thanks.'

'On the wagon?'

'On duty.'

'That's good.' He poured one for himself. 'You and I are going to need to have a few together before this business is through.'

He sat down opposite me nursing his glass and swinging one long bare leg over the other knee.

'You're a professional, right?'

'Right.'

'So I can say anything to you, right?'

'Right.'

'As if you were a doctor.'

'Right.' What horror was he going to disclose? Film stars have had VD before, and it doesn't need a nurse.

'Well, it's like this, Richard Hayes.' He uncrossed his legs and leaned forward. 'It's surgery. What's that they call it? Cosmetic. Yes. Cosmetic surgery.'

'Good idea.'

'What do you mean, good idea? You think I look so terrible?'

'No, but I mean –' he was suddenly so angry that I was afraid I had lost the job already '– I mean, I thought everyone in Hollywood had that done sooner or later. Don't they?'

'I am not everyone in Hollywood, kid. I'm Budd Malone, who always looks so great, how does he do it? I want them to go on saying that, and I don't want them ever to know how he is going to do it.'

'How?' I risked, since the anger had swiftly passed.

'Bags under the eyes.' His face was very solemn. 'Goddam loose skin. Here.' He took off the dark glasses and stared at me without blinking. 'See what I mean?'

I saw the normally loose face of a well-boned, likeable man of about fifty – older than he looked on the screen – who had probably drunk too much over the years.

'What do you think, kid?' He stared at me as if I held all truth.

What did he want me to say? That his face looked marvellous, and did not need plastic surgery on the eyelids or anywhere else? Or that the slack top lids and baggy lower ones looked ghastly, and did?

So I asked him, 'What do you want me to say, sir?'

He sighed, relaxed, and put on the very dark glasses again; he took a drink and set down the glass.

'Good answer, Richard Hayes. You're hired.'

He wanted me to unpack for him, and because I liked him and wanted this job, I did not tell him I was not a valet. I did everything he asked me, including going out to shop for him, writing a letter, and making two or three telephone calls. One of them was transatlantic.

'I'm calling for Mr Budd Malone. He won't be able to keep his appointment next week. I'm sorry. I can't tell you where he is staying. He's working, yes. Top secret.'

You should see me now, Sister Winifred Cogswell, who bellowed down a ward full of patients and a surgeon doing his rounds with a clutch of sycophantic students, 'Mr Hayes! If any examiner is ever insane enough to pass you, it will be a disaster for the nursing profession!'

Later, when he started to call me Dicky and we were old buddies, with steak and booze sent up, I asked him, 'When you took off your glasses, what *did* you want me to say?'

'That's just it, kid. I don't know. If people said, "You don't need a thing done", they'd be condemning me to middle-aged parts. Like my agent and some of the producers. They say, "There'll be more and more parts for you as you age interestingly. Character parts. Meaty ones. Look at John Wayne. Look at George C. Scott. Look at Shelley Winters." I don't want to look at John Wayne and George C. Scott and Shelley Winters. When I look in the mirror, or at my face up there on that big screen, I don't want to see Budd Malone ageing interestingly, and telling the girl with the tits, "Go to him, Celia, he wants you." I want to see Budd taut and virile, saying, "Come here to me, Celia. I want you." '

'So did you want me to say, "Of course you must have the eyelid operation"?'

He leaned his elbows on the table the waiter had wheeled in, sank his chin in his hands and looked very old, like a blind beggar in his dark glasses.

'No, because that would imply how terrible I look now — have done for years. When you have to go to make-up an hour earlier than anyone else ...when you have to have your own lighting man ...' He brooded, 'When I told my wife I was going to have my eyes lopped, you know what she said? She said, "Why stop at the eyes? Why not have the whole goddam mess lifted?" ·

'Why not?'

'You too, Brutus. You know what they do? I saw a TV beastly about it. Pal of mine was the saintly doctor, prostituting his gifts on the faces of rich old bitches to get money for his free clinic for ghetto babies with sickle cell anaemia. This is what they do. They get a paring knife, and lift the skin right off the bones and muscle, right off. They skin you alive. Then they haul it up and pin it back behind your ears, and in a few years, unless you don't talk or eat or crack a smile any more, the whole lousy lot sags down, and you have to be skinned and hauled all over again.'

He had decided to have the operation done anyway, whatever I or anyone else said. He had come to England to avoid Hollywood gossip, and because he had an English friend who was a plastic surgeon. The operation was tomorrow. It would be done under local anaesthetic. He did not need nor want to stay in the hospital. His wife had not come with him, and his girl friend was filming in Finland; because he was lonely, like so many public people, for the type of friend who would see him through a thing like this, he had hired me.

I was to stay in the suite with him.

'Not tonight?'

'Sure, tonight. I may get the horrors and need someone to talk to.'

'It's not very convenient.' I was aching for Fanny. 'You could ring me at my flat if you can't sleep and want to talk in the night.'

'OK.' He laughed at me. 'And I might just do that.'

19

I packed a bag next day. I did not want to leave, even for the few days it would take to help Budd Malone to adjust to the loss of his eye bags. But Fanny said, 'Perhaps it's a good thing. We didn't want to get tied down. You said you wanted to stay free, remember?'

'You said so.'

'And I do.'

She wanted to pretend that we were still independent, that desire had not brought more desire. Why? I should have slugged her, or chained her to the wall. If I had not had a job I don't know what I would have done. As it was I took my bag to the hotel and went with Budd Malone to the hospital.

He was making as big a production of it as if he were going to have a major internal operation. He would not eat breakfast, 'In case I throw up.'

'It's a local anaesthetic.'

'I can throw up on a local.'

He spent an hour in the bath, filing the corners of his toenails, cleaning his navel with an orange stick, pumice-stoning the soles of his feet. He washed his hair, rubbed in a darkening rinse, and sprayed it with a little light lacquer where it tended to turn up at the sides. He scrubbed his teeth three times, went round them with dental floss, and gargled with undiluted mouthwash that scorched the inside of his lips.

'For the nurses,' he said, with simple courage.

He changed his clothes three times before he decided what he would wear. He finally came out of his room in white slacks – 'that hospital look' – and a black polo neck with a stark lead medal on a chain. I pointed out that the polo neck would be impossible to put on again after the operation, so he went back once more and came out in a dark red silk shirt with white stitching and his initials on the pocket.

The custodian of the glass cage took us down in the baggage lift. He was very discreet, and did not speak. This made Budd more nervous than if he had. Outside the staff entrance a limousine and chauffeur were waiting, also discreetly.

Whether they had been primed or not, people must have recognized Budd, even in dark glasses, but they said nothing. Although he wanted privacy this made him feel more insecure than if he had been mobbed by fans squealing, 'Budd Malone!'

At the hospital they were also very discreet. A girl at the reception desk steered us through the corridors to the surgeon's office, making a prissy mouth. Mr Manderson's secretary stood up, carefully not quite looking at Budd, and said, 'Good morning, Mr Riley. You're in nice time. You can come along to theatre right away.'

'Aren't I going to be wheeled in?' The simplicity of it all scared him more than big drama.

'It's only just across the corridor.'

'OK. Come on then, Dicky. Here goes nothing.'

'Your friend can stay here,' the secretary said.

'He's my nurse.'

'Mr Manderson has his own theatre staff.'

'Either Dicky comes with me, or I don't go.'

'All right then. Come along.'

The telephone rang and while she turned to answer it Budd looked as if he might escape. 'I'll ring you back.' She put it down and took Budd's arm, and steered him – a small-breasted, heavy-hipped gaoler – firmly out of the office and through swing doors into the theatre wing.

She put us into a dressing-room and Budd changed into a green operation gown and rubber slippers. He was so nervous that I had to help him as if he were a sick man. I stored the beautiful trousers and shirt in a tiny locker and put the lead medallion in my pocket.

'And this, you have to wear.' I handed him the green plastic shower cap which had been left with the gown and slippers.

'To my grave.'

'You'll have to have something over your hair.'

'Never that.'

A young nurse came in briskly, gave him half a look, and said, 'That's right. Put on the cap and come with me. The cap,' she said again at the door.

Budd put it on, lower on his brow than necessary, to make the worst of it.

'How do I look?' he asked me.

'Terrible.' He wanted truth and pity, not jolly bolstering.

The nurse told him to lie on a trolley that was standing against a wall in the corridor and went away fast. People passed back and forth, talking, studying notes, pushing drums and cylinders.

'Public exposure.' Budd turned tragic eyes on me under the ridiculous cap, then shut them and began to do deep breathing through wide hairy nostrils, to calm himself. I was reminded of the Major telling us in the pub about the old pneumonias, pushed out into a draughty passage to die.

People went on passing by. Budd shielded his face with his arm but they were not looking at him.

'If they only knew,' he said. 'I was afraid I would be mobbed for autographs.'

'Do you want them to know or not?' A lot of our conversation was like this. He had decided that honesty was his theme with me and my role was to help him examine his motives.

'No,' he said. Then after a few moments: 'but in case, have you got a pen on you, Dicky?'

His friend the surgeon came, with small magnifying glasses fitted on to his spectacles.

'This is it then,' Budd said.

'This is it, pal.' The surgeon knew the dialogue.

He made some lines in soft pencil on the famous face, marking where he was going to make his incisions, and how much skin would be removed.

'My secretary told me you'd brought your own nurse,' he said. 'I thought it would be some bird.'

'Not when I'm struck low,' Budd said.

'Good.' Mr Manderson marked in the last line. 'He can hold you down on the table.'

He told me where to get a gown and mask. When I came back to my patient he had his head turned to the wall, with closed eyes and slack lips, and I thought he might have passed out.

'I'm pretending they've already put me under,' he said.

'They're not going to put you under.'

'I'm pretending they are.' He opened his eyes and turned his head, just as an operation case was wheeled through the swing doors from the theatres, full of tubes, its red, suffused face turned sideways towards us with an airway in its mouth.

'Dicky.' Budd put out a hand to me. 'I wish I hadn't come.'

'Well, hello there!' A cheerful porter with an Afro and some gold teeth came up to take one end of the trolley. I took the other. After we had wheeled him into a small side room and shifted him on to the table, and the porter had wheeled out the trolley – 'See you later, man!' – Budd held on to my hand from then on. He raised his head to goggle at Mr Manderson coming from the sink with dripping hands and arms raised – 'By God, you've been watching afternoon TV, Pete' – swivelled his eyes round to the instrument trolley just as the scrub nurse raised the towel with tongs to let the surgeon check it, swivelled them quickly back again and closed them tight.

Someone with a clipboard looked round the door. 'What operation is this?'

'Plastic revision of eyelid deformity.'

Budd groaned.

'Relax,' Mr Manderson said. 'This is the worst part.'

'So you tell me to –' Budd drew in a gasping breath and crushed my hand in the paw that had caressed fabled actresses, as the first tiny needle went in. Several gasps later he did begin to relax into a beatific smile as the numbness spread.

The smile was covered with towels, then sterile towels.

'How do I breathe?'

'Through this.' The surgeon tapped him on the nose with his elbow. 'Shut up now, old Buddy. I'll tell you when you can talk.'

'Just one word.'

'What?'

The nurse handed a scalpel.

'I don't want to have it done.'

Whistling softly under his mask, Mr Manderson cut and snipped away the folds of flesh and pieces of loose fatty tissue. He did not talk to Budd, but when he invited the nurse and me to admire the lacrimal part of the orbicularis oculi muscle, Budd muttered, 'Don't forget I'm not asleep.'

The surgeon removed some of the spare flesh with a cautery, making a smell like a blacksmith's shop.

'May I say something?' Budd asked under the towels.

'Go ahead.'

'I'll need another shot of that dope before you hammer the nails in.'

When it was time to sew up, the time when everyone in the theatre relaxes, Budd and Mr Manderson chatted about the war, which was where they had met each other, as orderlies in an Allied hospital. I was proud of Budd. I had thought he would struggle and gripe all through the tricky and unpleasant operation, but he lay still as a crusader on a tomb, only the pressure of his strong dry hand telling me things.

The surgeon put some ointment in his eyes and told him it might blur his vision.

'Vision, what vision?' Budd tried to open his battered eyes. He looked like a giant panda, with black stitches all round each eye, and the redness already darkening to bruises among the crusted blood.

'Lie flat and keep ice on it,' Mr Manderson said, 'and you'll get less bruising and it won't look so bad for so long.'

'I don't care what it looks like,' Budd said unhappily. I could see that the nerve ends were beginning to wake to pain. 'I'm not going anywhere or seeing anyone, ever again in the whole of my life.'

'OK,' his friend said, 'but ice will help the pain.'

'What are you giving me for that – Demarol? Percodon?' Budd asked, with an American eagerness for the pharmacopoeia.

'Aspirin will do it.'

'Aspirin!' It was an insult.

'So long, Buddy. Come and see me in four days and we'll take out the first stitches.'

'Where are you going?' Budd turned his blind face anxiously to him.

'Got to carve up someone else. Lady with deformity of umbilicus. Wants to wear a bikini. She's seventy.'

'Join the club, old girl,' Budd said weakly.

I got ice cubes in a plastic bag and found the porter sitting on the trolley, swinging his legs. He and I helped Budd on to it and wheeled him back through the swing doors to the busy corridor.

'What do I look like?' he asked me.

'Fine.'

He held the icebag over his eyes and said, 'Can't see a thing.'

I got him off the trolley and into the dressing-room and helped him to take off the gown and put on his own clothes. He was like a passive baby, the fine tanned chest and muscular arms powerless to defend his drooping spirit. At one point I thought he was going to cry. The porter brought in a wheel-chair and sat in it, clicking gum in and out of a hollow tooth. He did not get up when Budd was ready.

'Do I get to wheel you, or you wheel me?' Budd asked him.

'Take your choice.'

I got the porter out of the chair by tact, since I was alien in this hospital, and he pushed Budd out to the hall while I went to get the car. When I came back Budd was sitting by the door holding the bag to his eyes with both hands. It was leaking slightly. It looked as if he were crying.

The chauffeur went on being discreet. He stood back while I helped Budd from the chair into the car, then he put a rug over his knees and shut the door without looking at him. At the back of the hotel I led my blind man, clinging to my arm, through the staff door and into the lift, the door-keeper putting his bulk between Budd and a couple of chambermaids who goggled at him as they stepped out of the lift.

Safe in our luxurious crow's nest, Budd lay down at once, without waiting for me to undress him. I put a wet cloth over his eyes and a bowl of ice beside him. My job was to keep cooling the cloth in the ice and laying it over his poor martyred eyes. Bruising was beginning to darken and spread.

I made him a giant martini to take his aspirin with and he felt better.

'Want to see yourself, Mr Malone?'

'God, no.' When he got up to go to the bathroom, he held his hands in front of his face as he passed the mirror.

He could not see anyway. Very early the next morning I was woken by a yell through the half-open door between our rooms.

'Dicky!' Desperate. 'Come here – come quick!'

He was standing in front of the mirror with his pyjama jacket open over his hairy California chest, trousers slipping down over the slight paunch he normally kept tucked in, toes curling.

'It's not that bad.' I looked at his reflection. The giant panda after a three-day bender. 'What do you want me to –'

He did not want to play the honesty game.

'That's not it.' He waved his arms frantically. 'I can't see. I've gone blind.'

'It's the ointment ... the stitches ... the anaesthetic ...' I tried everything, but he insisted I ring the surgeon at home.

'Peter!' Budd flung out a hand, felt down my arm and took the telephone from me. 'You cut the optic nerve.'

'Oh dear.' I could hear Mr Manderson's voice. 'Mother told me never to do that.'

'I'm not joking,' Budd growled.

'OK, old son. Some of the nerves are bruised, that's all. You'll see all right in two or three days.'

'Why didn't you tell me I'd go blind?'

'Would it have made you feel better?'

'You're a dishonest operator. I may sue. How's the old lady's navel?'

'She can't see through it either.'

After the first shock, Budd almost enjoyed being blind. 'Now I know,' he said. 'I know how those guys feel.' He groped his way from room to room by the furniture, spilled soup down the front of his lustrous silk pyjamas, and asked me to feed him, opening his mouth wide like a chick in a nest.

When his wife rang from Los Angeles he told her, 'Tell Chater to talk to some writers. When I come back I want to play a man who suddenly goes blind.' He put down the receiver. 'She says Bette Davis already did it,' he told me. '*Dark Victory.*'

*

'It's not *Dark Victory*,' he said on the third day, when his vision cleared enough for him to see a blurred reflection of his stitched and battered face. 'It's *The Ghoul*.'

Even with the very dark glasses on, you could see the stitches at the sides, where the sagging skin had been tightened and fastened and clipped off. He would not see anyone. People were beginning to ring up. Somehow the word had got round that he was in London, although we managed to keep it from the Press.

'He's been ill. He's got flu. He's very tired. He's resting. He's had a wisdom tooth out.' Part of my job was to invent plausible excuses. 'He had to have a minor operation.'

'Don't say that,' Budd called from the next room. 'They'll think it's haemorrhoids.'

Flowers came, great structured vases of them which died too soon, taken from a refrigerator to our suite, which had the heat on in June. Letters came, and mammoth cards with comic jokes he could not read. Read out by me they were not very comic. Boxes of chocolates came, and towering baskets of fruit.

I took some of the fruit and chocolate for Fanny and Miss Barrow when I took a couple of hours off to go home. Fanny was not at the flat. The smell of her was. Our bed. Our view. Our kitchen, with the mug I had used last still upside down on the draining board.

I left a note about love with some of the fruit and chocolates, and took the rest to Miss Barrow. She was coming back from the shops with Maud on a lead, fouling the pavement exactly under a notice about what it would cost you if your dog fouled the pavement.

'Bless her,' Miss Barrow said, and I saw that Maud had won her.

The old girl (Maud, not Miss Barrow) would not pay any attention to me, or even look at me, or check my legs for other dogs, as she usually did with a censorious air when I had been away from her. Her stomach and sides were swollen but the rest of her looked rather thin. When I asked Miss Barrow if she should see a vet, she said that she had handled socially prominent American mothers who had got themselves pregnant again as soon as they had Miss Barrow in charge of the baby. She could handle Maud too.

I felt a bit jealous, seeing Maud standing sycophantically by Miss Barrow's legs, not mine. As soon as the job with Budd Malone was over, Fanny and I would find a place where we could have Maud and her pups.

As Miss Barrow turned to go into the house I asked if she had seen Fanny.

'Not today. Oh yes, I have.' She turned back. 'I saw her getting into her car this morning.'

'Where was she going?'

'Search me. She had a gentleman with her. I don't pry,' said Miss Barrow, who knew everything that everybody did in this street.

A gentleman? I trusted Fanny and the love we had. So why did I suddenly feel depressed?

*

When I got back to the hotel suite I could not open the door with my key.

'Who is it?' Budd's voice on the other side of the door.

'Dicky.'

'Thank God.' Budd unfastened the chain and let me in. 'I'm starving, but I wasn't going to risk the waiter seeing me.'

His vision was clearing slightly, but he still wanted to have his food cut up, and to take his whisky through a straw. It was not exactly that he was childish, although he was a bit, in the way that people are when they are sealed off from reality by something like films. It was because, having assented to the ordeal, he must extract from it all possible importance and drama.

'When people tell you how marvellous you look,' I asked him at lunch, 'what will you tell them?'

'I'll smile and say "Gee, thanks", and they'll wonder if I always looked this way.'

'Do you want them to notice a difference?' I fed him one of his honesty questions.

He chewed slowly for a moment, then said, 'Yes.' Then, 'I think so.' Then, 'But if they're too amazed, I'll worry about what I looked like before.'

'That won't matter.'

'Like hell it will.' If Budd had nothing to worry about in the present or future, he made do with the past.

The limousine came in the afternoon and I took him to the hospital to have the first stitches out, wearing dark glasses with sides on them, and a cap pulled over his face.

He wanted a wheelchair to take him to Mr Manderson's office but I persuaded him to take my arm and we travelled the middle of the corridors, with the streams of people dividing round us.

Outside the door he pulled me back and asked, 'Do you think Pete will think I look better than anybody else so soon after the operation?'

'Of course.'

There were other people in the waiting-room. Budd went in sideways to them and sat with a magazine in front of his face. When we went into the surgery and Mr Manderson said, 'Take off the glasses,' Budd took a deep breath, removed them carefully, and finished the gesture with wide-flung arms, and a face bravely tipped to the light.

'Mm.' The surgeon looked. 'OK.'

'Is that all?'

'What else?'

'Don't I look better than anyone else so soon after the operation?'

'Of course.' He was busy. 'Get on the table and we'll make you look even better.'

He took out some of the corner stitches. It hurt. Budd nearly broke my fingers.

After I had cleaned him up he opened his eyes and said, 'My God. My *God*.'

'What?' Mr Manderson turned round from the sink.

'I can see.'

'Some of the tension is off.'

'I can see.' Budd swung down his legs and went round the surgery touching things, looking out of the window, examining his own hands, as if he had been blind all his life and had undergone a miracle in the last reel.

In the corridor he took my arm then straightened up and walked alone in his cap and dark glasses.

He could manage pretty well without me now, but he wanted me to stay, so I did. He still would not see anyone or go out, although the glasses hid almost all the fading bruises.

I went shopping for him. I enjoyed buying things in Piccadilly with wads of his money, and a free choice of presents for his wife and his girlfriend. Coming along the side of the hotel to the staff entrance, feet hurried up behind me. It was Fanny. She clutched me and kissed me passionately in the middle of the pavement.

When she unwrapped the embrace I saw that she was carrying the tape recorder. That was what had hit me in the back when she flung her arms round me.

'What's that for?'

'Listen.' Fanny's eyes had blue excitement in them. 'I want to talk to Budd Malone.'

'Nothing doing.'

'I know a man who'd pay well, if I could get an interview.'

'He's not giving any.'

'You could persuade him.'

'He's seeing no one.'

'He sees you. Don't be selfish.'

'It's my job.'

'Don't be smug.'

'Leave me alone.'

We looked at each other without love. All of a sudden she seemed cheap to me. Just any old girl. Her hair was greasy. The bright lipstick was wrong. Her pants were too tight. I had never looked at her like this. It was horrible.

'Who was in your car yesterday?' I could not ask it without sounding possessive.

'Where? Oh – Jeffrey Turner. The cinema man. He came up to look at stuff for the walls, and I drove him back.'

'Why can't he drive himself?'

'He lost his licence. He had a sort of blackout last year, and hit someone.'

'So you're sorry for him.'

'That's it. So can I see Budd Malone?'

'No.'

'I'm out of a job. I need the money.'

'I'll give you some.'

'No thanks.'

I walked away from her and she followed me and came through the staff entrance, telling the man on the door that she was with me. I was not going to make a scene in front of him, so

I let her follow us into the lift, and we rose like strangers, not looking at each other. When the man put us out and sank out of sight. I said, 'Go away', but she followed me round the three sides of the tower and ran up the stairs beside the small slow lift. I could hear her pattering round me as I went up.

At the door to the suite she said, 'Just ask him, that's all.'

'No.'

'Then let me.'

Once she got in we would never get her out. I opened the door a little way and looked round it, blocking Fanny behind me.

'Mr Malone!'

'Come in, I need you. I can't find anything. Where in hell have you put everything?'

'Mr Malone, there's a girl out here called Fanny Runyon, with a tape recorder and a rather suspicious claim to come from the BBC. Will you see her?'

'Oh hell, I don't know.' He came out of the bedroom, putting on his dark glasses. Fanny was the first reporter to find him. He had been dreading them, and missing them. 'Is she pretty?'

'What do you want me to say?'

'If she's not, I don't want to see her. If she is,' he lowered his voice, 'I don't want her to see me.'

'So it's no either way.'

'Yeah. I guess so.' He sat down and began to bite his nails, diligently, in the way he had, as if it were a form of care.

'I'm sorry, darling.'

Winning dispelled my anger. I turned round and gave Fanny's anxious little doggy face a brief kiss, before I shut the door on her gently. It felt like shutting the door on an only half-discovered mystery, something I would never quite understand.

'I feel depressed,' Budd said, as I crossed the little hall into the room (*he* felt depressed). 'Come and cheer me up with disgusting tales of what goes on in hospital. Two-headed babies. Grafting dogs' brains into condemned psychopaths.'

'Can I have a drink?'

'Help yourself.'

*

Even after his last stitches were out, and he could read prop-erly, and go anywhere with dark glasses hiding the remains of the scars and bruising, he still kept me on at private nurse's rates to order meals and organize his laundry and go with him to dark bars and cinemas.

On the evening before Budd was to fly back to Los Angeles, the surgeon came up to our suite for a drink. He brought the pictures that he had taken before the operation in a harsh light that brutally emphasized every fold and furrow.

'Do I want to see them or not?' Budd worried.

'I want you to.' Mr Manderson put the pictures before him. 'I want you to see the miracle I've wrought.'

'Good God.' Budd studied the photographs in stricken silence. 'You need a lighting expert, Pete. No.' He put his hand on the pictures as Mr Manderson reached for them. 'I'll keep these.'

'I need them for my files. When the bruising and swelling is gone, get some close-ups done for me – without make-up – so I'll have a before and after set.'

'And sell them for a fortune to *Screen Play*. No thanks.'

'I won't need to if you pay your bill.'

Budd went to the desk and wrote out the cheque. While he was there he wrote out another one for me, extra to what he had paid the agency.

'No, I can't.' I had already made enough off Budd to keep me idle for some time. If I only knew where I was going to be idle, and who with.

'If you refuse,' Budd played our honesty game for the last time, 'you'll feel noble. If you take it, you'll feel rich.'

I took it.

20

Fanny had gone to stay with Melody and her father. She had given up the flat without telling me, our room, with the chimneys and steep roofs marking the night for us.

With money in the bank and a hollow in my normally exuberant heart, I went home to stay with my parents.

'How's that nice girl, what was her name?'

'Fanny? I haven't seen her for a few days.'

'Must be about time for the end of that one.' My brother was there. He was only thirty-six, but his humour was already weighted with the repetitiveness of middle age. He had always made ponderous jokes about my short-lived girls. When I told him I would marry Millie one day, he had said, 'I give her about a month.'

That was about all she did have. When she was killed my brother was in Hamburg, trying to sell something to the Germans. He rang me up and wasted ten expensive minutes not knowing what to say. I hope he charged it to the firm.

'I liked her,' my mother said hopefully.

When Millie and I were talking of marriage everybody said we were too young. With Millie gone, I was too old not to be planning marriage. I could see that my mother wanted to ask me if anything was wrong, but the poor woman had trained herself to leave us alone, even before we were grown up. There had been many times, as now, when we might have talked, but neither of us knew how to start.

While I was at my quiet home, painting my mother's kitchen and rebuilding the coal shed with my father, I got a telephone call from the woman who had brought Mrs Turner to see Melody about the job at Small World: Mrs Dent, who had the son with Guillain-Barré syndrome.

She wanted to have Robin home, and the doctors had agreed to discharge him if she could find a competent nurse who understood the rehabilitation care of this type of patient. Would I be interested?

Very. Challenging private cases which need specialized nursing are hard to come by.

'Are you sure you could cope?' I remembered Mrs Dent as a commanding woman with tightly sprung calves and one of those noses set on high that spell sinus. Her voice matched the memory.

'I took a neurology course this year and we did quite a bit on this kind of care.'

'I know. Fanny told me.'

Fanny had got me the job. Fanny wanted me near her. My empty heart was filled immediately with a fresh bright stream of hope. From strangers like Mrs Dent with her polyradiculo-neurotic son come the earth-shaking items of news.

*

The following week, when I stopped at Melody's house on the way to see Robin in hospital, Fanny was out. She had a job. She was working for Jeffrey Turner at the cinema.

'What's the matter?' Melody, all bottom and ankle bone in her shrunk jeans, stared at me curiously over the ironing-board where she was going at shirts in a slapdash way. 'Didn't she tell you?'

'I haven't talked to her lately.'

'Is something wrong?'

My mother would never have asked a question like that. But Melody weighed in with what she thought, so one was able to be honest back.

'We had a sort of fight in the street. Then she gave up the flat.'

'It cost too much,' Melody said. 'But I thought you were there together.'

'Sort of. But Fanny doesn't like to be tied down.'

'What is she afraid of?' Melody put down the iron and turned to get her coffee. 'Her marriage was a disaster. She was better out of it. But it still hurts her, being dropped by her husband.'

Instead of saying, 'Poor Fanny,' she said, 'Poor Dick,' and put a hand on my arm, a large hand, a man's friendly touch.

She had put the iron face down on the board. It began to

burn through the cover and she snatched it up with a yell.

*

Fanny had brought Maud to Melody, who would not mind a few more puppies. Maud had taken a quick tour of the house and garden and gone quite flat overnight. Everyone, including Maud, went looking under furniture and hedges. But where was her milk, and where were her pups?

Poor old Maud, frustrated wishful thinker, had had a phantom pregnancy. Everything at the farm had been giving birth when she was there. She must have started cooking something up by herself, since her swinging affair with the sheepdogs had been no more than fantasy.

Melody had several dogs who sat under the chopping board, tore into bags of garbage, upset dustbins, and bit the nursery-school children. Maud was harried. That was why she had gone flat.

I took her to the Dents who had no dog. She and Robin did not like each other, but she was willing to sit by the wheel-chair, one ear up, one down, while homecoming pictures were taken of Robin squinting under his hair into the sun. When I put him into the hammock with a book, Mrs Dent thought it looked quite nice, if people came, to have old Maud lying in his shade underneath.

*

Guillain-Barré syndrome, named for two French neurologists, is a severe type of polyneuritis of unknown origin. It invariably starts some time after an upper respiratory infection, leads rather quickly to paralysis, and sometimes death.

'*Acute post-infectious polyneuritis of unknown etiology, characterized by sensory and motor disturbances, and marked increase in level of spinal fluid protein.*' I looked it up again before I went to the hospital, in case anybody asked me.

With Robin Dent, it had started with flu, treated casually by the nurse at his boarding-school.

'Old bag.' Robin told me the tale in his own way, after the specialist with his silky Vandyke and modish wire spectacles had given me the technical talk. Robin spoke rather slowly, with pauses, a legacy of the speech disability he had suffered when the disease involved the cranial nerves. 'Initiates virgins.

For a small fee.' He sighed. 'Only the little kids are desperate enough for that.'

He was about fifteen, a skinny pale boy with lanky hair and spots, very weak and floppy in a wheelchair. The first thing he said to me was, 'I'll never walk again, you know.'

'Rubbish, of course you will.' Mrs Dent had come to the hospital with me, her large trunk corseted, her body and brain unsupple, a mother impossible to imagine in the act of parturition, let alone of conceiving.

'I won't.' When Robin spoke to his mother a limp lock of hair fell forward like a shutter.

'Old bag said I was neurotic.' Robin did not talk to me until his mother had left. 'I felt lousy, I always do at school.'

'Ill?' I sat on the bed, he below me, drooping in the chair. It was a nasty room, with crude furniture and a view of a steamy shaft between buildings. The sooner I got him home the better.

'Depressed . . . you know?' He looked up at me with a squinting grimace, like a fussy boy objecting to sun in his eyes. There were still traces of his facial paralysis. 'My father went there. He hated it too. But he still sent me.' He thought for a moment. 'They made me play cricket. That started it.'

'It would have started anyway, wouldn't it, if the infection was there.' I didn't know yet whether he wanted me to be all nurse, or all friend, or a mixture of both. I was feeling my way.

'No,' he said petulantly. 'I stood in the long grass. My legs went to sleep. I got behind the hedge and dragged myself in somehow. To bed. Bits of me hurt. Bits I couldn't feel. I got scared. Polio, you see? Someone came and said, "You're breathing funny." They got the old bag. She thought I was fa-faking. A hysteric, she told the doctor. "These boys – all neurotic." "Nonsense, woman." ' He paused, breathing with difficulty. ' "This boy is very ill." Sweet words.'

They had put Robin in the hospital near the school, which naturally was at the other end of England from his home. After he became paralysed, and had a tracheostomy, and prayers chanted in the school chapel, they brought him nearer home.

I looked after him in the hospital for a day or two, learning the routine of care and exercises from the nurses and the physiotherapist. Sometimes he talked to me. Sometimes he didn't. The speech therapist had thick, distorting glasses and a mouth that went, 'Oh – ohh', like an astounded frog. Robin would not talk to her at all. He slept a lot and woke heavily. Much of the time he was quite depressed and apathetic.

The ward sister agreed with the specialist that Robin would do better at home, 'with the right kind of nursing'. A warning that reminded me of Sister Hawley on Men's Surgical, who bequeathed you a moribund patient at night with, 'If that man dies before morning, I shall hold you entirely responsible.'

*

So I moved into the Dents' boring smug house. Fanny was only a few miles away but it might have been a hundred. She said she was busy. We hardly met. Her voice on the telephone was breathless and warm at first, then it remembered she was fighting for independence, and cooled. I waited.

Robin was better at home, although when his mother was about he would slip defensively back a few notches, and even cry, if he could manufacture enough self-pity.

She was not a bad woman, but she had been traumatized too, by suddenly hearing that her son's lungs were packing in, and she had better come and look at him, in case it was for the last time. Robin could talk about the terror of it. She could not. Nor could Mr Dent, an ossified man the same shape as his wife, allowing for sex differences, who ran some large concern that covered acres of sweet land with efficient glass buildings and belched clean smoke between us and the view.

Actually, they did not talk about much at all. I never heard them have a proper conversation all the time I was in their house. We had meals together – Robin lifted into a dining-room chair from his wheelchair – and the dialogue went like this:

MR DENT: I saw Bill Matson today. Looks ten years younger.
MRS DENT: Ten years younger? I don't think so at *all*.
RICHARD HAYES: (*I was Richard again, since Mrs Dent had a nephew called Dick who had gone to the bad in Leicester and was not talked about.*) Are you going to have macaroni cheese, Robin?
ROBIN: Yuck.

MRS DENT: It's on your diet.

ROBIN: Yuck my diet.

MRS DENT: Richard, make him stick to his diet.

MR DENT: Leave the boy alone. He's putting on weight.

MRS DENT: (*looking at him over her high nose as if thirty years of marriage had been the ghastly mistake that it had*) Do you think so? I don't think so at *all*.

RICHARD: I'll show you his chart.

MRS DENT: Those scales aren't true.

MR DENT: I bought new ones.

MRS DENT: From Eades, or the ironmongers?

MR DENT: From Eades.

MRS DENT: Their son came home. I think he's been in prison.

MR DENT: High time.

MRS DENT: What do you mean?

MR DENT: Do him a power of good.

MRS DENT: (*who had been ready to approve of gaol for Eade jr, if her husband had not done it first*) Rubbish.

Robin and I contributed very little. I sat and thought about the bed under the window in Fanny's flat and tried to imagine the Dents' sex life. Robin sat and let his hair flop, and since his neck was too weak to shake it back, I put it back for him.

Such was the pattern in that house, enlivened occasionally by visits from other sons and daughters who, having escaped to marriage and careers, did not stay longer than they thought that Robin needed them. He did not seem to need them at all. He was still quite depressed and withdrawn and wished that they would all go away and that he and I could have the house to ourselves.

He was a strange, lonely boy. Even before his illness he had always been a solitary. He seemed to have no young friends, and his room was a sort of cave of books, small treasures, and a stereo set which he listened to loud, to insulate himself, but did not share. He did not like me to be in the room when he was listening to music.

He would not agree to a ground-floor room. He wanted his old cave so, until he could manage stairs on his crutches, I carried him up and down, listless as a bunch of dead flowers, one hand dangling down my back, the other playing with the rubber ball with which he exercised his fingers.

I had a room next door to his, and the room beyond that had been fitted up for his exercises, with parallel bars and pulleys and various devices the therapist had suggested and the Dents bought at once. They could express themselves with money, if not with emotional verve.

As Robin's arms grew stronger he could shuffle on a walking frame, and I was starting him on crutches, which he hated. He saw them as a step back, although they were a huge advance on a wheelchair.

On a good day we worked outside. He had sweated the length of the terrace, grumbling at me while I exhorted and supported and cajoled him (in this kind of care, you do as much work as the patient).

Mrs Dent opened a window. 'I watched you every step of the way, Rob.' She leaned out, her hair like machinery, since she did not brush it out for two days after going to the hairdresser. 'Mrs Sisson is here. She didn't see. Do it again for Mrs Sisson.'

Robin told her where Mrs Sisson could put it, collapsed into his wheelchair and would not get out of it for days.

As well as recurrent bouts of pain in the limbs that had been affected, he had occasional overall relapses, when I could do nothing with him. He tolerated me. He was not fond of me, or anything like that. I had not seen him show fondness for anyone. I was an acceptable alternative to the hospital or his mother. When he was depressed, he would passively allow me to nurse him, nothing more.

My job here was to get him going into full life again. No progress felt like my failure. The ward sister at the local hospital might have said, in the words of Sister Hawley when she found the dying man's bed empty in the morning and the mattress gone for fumigation, 'I knew it.'

When I had a day off, a violent Irish girl with a loud laugh and run-down shoes took over Robin, who withdrew what little you could see of his personality completely, like a cautious snail.

I went home the first two weeks, because my father was ill. The next week Fanny was going to fetch me, but she was busy at the cinema, so I walked the few miles to the Runyons' house.

Marigold Turner was on the side lawn, making daisy chains with a covey of little girls. She looked happier than when she first came over. She and Jeffrey lived in a tottery cottage at the crummier end of the village in which the Dents had converted a row of three houses to dominate the choicer end. Jeffrey had been away learning to be a projectionist, but I had seen Marigold occasionally in the post office or the little shop. Once I had thumbed her for a lift, walking home in the rain, but she had speeded up in alarm, not recognizing me.

She knew me today. When she looked up and saw me she did not blush. She put her soft pale hair back behind her ears and smiled and said 'Hullo', and the little girls fell all over her to get back her attention.

'Come on, Dove. Here's my flowers, Dove. No, mine. Look at me, Dove.'

I sat on the weedy grass with them. I liked this so much better than the Dents' stiff garden, which an arthritic gardener tried to disguise as one of the municipal parks in which he used to work.

'Why do you call her Dove?' I asked.

'Because she is so lovey-dovey.' They stroked her hair, and sat in her lap, and brought her infinitesimal wounds on their tiny fat knees and fingers to be kissed. This was her place, with children. Perhaps that was why she had married juvenile Jeffrey Turner.

As the Nickelodeon Cinema neared completion he seemed to be falling apart. His face got longer, his hair and moustache thinner and wilder. His clothes looked flung at him, as if from a distance. His gym shoes sprang new holes at the tubercle of the fifth metatarsal. He jerked and picked and fiddled and flung himself about prophesying despair.

Fanny told me that when he was in the office she could not get any work done, and when he was out of it he rang her every half hour to find out what had gone wrong.

'Nothing. Why should it?'

'Something always goes wrong when I'm not there.'

When he was there pipes leaked, machinery failed, lights fused, and a section of the fibreglass drapery Fanny had helped to pleat and hammer to the walls collapsed on to where rows four through ten would be when the seats arrived.

Melody's son Carl, home from university, was learning to be an extra projectionist. His girlfriend, famous for being able to sit on her long red hair, would help Fanny to sell the tickets and clean. They were all more enthusiastic about the cinema than Jeff was. He had family money to back it, but he foresaw ruin.

He was a depressing person. I hoped that Fanny would find another job soon. Evidently she was still sorry for Jeffrey.

When I went in from the garden I surprised him in the kitchen, nicking something from the refrigerator. He turned round with a profanity and trod on a profane cat. He had been eating egg salad with his fingers. He wiped his mouth with the back of his hand and left egg on the sad moustache.

I did not know whether to ask him about the cinema. Sometimes he got paranoid if you didn't. Sometimes, like today, he flung his hands into his hair and cried, 'Don't talk about it, for Christ's sake!'

'He doesn't want to talk about it just now.' Dove came into the kitchen with some children for snacks. 'It's too near opening date.'

'We'll never open.' Jeff flung himself into a chair with his legs stuck out and a little boy came to stand between his knees and stare into his gloomy face. 'This thing will ruin us all.'

'Don't be silly.' Dove gave him a plastic cup of blackcurrant juice along with the children.

'You've got purple round your mouth,' the small boy told him.

'So have you,' Jeff said.

When the children had gone, Dove took her husband to the cinema, where he had forgotten to go, which was why Fanny had not fetched me. Melody gave Maud and me one of her good scratch meals, that somehow survived experiments and spills and near combustion on their way to your plate.

Fanny came home at last and sat opposite me at the kitchen table and picked bits out of my salad. She was tired and fed up with Jeffrey Turner.

'Get out,' I said.

'Not before opening night.'

'It's making your skin grey.'

It wasn't, but she got up at once and went to check her bright face in Mel's steamy wall mirror.

I stood behind her. 'Let's go upstairs.'

We went up to her room. But the telephone rang, and it was Jeffrey wanting Fanny back in the office for a crisis.

'He's desperate,' Melody called through the door.

So was I, but Fanny got off the bed with a sigh and went to brush her hair.

'Who comes first?' I said.

'He does need help.'

'Instant Jesus.'

'Nurse Hayes. You're not the only one who can help people.'

In those days, we scrapped back and forth at each other idly, in a way we never had before.

21

Although from time to time I got one of my spells when I wanted to go back and be part of the gossipy, purposeful life of hospital, there was enough real therapeutic nursing at the Dents to keep me busy, and enough challenge in dragging poor unwilling Robin back into life.

And Fanny was near me. Still not mine. I never could possess her in the selfish, old-fashioned way I wanted. But she was near. I could wait. I might as well dig myself in here for the winter and wait. I enrolled in a psychology course at Cambridge, got some books and made my room a cave each night, when Robin was bedded in his own cave.

Phyllis Runyon would have lopped a chunk off my pay for extra electricity, but the Dents, though limited in vision to a small, foggy area that stopped short of the greater joys of life, had always had enough unearned money not to be mean. They

179

paid me well, and without, like Phyllis, making bitter little references to overpriced professions.

Since Mrs Hewlett-Bye had always been fair to me, as far as her nature understood the meaning of the work, I let her take commission off the Dents, although I had not got the job through her agency.

'Polynewditis. Ah, yes.' She claimed to have restored many sufferers by her rare skills.

'Then if I say Guillain-Barré, H.B., you'll know the sad story.'

'Guillain-Bahdé . . . alas yes, I knew him well.'

The Dents had more money than charm. As well as this comfortable country house of no character, they owned a place on a small island in the Bahamas where they usually spent most of the winter. Mr Dent was the kind of Board Chairman who can be spared by the firm for long periods.

This year he had bought a new boat and was itching to go and sail it. Robin should go too, and finish his convalescence out there in the sun and blue water. But by the end of October the specialist did not think he was ready to go so far.

Thus Mrs Dent, loyal to everybody, from habit rather than emotion, was caught in the old conventional dilemma between husband and child.

Mr Dent, like many inattentive husbands, became uxorious only when it was least convenient. He would not hear of opening the Bahamas house without his wife, although there were maids and gardeners and a boatman called Willie, who was talked about as a cross between Jeeves and Little Black Sambo, his comic sayings requoted, his natural wisdom reverenced.

Mrs Dent wanted to go to the Bahamas, not necessarily to be with Mr Dent, but because she led an even less fruitful life out there than she did in England, with nothing to do all day, Robin told me, until the five-thirty round of who was having who over for drinks. But how could she leave her son?

'With me,' I said. 'We'll be all right.' Even better, since she contributed little to Robin's rehabilitation except annoyance.

'I couldn't leave you alone in the house,' Mrs Dent gonged through her nasal cavities.

'Why not? I wouldn't steal the spoons.'

'I didn't say you would.'

My jokes always fell flat in this house. Mr Dent did not listen to them and Mrs Dent took them seriously. Robin only laughed at sick jokes.

Dialogue at lunch:

MR DENT: I got Betty to ring up the travel agent. We can get an Out Islands reservation if we get the Nassau flight next Monday.

MRS DENT: I can't possibly go on Monday.

MR DENT: Yes, you can.

MRS DENT: I haven't begun to think about clothes.

MR DENT: You've got cupboards full out there.

MRS DENT: And I can't leave Robin.

(*She is eating peas neatly, four at a time, one on each tine of her fork. Mr Dent is drinking wine in a patriarchal way, with one finger up the side of his glass. Robin's neck has gone wonky and his flop of hair is almost in the gravy. I put my hand under his chin and lift everything back in place, but it flops again, so I take away his plate, since his mouth is folded, lower lip inside, which means he is not going to eat any more.*)

MRS DENT: You go, dear, and I'll follow with Robin later.

MR DENT: You're coming with me.

MRS DENT: Arnold, I am not. (*puts down knife and fork*)

MR DENT: Then I'll stay here.

MRS DENT: Stay here.

MR DENT: And miss the races.

MRS DENT: The races. You must go.

MR DENT: Not without you.

It was the nearest we came to great drama all the time I was in that house.

Into the middle of it, bumbling into trouble like a goat in a chicken hatchery, Melody Runyon stopped on her way from taking Dove home, to see how Robin was.

Mr Dent offered her some hock and she said, 'If I'm not in the way. Are you having a row?' She looked round the faces.

The Dents said, 'Of course not.'

Robin said, 'Yes, they are. He wants her to go to Cat Island. She wants to stay with me.'

'Not want,' her mother began. 'Yes, of course it is want. I can't leave you.'

'I'll be better off without you,' Robin said, through his hair but clearly.

'Hnthere. Hnyou hnthee?' Mrs Dent wheezed in affront.

'He meant he'd have to be more independent.' Melody tried to appease.

'No, I didn't.' Robin thumped the tablecloth with his rubber ball. 'I meant I'd be better off without her.'

'Look,' said Melody. 'You go, Lettice, and Robin and Dick can stay with me. We'd all love it. The tutor can come to my house just as well, and so can the physio. Maud too. There's loads of room. They can have the rooms in the corner that have their own bath. What do you say?'

'Well ...' the Dents began, and, 'I don't think ...', but Melody was looking at Robin and me. We nodded. Robin was beginning a smile. My face had stretched sideways so far that the Dents could have fired me for insolence.

*

Robin was better without his mother, poor woman. It was not only her fault for inhibiting him. It was partly his fault for letting himself be inhibited and for deliberately not trying because that would have pleased her.

When he told me, 'I'll never walk again,' that was meant for his mother.

Once at his house, when he was whining about his exercises, and wanted to spend the rest of the day in bed, I had asked him quite roughly whether he thought it was worth being a cripple for life, to spite his mother.

'I'll report you,' he said. He did report me sometimes, to his GP, who went, 'Dear, dear,' and winked at me. 'I've been very ill. I almost died.'

'And so sometimes you think,' I pursued, '*I wish I had died. It would have served her right.*'

'Shut up.' His way of ending any conversation he did not like.

In Melody's house, with our own rooms at the back corner, and one of the Small World rooms cleared for his equipment, which the children climbed and bounced and bicycled on, shrieking with joy, Robin made progress. He worked with his crutches every day, put on weight and slept well, without calling me as soon as he saw my light go out when I was falling asleep over a textbook.

Fanny and I made progress too, cautiously happy, sometimes sparring, increasingly often in harmony, among Melody's clutter.

*

The hayfield cinema, christened the Nickelodeon, was almost ready to open. There were no seats yet, but on Robin's sixteenth birthday, Jeffrey got his booker in London to send an old James Bond film, and Melody and Mr Runyon and Dove and Robin and Fanny and I took pillows and cushions and watched it from the floor. Carl's girl friend Hildur, name re-spelled now that she was involved with the arts, sat on her long red hair on the sloping concrete.

Jeff ran the projectors, although Carl was already more skilful. There were gaps between reels, when we saw F-I-N-I-S-H 1-2-3-4, but otherwise he did not get himself tangled in film or set the place on fire. When Dove stood on tiptoe after the film to kiss him proudly, he flung away and said, 'Don't humour me. It was a lousy job.'

'Yes, it was.' Fanny's father had come under protest.

'What do you know about it?' Jeffrey walked out and waited in the car while Dove helped to pick up cushions and turn out the lights and lock up.

*

One afternoon Maud and I went for a long, cold walk over the hill and down the track at the edge of the ploughed field.

The old girl liked to get away from the house. Indoors, she stuck close to me, away from the other dogs. When they rioted out after a cat, or roamed away to hunt, she stayed primly at home with her paws on the window-sill and watched them go.

Something had gone out of her with the lost phantom puppies. That trauma, on top of her ordeal of abandonment in the flat had taken the stuffing out of our poor old Maud. She was still our dog, mine and Fanny's, the only thing, since Fanny forgot to take our sea poster when she gave up the flat, that we had owned together.

On walks alone with me Maud's old tramping blood revived, and she would wander, casting for elusive prey with her brown snout. She had disappeared when I reached the bottom of the plough and I turned into the lane and walked back up it to see if she had gone into the wood on the other side.

A chill, blowing rain had started. When a small car came slowly up behind me, I thought of stopping it for a lift. It stopped anyway.

It was Dove, looking cold and pale, with her long blonde hair tucked under a childish stocking cap, and a pair of rather pathetic fur gloves, like little paws, clutching the wheel as if the car were a runaway pony. She leaned across to open the door for me and I got in.

She did not talk, and I did not know what to talk about. I was hardly ever alone with her. She was always either busy with the children, or chasing after Jeffrey, or sitting among people, not tongue-tied, but choosing silence.

At the edge of the wood, Maud was waiting, soaking wet, one paw up, one ear up, looking anxiously down the road for me. Dove stopped, and I took Maud into the front, since the back seat was covered with boxes and papers and clothes and an exhausted pair of mountain boots, gaping through knotted laces. Maud sat on my feet and shivered and drenched my legs, and I put a newspaper over her.

Before we reached the wider road that led towards the town, Dove turned her pale, pointed face to me and said, 'I've got to talk to you.'

'What about?' I had never heard her sound so positive. Usually she was tentative and self-effacing.

'Oh, it's nothing really.' She thought better of it and looked back at the rising road.

'No, come on. Before we get home.' Carl and Hildur were rehearsing for a folk festival and the house was full of beards and banjos.

'All right.'

Dove pulled the car off the road into a gateway and sat with the paws on the wheel, biting her lips. Her pale waterfall of hair usually hid much of her face. With the hair confined by the funny red stocking cap, her face was bare and vulnerable, the temples laced with faint blue, the facial artery throbbing where it crossed the pure bone of the jaw, a pulse moving in her fragile neck.

Neither of us spoke. Her shyness made me shy. Would we sit in the little car for ever, rocked by wind and rain? I was seeking for some way to hint that I should get back to Robin when Dove said quickly and quietly, 'I'm pregnant.'

When a girl says that to you – unless you are the father – you have to wait and see whether you're supposed to reply, 'That's wonderful', or, 'Bad luck'.

If you are a nurse, the appropriate response is usually, 'Bad luck', since the next remark is likely to be, 'Can you help me?'

But Dove was married, so I said, 'Is Jeffrey pleased?'

'He doesn't know yet.'

Silence. More lip-biting. She had the kind of pale, turned-out lips that crack and flake on a bad day.

'Will he be pleased?'

'No.'

'Oh. Are you pleased?'

'I don't know.'

She shook her head and the tail of the stocking cap flicked its tassel from her back to the front of her shoulder.

'Oh come on, Dove.' A baby might be just the job to strengthen this feeble marriage. 'Even if he thought he didn't want children, once the baby's there, he'll love it.'

'You don't understand,' she said flatly. 'It's not his child.'

'Oh.'

It was all I could manage. Meek little Dove, gentle, patient, shy little Dove. But it did explain why she could put up with the inadequacies of Jeffrey Turner. Because she was getting it somewhere else.

Before I could say anything more, Dove suddenly caught her breath and turned to me with such vehemence that Maud pulled back against my legs, damp and shivering and smelly.

'Help me.' Her wide grey eyes were stretched with pain. 'I want to have it. I want my baby. But I can't. Help me.'

'What do you want me to do?'

185

'I don't know. But I thought – you're a nurse–'

'Oh no.' Abortion counselling for someone who doesn't know what they want to do – that's dangerous. 'Ask your doctor.'

'He's Catholic.'

'Ask another one.'

It was all I could think of. I felt stupid. I wanted to yawn, even in the face of Dove's dilemma, and I did yawn, right in Dove's anxious little face, which was beginning to look as cloudy and stupid as mine. She had left the engine running to work the inadequate heater. There must have been an exhaust leak somewhere, because my nose told me, and then my clouding brain realized that we were being quietly asphyxiated.

'Get out!' I switched off the engine and banged open my door and got out, dragging Maud. I took a couple of gulps of wet, wintry air, and went round to open Dove's door.

It was stuck. It was a mean little car, this one, nothing working properly. I had to go round to the other side, reach over and somehow pull Dove over the gear lever and seat and out into the muddy gateway. She lurched against me. I helped her and turned her face up to the driving rain. She spluttered and choked, then she began to breathe properly, limp against me with her eyes closed.

'All right?'

She opened her eyes and stared at me, then stood upright, swaying.

'Better get that exhaust looked at,' I said. 'You'll kill yourself.'

'I drive with the window open,' she whispered.

'Then don't park with men.'

She did not smile. Her teeth began to chatter. I put her back into the car with Maud, who had survived carbon monoxide poisoning, as so many other hazards in her chancy life, and got into the driver's seat.

'I'll take you home.'

'Jeff's there.' She was crying. 'Not like this.'

I took her to Melody's house. Mel and Fanny were out. Hildur and Carl and Co were all over the ground floor with music. I got Dove through the kitchen without meeting anyone except a boy in a sleeveless leather jacket with Indian beads round his hair, who helped me carry her up to my room when she collapsed at the foot of the backstairs.

Robin, who was having one of his brief relapses of muscular tenderness and mild parasthesia, was in his bedroom with the physiotherapist. I could hear her healthy voice beyond the wall: 'Up, down, in, out, push, pull, come on, try harder,' and Robin belly-aching, 'I can't.'

Dove lay on my bed and wept painfully. I thought she might be aborting now. I put my hand on her to see if there were any contractions and she clutched on to my hand so tightly that I had to kneel by the bed and stay with her.

'Dove,' I said. 'What have you done?'

Not having worked on Gynae, I had never dealt with anything like this. A female nurse is prepared for all kinds of male crises. A male nurse is at sea, with old wives' tales of knitting needles, visions of great haemorrhagic floodings.

I was mentally tearing up the sheets when the door opened and Fanny came in.

'What on earth?'

'I think she's miscarrying.'

'No, I'm not.' Dove opened her eyes on a great sob. 'I wish I was.'

'Oh, darling.' Fanny's marvellous face was swept with a beauty of tenderness that it might never wear for me. She rushed to the bed. Dove let go of my hand and I got up and went next door to Robin and the physiotherapist.

'Up, down, in, out.'

'I'm tired.'

'Once more, range of motion with the left.'

'Make her stop, Dick. She's killing me.'

*

For the grand opening of the Nickelodeon Cinema Jeffrey had booked Charlie Chaplin's *Gold Rush* and invited about a hundred people he knew, or knew of.

Carl and Hildur and Fanny laid the carpet just in time. Jeffrey got stomach cramp from kneeling, and left them to it. The painting would have to be finished later. The car park was still wet grass and mud. The seats were delivered only two days before by one small square man, with a plastic cover buttoned over his hat. He and Carl and Jeff and I, and Mr Runyon when he came home from the office, worked a day and most of a night assembling them and bolting them to the floor.

By opening day everyone was exhausted and bitchy. Robin was bitchy too. He told me, with a nastiness much too mature for his sixteen years, that I was paid to work for him, not Jeffrey.

Breakfast, after a night of almost no sleep, felt like those unreal breakfasts in hospital after night duty. At the Essex they used to give the night nurses what the day staff had had for supper the night before, things like sheep's hearts and grey codfish balls. I can taste them now.

Melody and Dove were at it with the infants in the front room, with Dove going tinkly, tinkly on the old upright, and Mel loudly off key, leading a scratchy chorus, while the small feet stamped.

Jeffrey, who had kept a bottle of whisky going all night while he sweated over the seats, bruising his fingers with the hammer, and pinching the pads of his thumbs with the pliers, was hunched over a mug of coffee, eyes closed and forehead loosely corrugated.

When his wife came into the kitchen with a child who had been sick down the bib of its overalls, he said, 'Do you have to make that bloody racket?'

'It's sing-along time.' Dove opened her clear, wide-spaced eyes at him innocently. 'They love it.'

'I hate it.'

'Why don't you go home and get some sleep?' She stood the child in the sink to strip it.

'Because you won't take me.'

'Oh, Jeff.' Dove turned round in distress, while the child sat patiently on the draining board and waited to be cleaned. 'You know I can't leave now.'

'You give those puking kids more time than me.'

'It's my job.'

'And if I wasn't such a failure you wouldn't need it.'

'Oh, Jeff.' Dove sighed helplessly, and turned back to the child.

'Castrator,' Jeff said, without conviction, to her slender back.

Her front was still slender too, but she was going to have to make some decisions pretty soon.

Carl and Hildur were young enough to look unmarked by the night, but they were fighting. They fought a lot, physically, since their love was more physical than anything else. This morning, when she would not cook eggs for him, Carl took her long red plait of hair and wound it round her throat until her eyes bulged.

I read the newspaper and tried to imagine I was alone in that hill cabin to which I retreated mentally with Maud, no one but Fanny coming to visit us up the path between the tall wild flowers.

Robin, who had breakfast in bed, rang his bell. I had said he did not want bacon. The bell meant he did. He rang again but I had seen something in the newspaper.

Budd Malone was in London to talk about his new film and air his plastically revised eyelids on television.

'Carl,' I said. 'I'm going to ring him up and ask him if he'll come down for the opening. He's not on the box till late to-night.'

'You think he'd come?' Carl let go of Hildur's hair and she went back to her yoghourt. 'That would get us the front page of all the local papers.'

'And the London press as well,' I said. 'I'm going to try.'

Budd was in the same hotel. At first they denied it. I rang again and asked to be put through to the old suite number in the tower. That worked. Budd answered the telephone in a disguised voice. ''Ullo?'

'Is zat zee famous movie star wot 'ad 'is face lifted?'

'What in hell are you – Dicky!' He sounded really pleased to hear me. 'Where the hell are you? Come round right away. Some idiot on the coast packed all the wrong shirts for me and I can't show my face on Piccadilly to hunt up some more.'

'Does it look so awful?'

'No, jerk, it looks great. I think. As long as I look in the mirror without my glasses. I mean, they'll mob me, the natives.'

'They won't.'

'Don't they care?'

'Londoners don't mob film stars any more.'

'Too bad,' Budd said. 'When am I going to see you, old Dicky?'

'Tonight.'

I told him about the Nickelodeon and it caught his fancy. Underneath the foolery he was a pretty kind man. The charities which he got tax credits for supporting were not all the fashionable ones, and I knew of one failed friend, at least, who never touched him in vain for a so-called loan.

He liked the idea of the lion helping the mouse. He would be on hand to make a speech before the film. He would have his agent call all the papers. What should he wear?

'Anything.'

'I've got bags full of clothes, and I hate 'em all. Come on up and pick out something for me.'

'I can't. I've got a patient here.'

'A *patient*? I thought I'd paid you enough to retire on.'

'I work for the love of humanity.'

'Bullshit. How's that girl of yours?' Budd asked. 'The one with the tape recorder.' He was pretty shrewd, old Budd. He had guessed, although he had not said, that Fanny was the one.

'She's here,' I said.

'I'll be there.'

I should have gone to London and brought him back. He never did turn up for the opening of the Nickelodeon. Nor did the Press. Nor did Charlie Chaplin, the whole of him. When Jeffrey took delivery of the film the first and last reels were missing. He showed the middle three. The heavens opened in a cloudburst and only half a dozen of the invited guests showed up.

'Just as well.' Carl was indestructible. He got that from Melody.

Jeff said he would cut his throat. Any operation he started was doomed to disaster. He turned up his collar and ran out into the teeming night, while Dove was helping Hildur to pick up the pitifully small amount of litter left by the sparse audience.

She got into the car and went after him. We watched her up the road. In the weak beam of the headlights, we saw Jeff running ahead, with his head thrown back and his elbows going. He ran on. Dove slowed and drove behind him.

We went home and turned on the television. Budd was splendid. He did his slow, drawling, joky bit, and told charmingly scurrilous stories, and deepened his famous voice to give sincere credit to everyone else in the new film but himself. The make-up and lighting were good — he would not have done the programme otherwise — and his reconstructed face looked vigorous.

'What's he done to himself?' Carl leaned forward to the set. 'He looks different.'

'Had his face lifted,' Robin said. 'And about time, poor old relic.'

I said nothing. You could not be angry with Budd for forgetting the Nickelodeon. He had genuinely meant to come and help us. That was enough.

22

Fr R. Hayes. Confessions heard, afts and eves. No appt nec. Spanish not spkn.

A week later, while still digesting Dove's revelation, I got a basinful from Jeffrey Turner.

Carl and Hildur were playing drums and guitar at someone's party. Fanny had gone to see her mother. Dove had come over queer on Small World Parents' Day, and thrown up the fruit punch and some macaroons. Melody offered to settle Robin for the night so that I could help Jeffrey at the cinema.

While he went into the booth to put the first two reels on to the projectors, I sat on the stool where Hildur perched behind the counter, and sold tickets and chocolates and peanuts to about thirty people — mostly young, since we were showing an old Beatles film.

When they had gone inside, I left a girl I knew to watch

the cash desk, and nipped up the stairs to the hot little hutch where the two projectors waited with their reels of film on high.

Jeffrey was fidgeting about in a torn sweatshirt and jeans shrunk high above his bony ankles. His feet were bare. Long yellow feet with sharp toenails. Whatever people think about nurses I could never be queer. I have this thing about men's feet. Blanket baths are my penance, and geriatric toenails my Waterloo. Jeff was biting his fingernails and picking his long crooked nose. He was still nervous of the projectors and the arc lamps. When he was going to show a film he was as apprehensive as if he were going on stage to perform himself.

I had stayed up here with him once or twice to watch a film through the small window, only half hearing the words. When it was almost time to see the white dot in the corner of the screen that signalled a change of reels, Jeff would break into a sweat, rub his hands on the seat of his pants, and chew his ragged moustache sideways, as if it were stuck on crooked. The dot! He would jump like a startled doe to light the other lamp and start the projector, just a fraction too late to avoid a jerky changeover.

When I said, 'OK, Jeff, the kids are in,' he stopped pacing, rubbed his hands, and took breath like a diver.

'Let's see . . .' He flicked a switch. 'Start fan, that's it . . . get rid of the ozone the arc makes. Deadly poison,' he said to impress me. 'Got to know these things.'

'Ozone's not poisonous.' I had forgotten most of my chemistry, but I did know that.

'It is.'

'It's not.'

'You think you know everything.' Jeff was always suspicious of me for being professional. He carried a grudge against all training and schooling and would not let Dove go back to college for her degree. 'Know it all, don't you?'

'Start the film, for God's sake.'

'Shut up. Let's see – light lamp. Christ!' The spark jumped between the electrodes and the brilliant light flared behind the glass shield. 'Start reel . . . let her go!'

Jeff bent to peer through the little window. 'It worked.' He was quite surprised to see the credits dutifully rolling on the screen.

At the end of the film the small audience clomped out in bare feet and football boots, leaving a quantity of litter behind them that would do credit to a rock festival. I took the dustbin and began to pick up the motley mess. It was mostly paper and empty packets, with occasional more interesting items, like knives and bottles and a pair of panties embroidered 'Monday'. This was Thursday.

When he had rewound the last reel, Jeff joined me, but after stooping along one row, he got sick of it, and slumped into a seat with his bare feet over the back of the seat in front.

'Knock it off, Dick,' he said irritably. 'It's disgusting.'

'The girls have to do it.'

'Don't be bloody noble. They don't mind. Have a drink.' He took out a flat whisky bottle. 'My supper.'

I left the dustbin and sat beside him. 'No wonder you get gastralgia.'

'What's that?'

'Cramps.'

'Dr Hayes. You think you know everything.' This seemed to be his theme for the night. 'Ozone's not poisonous, he says.'

'It's not. They're using it in France to unpollute the Seine.'

'Always got to know everything. Always got to be right.' He grumbled on. 'Gastralgia. What use is it to know that?'

'Not much.' I wiped the neck of the bottle with my thumb and passed it back.

'No help to me.'

'What's the matter?'

It couldn't be pregnancy, but he groaned, as if he were going into labour in the third row from the back at the Nickelodeon.

'Everything. I'm sick of everything. No point any more. If there ever was.'

'Have you talked to your doctor?'

'Doctors.' He took a long drink and was silent, staring empty-eyed at the empty screen, as if he were watching a film of his own gloom.

'Anti-depressants could help.'

'Pill pusher. Just like the rest of them. A nurse.' He champed on this, his moustache lifting and settling. 'I've never met a man who was a nurse.'

If I could have a shilling, as they used to say, for everyone who said that, including my brother's wife Cecily when he first brought her home, I would be a rich nurse, and able to retire and run my own Home and shove people like the Major out into the corridor with pneumonia.

'A nurse, of all things.'

'You thought all male nurses were queer.' I said it for him, to spare myself the boredom.

'So why do I tell you this?'

'What?'

We sat side by side, with our feet over the chairs in front, and finally Jeff sighed and said, 'It's Dove.'

He knew.

'She thinks I've gone off her.'

He didn't know.

'Just because I – well, God, when you don't feel like it, but you try anyway, and you can't get the bloody thing up—'

He'd have to know.

He dropped his feet, got up and stumbled up the aisle, and the swing door sighed behind him. I found him treading into the remnants of his gym shoes. He was crying, so I did not look at him, or say anything. I took him home.

Outside his cottage, where the lights were on, and Dove's small face looked out between her hair and the curtains, he got out, and that slight odour of depression, sensed rather than smelled, went with him.

Father R. Hayes. Confessions heard. No solace given.

*

I did not see Jeff again until a few nights later. He had somehow got hold of a tattered print of *King of Hearts* and I went to the cinema.

It was a fascinating film – the first reel of it. I had slightly spoiled my film-going by watching for the little white dots to see how cleverly they had cut the film. There it was. Man walking down the road. You would not notice that he suddenly got a bit farther away.

The picture left the screen. F-I-N-I-S-H in black and

white. 1-2-3-4. A faint clicking of sprockets. Then nothing. White light. Blank screen. No sound. You could hear the hum of the projector.

'Oh come on, Jeff.' Carl looked round angrily. A man laughed. Girls giggled. Someone in the front started a slow handclap and then feet began to stamp. Carl got up and I followed him up the aisle. He pushed the swing door, ran across the foyer and up the stairs, and through the heavy fireproof door of the booth. One projector had a full back reel, going busily round with the arc light still burning. Jeffrey was on hands and knees on the floor, sagging, eyes closed. It was very hot, and there was a strong electric smell, like tube trains. The smell of ozone.

Jeffrey had forgotten to switch on the fan that blew the exhaust from the arc light up the chimney and it was seeping out into the room where he knelt, breathing in – not death. A small amount of ozone would not kill him. Did he hope it would?

Carl flicked switches and we pulled Jeff upright and got him outside into the hayfield. He was breathing in gasps, with his eyes still closed, but his colour was all right, as far as I could see in the light from the cinema entrance. Was he faking? I gave him a bit of artificial respiration anyway, while Carl ran back to start the second reel, before the audience came out to see what was wrong.

'Get off my back,' Jeff said into the grass. I sat on my heels, and he rolled over and blinked up at me, contorting his moustache as if he had swallowed something foul.

I felt desperately sorry for him. I wanted to say that. But I asked, like a stupid nurse, 'How do you feel?'

'Lousy.' He sat up, coughed, spat, then turned away from me and leaned over to vomit into the clover. When he could speak again, he said, 'You see, you don't know everything. Ozone *is* poisonous.'

23

'But it isn't poisonous. Ozone O_3. Only lethal in large concentrations, when it may oxidize healthy tissue. I looked it up, in case I was wrong after all.'

'Thank God you weren't,' Fanny said.

Dove and everyone else thought it had been an accident, but I was not so sure. When Fanny came back, with her laughter and colour and bright stunning eyes, I told her what Jeffrey had said in the third row from the back at the Nickelodeon. I always told her everything.

'He does need help,' I said.

'I'll do what I can.'

'I mean medical. He's very depressed.'

'Wait till he finds out about Dove.'

'What's she going to do?'

'She doesn't know.'

At two months' pregnant, Dove did not have much longer to decide. It was a mess either way, Fanny and I agreed, making those calm, wise, decisive statements about other people's problems that solve nothing.

'I dread telling him I can't work for him much longer,' Fanny said, with the face that goes with the calm, wise statements.

She had told her mother that she wanted to study something. Phyllis had said, 'About time,' and, 'Don't look at me for fees.'

*

'I'm going to give up work and learn something,' Fanny told Robin. 'I'll go to college.'

'You wouldn't get in.' Robin made one of his sneery faces, the side of the top lip hitched up.

'Perhaps I'll be a nurse.'

'Bit late to start, old girl.' Robin sneered on the other side. It must have been torture for him when he had had the facial paralysis in hospital. He liked to make terrible faces at people. Half the time he looked like a gargoyle, although when he was asleep he was not bad looking, in a raw, bony way.

Fanny threw a book at him, which I caught. A book was too hard to throw at someone recovering from polyneuritis who could not move quickly.

Robin and Fanny had known each other off and on since Mr Runyon and Melody moved here when Robin was quite small. They were familiar together. She teased and he insulted. She played at flirting with him and I wanted to tell her not to. He was not a child. He was excited by her.

But she was good therapy for him. He had brightened since he had been here. He stopped droning, 'I'm crippled for life', and even tried a cane instead of crutches, which I had not been able to get him to do. Perhaps he should have had a girl nurse, not me.

'Anyway, you'd never pass the exams.' His insults to Fanny had less precocious malice than his jabs at other people.

'If Dick could, I could.'

'He cheated.'

'Or it was easier in those days.'

'Before penicillin.'

Fanny was the same age as me, but she laughed and fooled with Robin as if she were a kid, and I was the stuffy old Nanny.

I did not mind. Rob did not know it, but these days she was all mine again.

*

Our rooms were at opposite ends of the house, with Fanny half a flight lower in a room that had been built over the garage. I don't suppose anybody in the house – except possibly Robin – would have minded us sleeping together, but unless you are in your own home, it's more fun to be clandestine.

I went to stay with a girl once – Alison, her name was, she had big ears – and because the house was full for the weekend, with bodies on sofas and floors, her mother said to me after the fourth gin, 'Share Alison's room.' Loose Martini wink. 'I don't care.'

The upshot was that Alison went for a walk with a man who had sideburns like razor shells and never came back and I slept on two chairs in the dining-room. Someone else was in Alison's bed right over my head. It squeaked rhythmically. No doubt her mother was listening.

I did not have to be on call for Robin now. To get to Fanny's room I went past his door, where the light would often still be on and music playing. If I opened the door and said, 'Go to sleep,' he would make a rude noise, or say, 'You're not my keeper.'

Along the corridor, round a corner, under an arch, and down the short flight of stairs that led to the room above the garage. There were loose treads here, and if they creaked, three or four dogs who slept in Melody's room would bark.

'Shut up!' Mr Runyon under bedclothes.

'They hear something.'

'For God's sake, Mel.'

'I'll go and see. Come on, dogs.'

'Get back into bed.'

'And wait for rape?'

'Good luck.'

I took to going downstairs, out of the back door and round the side of the house to the toolshed, where I picked up a stepladder, put it against the garage wall, and climbed into the room where Fanny waited for me, sitting on the floor by the window in a white nightdress cut square over the tender white foothills of her breasts.

The birds woke us early and I would go back the same way, before Melody came out with the dogs and her huge bare feet, kicking spurts of dew out of the silvery grass.

The trouble with Melody was that she never went to bed. What casual housework she did was usually at night. She would racket about, doing jobs like scrubbing floors or making casseroles, that most women do in the morning. I could not always get out of the back door.

One night when she was wallpapering the pantry, I got out into the garden, but I could not get the ladder, since the toolshed was opposite the pantry window, in the staring light of a full moon.

When I stood on the back lawn and turned up my face I could imagine that the chill autumn moon was warm. It shone on my face as benignly as the sun. More benign, since the sun, like God, is too dazzling to confront, but you can stare at the moon with your eyes wide open.

Small clouds moved their shapes across the bald, astonished face of this full moon, its mouth open in that O with which it beholds the dark earth. As I stared, the face grew glummer, then disappeared. I squinted to make two moons. One small travelling cloud passed over the first moon, then over the second. Two moons, one cloud. I had created the second moon, with its own place in the sky.

I sneaked through the shrubbery to the garage to call under Fanny's window to come down and see if she could do it too.

The sharpest of Melody's dogs barked. Mel stuck her head out of the pantry window. 'Who's there?' If it had been a man with a gun she'd have got her head blown off. Fanny hung from the window-sill and dropped down to me in her white nightdress on the grass.

All this was ages ago, last year when I was young. It was the most marvellous thing that ever happened to me.

It did not last. Robin did not need me now, although he was still dependent on me as long as I was there. His doctor said that he could go back to school for the rest of the term, before flying out to the Bahamas.

'Traitor.' He sulked at the doctor under the hair that was lank, however often I made him wash it.

'They can't make you play games though, old chap,' the doctor jollied.

'Then they'll make me do library, or some crap like that.' Robin's lip hung. When he wanted to sulk it was a waste of breath to try and jolly him.

I rang Mrs Hewlett-Bye and told her that I would soon be on the market again.

'How's it gone, Hditchahd?'

'Pretty good. I've learned a lot about old Guillain-Barré.'

'Come in for tea some time, and tell me all the dirt.'

'Will do, H.B.'

'Hdodger.'

*

Fanny went to London to find out whether she could train as a nurse at her advanced age. I took Robin back to school in the Dents' car.

From his descriptions, I had imagined a grim, windswept

prison, full of fascist perverts. It turned out to be a rather charming collection of faded red-brick buildings on the edge of a quiet market town in a shallow wooded dent between green hills.

The school nurse, the old bag who had labelled the onset of Robin's near-fatal illness as hysteria, turned out to be a soft, amiable lady in glinting spectacles, who welcomed Robin back with a warm relief born of remorse.

'It's terrible,' she told me, as we sat in the infirmary for our little professional chat over sherry brought out of the D.D. cupboard. 'I'm so afraid of missing something again, I don't even take their temperatures before I give out exemption slips for games or an exam.'

'Don't baby Rob,' I said. 'He's all right now.'

'No thanks to you,' Robin said automatically.

When I left him at his dormitory he moved forward as if he wanted to put his arms round me but then dropped his hands and sat down on the bed in his tiny cell, with another boy's girlie pictures on the wall.

'So long,' I said.

'So long. And—'

Two boys banged in. 'My God, you're back, everyone thought you were dead,' and I left.

*

On my way south, I detoured out to the coast to see a friend of mine who was in charge of the medical wing of a small hospital that used to be a sanatorium in the days when TB was only treatable by environment. The hospital buildings stood on different levels on the back slope of cliffs that faced a cold, blown sea. The turf was short and harsh, like crew-cut hair. Trees all leaned the same way. The air was marvellous.

I found my friend in the same kind of Charge Nurse's office he had been in at the Essex, surrounded by the same path lab baskets and pictures of antique surgeons and benefactors, with the same view of the boiler room wall, and what looked like the same very young nurses – only ruder – charging in and out with complaints, demands and plain statements of calamity.

'Aren't you sick of it?'

'I don't know.' He shut the door on a quarrel between a ward

maid and a laundry porter in the corridor and poured out the
same kind of tea that had been stewing in hospitals since I first
went to the Essex in a state of high adventure. 'Aren't you sick
of privates?'

'I don't know. When I get the smell of this place – carbolic,
ether, floor polish, steamed fish – I want to be in a hospital
again.'

'When I see you driving round the country in someone else's
car in the middle of the week I want to get out of this drudgery.
I'm going to anyway, I told them last week, they could start
looking for someone for this job pretty soon. Be all right for
someone with a wife, but for me it's too far from the action.'

He had never been a part of any action that I could see but he
liked to think that he was in midstream.

Since I was not going anywhere I waited about until he was
off duty, and he showed me where he lived, at the end of a row
of white cottages that ran downhill from the hospital, with tiny
gardens in steps. The windows looked over a dizzying descend-
ing landscape of patterned fields and far-away spires, disappearing into a limitless haze, as if England were enormous. His
rooms were rather bleak. Two or three chairs, television, obvious
paperbacks, a bed, an inconvenient little kitchen. He had made
nothing of them, the rooms of a bachelor by circumstance, not
choice.

'If you're leaving,' I said, 'I might go after your job. Have
they advertised it?'

'Not yet.'

'Think I might get it?'

'You might.'

                                    *

I went back to Fanny. I could not get there fast enough. This
could be the answer for us. The dream had begun. This was
what we had been waiting for. This was what was round all the
corners that had beckoned me with such electric promise.

                                    *

Fanny said no. She would not go to the terraced cottage on the
back of the cliff with me, married or not.

'But it's so right for us. You could do your training in Nor-
wich. If I can't get that job I'll look for another somewhere like

it. We could have Maud –'. I did not like the sound of my pleading voice.

'No, Dick.' Fanny looked trapped. She actually glanced round the room, as if she were physically trapped. 'Don't try to tie me down.'

'Don't *say* that! Don't keep on saying it.' She was like a bloody gramophone.'

'It's how I feel.'

'It's so bloody immature.' I was furious with her for disappointing me. 'Grow up. Stop being so childish.'

'I'm older than you.' (She wasn't.) 'I've been married. And divorced.'

'It should have taught you more sense.' I turned away from her in bitterness.

'It did.'

I turned back to her, on the chance that she was, after all, beginning to make a joke of it, would laugh with me, leave the door open, as she had before, to whatever our relationship might become; and saw her again with those harsh edges, ungraced by love, any old girl.

*

I went back to London. I forgot about the hospital on the back slope of the cliff. I might have worked and lived there happily on my own, but hurting myself seemed somehow a way of hurting Fanny, so I went to London and found a room in a nasty slice of house near enough to Gloucester Road tube station to nourish my masochism.

With Fanny not there London had reverted to grey. The siren music which had once led me to her through the dogs' mess of the Kensington pavements was only traffic noise. The filthy lift gates which clanged me out at the tube station were the gates to Gloucester Road, nothing more.

I was very depressed. I had nothing to do. I spent hours in bed, wrapped in the cheap Indian print counterpane, and hours walking in back streets, going nowhere. I needed a job badly but I could not summon the energy even to ring Mrs Hewlett-Bye and be told, 'Nothing today, Hditchahd. Don't call us, we'll call you.'

I thought about Millie a lot. If Millie were alive we would be married by now. I would apply for the job on the cliff. We would move into the end cottage and whitewash it, like sterilizing a ward bed after the last occupant, and Millie could be the hospital physio.

If Millie were alive, we might have a child by now, grown miraculously somehow within her thinness. Millie. Millie. It was about this time of year that Millie had died. November. I thought about Millie more than about Fanny.

Although I thought I had got that nightmare out of my system, I found myself thinking again about Jack Judd's face, when I was afraid that Millie had come back to speak to me. Why afraid? I had run from her. The more I thought about that weird experience in the Place of Peace, the more it drew me back. In case. If I could reach a glimpse of Millie now I might stop feeling so desolate in this November.

I got up one day from the unwashed disorder of my bed and made myself into a nice clean, neat young man again. Francis Maude, back for a second sitting. As I was brushing my hair, damp in the vile bathroom at the end of the passage, I heard my telephone ring. I went back unhurriedly and when I picked it up, Jeffrey Turner said, 'Thank God. I was just going to ring off.'

'What's happened?'

He sounded as if something had happened. Fanny? Why should it be Jeff who rang me?

'She's gone.'

'Fanny?'

'What do you mean? Dove's gone. She – she's gone.' He was gasping, as if he had run half a mile.

'Gone where?'

'To her – to this – you know about it, Fanny said. She's gone.'

His utterly helpless despair, which should have touched me, was only annoying.

I said, 'She'll come back.'

'She won't.'

'Then you don't want her,' I said, stupid with selfishness.

'Dick, I –'

'Look, Jeff, I'm sorry. I've got to go out.'

He rang off before I did.

I put on my coat and went out. As my feet fell heavily down the stairs, step by step, as they did these days, I heard the telephone again, ringing, ringing in the empty flat.

24

When Ireen Judd opened the ochre door at the bottom of the steep stairs, her long face dropped lower. She remembered me.

'Oh, it's you,' she said without relish. But she took me upstairs to the cramped sitting-room to sit in front of the silent television, where four haunchy middle-aged women were pushing peanuts across the studio floor with their noses, exhorted by a frenzied puppet mouthing silently into a microphone.

She did not say anything, so after a while I asked if I could see the medium.

'My brother is in bed resting,' Ireen said.

'Too tired to see me?'

'You shouldn't have come.' Ireen looked at me. The thick grey coils over her ears were like airport headphones. Give her a couple of ping pong bats, and she could bring in a plane.

'I wanted – I wanted to see if the same thing would happen again.' Or did I? I wanted and dreaded it at the same time.

Ireen's shadowed eyes considered me gravely. 'It wasn't very nice,' she said, 'jumping up and shouting during the transfiguration.'

'I didn't like it. I thought I saw this girl, you see, who –'

'What you thought you saw,' Ireen said sternly, 'and what you saw, may be two very different things.'

'I didn't imagine it.'

'I daresay not.'

'Are you trying to tell me it was a fake?' I could not understand her.

'Are *you* trying to say that?'

'No. I'm trying to tell you I want to try it again.'

I could not seem to get through to her. I thought she was a bit potty. In those days, I was still young enough to label potty anyone I could not understand.

She would not disturb Jack Judd from his rest. I pictured him on his bed, the toes in thick grey socks turned up below the mounded pullover, transfiguring ceiling cracks into signs and portents.

I got up, still depressed and heavy. I wished I had not come. Millie was not here. Had never been. I only thought she had, because I was there, and she was still in me. Now she wasn't any longer. She had passed beyond that limbo where the dead hover politely before they go right away. Millie had deserted me too.

As I left I looked back before I followed Ireen down the stairs and saw Jack Judd cross the passage into the kitchen, fully dressed and shod, cradling a large brown teapot. He was not resting at all.

I went back to my room and back into my unmade bed. When the telephone woke me, hours later, and I heard Melody speaking to me, it was as if I knew what she was saying. It sounded like hearing the same story twice, like crossing your eyes and making two images out of one.

Getting no answer when he rang me back to ask me if I would go with him to where he thought Dove was, Jeffrey had asked Fanny. She agreed to drive him. It was quite a long way. When she got sleepy, Jeffrey would not wait while she pulled off the road and dozed. He insisted on driving. He had no licence but they were on back roads and it was night and there was not much traffic about. Not much, but some. Jeffrey got fed up driving behind a slow lorry, pulled out, hit a van, killed the man in it, and fractured the fourth cervical vertebra of Fanny's spine.

*

We moved her, after I got the Charge Nurse job, and she is now being cared for in the hospital behind the cliff, where I work. She is off the frame and in a body cast, and we may be married when the staff nurse of Fanny's ward comes back from her holiday. She does not want us to do it without her.

Later, when Fanny has recovered more use of her hands, we

205

shall be together in the whitewashed cottage. It is too soon to judge the lasting effects of the contusion and compression of the spinal cord. She may walk again. She may not. Anything may happen. We both still have that feeling of something just ahead, round the corner, an adventure, a promise of life.

Monica Dickens
Kate and Emma 70p

Kate is sixteen, a victim of cruelty, neglect and poverty. We meet her in a London court 'in need of care and protection'. Emma is a bare two years older, daughter of the presiding magistrate. A girl with a comfortable background, with a mind of her own.

Between these two an enduring, if turbulent, friendship is struck as Emma toils doggedly not only to lift Kate out of the mire, but also to make sense of her own life and love . . .

The Listeners 70p

The enthralling story of what happens when people at the end of their tether contact the Samaritans . . .

In this deeply felt, absorbingly told novel, Monica Dickens not only vividly portrays three would-be suicides, but also the Samaritans themselves.

A story in Monica Dickens's inimitable style – salted with humour and inspired by love.

The Landlord's Daughter 70p

Nobody (including herself) expected anything exciting to happen to Charlie, the innocent, coltish games mistress who was shy with men. Yet she was to lead a passionate secret life with a murderer on the run, before finding happiness . . .

Every page of this absorbing novel, which ranges from the Depression days of the thirties to the pop stars and 'dropouts' of today, is richly and compulsively readable – one of today's top-selling authors at the very top of her form.

Selected bestsellers

☐ **Jaws** Peter Benchley 70p

☐ **Let Sleeping Vets Lie** James Herriot 60p

☐ **If Only They Could Talk** James Herriot 60p

☐ **It Shouldn't Happen to a Vet** James Herriot 60p

☐ **Vet in Harness** James Herriot 60p

☐ **Tinker Tailor Soldier Spy** John le Carré 60p

☐ **Alive: The Story of the Andes Survivors** (illus)
  Piers Paul Read 75p

☐ **Gone with the Wind** Margaret Mitchell £1.50

☐ **Mandingo** Kyle Onstott 75p

☐ **Shout at the Devil** Wilbur Smith 70p

☐ **Cashelmara** Susan Howatch £1.25

☐ **Hotel** Arthur Hailey 80p

☐ **The Tower** Richard Martin Stern 70p
  (filmed as *The Towering Inferno*)

☐ **Bonecrack** Dick Francis 60p

☐ **Jonathan Livingston Seagull** Richard Bach 80p

☐ **The Fifth Estate** Robin Moore 75p

☐ **Royal Flash** George MacDonald Fraser 60p

☐ **The Nonesuch** Georgette Heyer 60p

☐ **Murder Most Royal** Jean Plaidy 80p

☐ **The Grapes of Wrath** John Steinbeck 95p

All these books are available at your bookshop or newsagent;
or can be obtained direct from the publisher
Just tick the titles you want and fill in the form below
Prices quoted are applicable in UK

Pan Books, Cavaye Place, London SW10 9PG
Send purchase price plus 15p for the first book and 5p for each
additional book, to allow for postage and packing

Name (block letters)_____

Address_____

_____

While every effort is made to keep prices low, it is sometimes
necessary to increase prices at short notice. Pan Books reserve the
right to show on covers new retail prices which may differ from
those advertised in the text or elsewhere